An Impractical Guide to Satyr Charming

Magical Husbandry: Book 1

Cynthia Diamond

www.cynthiadiamondauthor.com

Book Layout © 2017 BookDesignTemplates.com

An Impractical Guide to Satyr Charming/Cynthia Diamond-1sted.
ISBN 978-0-578-89709-7

This one is for Stacy, and her insatiable lust for men with horns and hooves.

Contents

Chapter 1

I vy's back hit the wall, almost knocking the wind out of her. Her pulse pounded as she gawked at the shattered remains of the chandelier. She'd barely had enough time to scream and roll out of the way before impact. Just seconds ago, she was mentally commenting on how ugly the damn thing was; a giant monstrosity comprised of dusty antlers that she was dreading cleaning.

Ancient lantern oil pooled at her feet and stung her nostrils with its musty scent. She rubbed the back of her neck, hands shaking as a tiny whimper squeaked from her clenched lips. Her couch was reduced to a pile of springs and stuffing.

Dammit, I loved that couch. Fuck the damn couch. That could have been *her* impaled by antlers. Her throat thickened, palms growing sweaty as thoughts raced at breakneck speed. *This was a mistake. This will never work. This is hopeless! You're going to fade away. You're going to die and... Oh My Gods, Ivy! Stop!*

She imagined a huge stop sign before her. The ruminating slowed. Ivy sucked in the stale air, searching for three sights to ground her; the huge stone fireplace in need of a good clean out, her beloved comfy chair that Auntie Dahlia proclaimed an eyesore, and the wall of boxes containing her spell books.

"I am safe. I am grounded," she murmured to herself, barely believing the words.

She counted her breaths, staring at the shattered pile of antlers. Sure, her cottage witchery had been strong before her "incident" but not anymore. Magic no longer surged through her veins. Her stomach twisted. Gods, breathing life back into this cabin would be like a root canal.

If you could even call it a cabin.

Mansion in the woods was more like it.

And it's your last hope if you want to live past the spring. Why couldn't she perform her ritual with a tiny bungalow? At least she'd stand a chance of saving herself with a smaller space. A surge of panic bubbled bile up her throat. She gulped it down, reaching into her purse. The reassuring rattle of her pill bottle made her heart slow. Oh yeah, her rescue drug was in order after that shock. *Don't fail me now, Atarax.*

Ivy flicked the lid off and popped the little white pill, swallowing it dry. The bitter metallic taste made her eyes water. She stood as still as a statue, concentrating on the cold air flowing in and out of her lungs. After a few minutes, her mind calmed, rationality returning.

This was a fluke, not an omen. It had to be. The most logical explanation for an old chandelier was that the rope holding it up was probably rotted, not that this abandoned cabin in the woods was overrun with demons. She stepped forward, toeing the debris that haloed the couch. Yeah, it was just a fluke. Nothing more than...

Eyes were upon her.

Ivy spun. Nothing was there. Her skin prickled, growing taut as the invisible stare grew stronger. Closer. Her lizard brain told her to run, to get the hell out, but her stupid feet remained glued to the floor as she called out, "Hello?"

She winced. *This is what dumbasses do in horror films, Ives.* And yet she called out again, her voice bouncing off the high ceiling. "Hello? Is someone here?"

A gentle clack-clack-clack whispered through the huge room. The hair on the back of her neck prickled. Movement flickered at the top of the grand staircase, rippling the atmosphere like heat on asphalt. The entity was tall, broad, air wavering around what could be horns. Ivy's brow creased.

Horns? Ghosts don't usually have horns.

And this didn't feel like a spirit. Ivy had encountered enough in her youth to know the cold empty touch of death. No. This was something corporal. Alive.

And unfortunately, invisible.

Curiosity overtook her fear and she stepped forward. The blur flinched, clacking as it moved back. What the hell, was it wearing tap shoes?

Ivy wet her lips. "So, hey." She pointed at the chandelier mess. "Was this...you?"

A growl bounced off the rafters and the blur flew down the stairs at breakneck speed. Ivy screamed, throwing out her hand to cast a shield on reflex. But no magic came from her fingertips.

"Shit!"

Ivy ran, the furious clacking gaining on her. The thing grabbed her shoulder, its claws tearing through her sweater. Oh God, it had claws. Razor sharp claws that pricked her flesh with warm tips.

"Shit shit shit!"

She slapped the invisible hand and the thing yelped, sounding more annoyed than hurt. Its hold released. Ivy dove out the front door, dashing down the porch stairs and stumbling to the rocky drive. She slapped her hands on the hood of her SUV as if it were home base, drawing a line in the dirt with her boot.

"No harm will cross this line! No harm! No harm!" she chanted, bending down to scribble runes beneath her barrier with a finger.

This won't keep it away, that terrified voice in her head moaned. *You have no magic to charge this ward. You think the symbols alone will hold it back? It has claws!*

"No fucking harm will cross, dammit!" Ivy whimpered.

The front door slammed.

Ivy dared a look over her shoulder. The cabin stared back, its wooden façade grayed with age, each board creaking as the biting autumn wind picked up. Its tall windows were boarded, but that didn't stop the feeling that it was watching her. Or maybe the invisible creature inside studied her. Either way, both were laughing at her; she could feel it. Mocking her. Finding her as pathetic as she felt.

You can't do this, her doubt whispered.

Ivy's hands shook. She wanted to get in her car and drive away, wanted to pretend she didn't have this idea in the first place. Just quietly die tucked away in her aunts' little guest house in downtown Big Bear. But she couldn't. She had to live. For Rowan. For Auntie Rosemary and Auntie Dahlia.

For Aster.

You let your sister down. Maybe this is the fate you deserve.

Tears burned her eyes, fury gathering tight under her ribs. She had to focus. Had to get angry, not scared.

Give up. Walk away. Try dying with dignity like a good little witch. Only fools try to fight the inevitable.

She picked up a rock and threw it at the cabin. Its harmless bounce off the porch wasn't enough to satisfy her so she threw a second, ricocheting the stone off the front door. She threw another, then another, hitting the porch swing with a loud crack, pinging the railings, and battering the window frames.

"Fuck you!" she screamed. "I'm coming back! Consider this a warning!"

Her knees went weak as the adrenaline rush faded. She fell back against her SUV, rubbing her spinning head. Her tantrum calmed her somewhat, even if it was embarrassing as hell. Thank the Gods her brother Rowan wasn't there to see it.

She glared at the house and whatever was inside it. This wasn't over. Oh, she was claiming that house. And even an invisible horned monster wasn't going to stop her.

She had no choice.

Chapter 2

F inn watched the female stumble down the porch steps. He grinned, kicking the door shut behind him. "Mission accomplished."

The human ran like she was on fire. Not that he was surprised, after all he had just dropped a chandelier on her. Well, beside her. He had no intentions of killing the female, just frightening her. It took timing to make sure she got out of the way, but he'd managed it.

Finn shook off his dimming spell, his form turning visible from hooves to horns. Now that the nonsense was over with, he could return to his exile in peace. A sharp crack hit the porch. He stiffened, his long ears swiveling back. Another crack, this one against the front door.

He peeked out through the crooked boards nailed over the front window. The female was pelting rocks, her cheeks puffed and eyes glassy. Finn hissed at her frustrated wails. She should have already disappeared down the road. Dammit, she was proving to have more back-bone than he thought. That did not bode well.

"Give up, human. Just go away." His claws dug into the windowsill, heart pounding as she paced in a little circle, then stared back at the house.

"Fuck You! I'm coming back! Consider this a warning!" She bellowed.

The female entered her vehicle. The engine roared, wheels crunched over dirt and soon she was gone.

But for how long? He bared his fangs. If she returned, he'd be ready. And next time he wouldn't be so nice.

"Finn?"

He turned to find Callum entering with a stormy gaze. His long tail lashing, the clacking of his hooves echoing off the high ceilings as he charged towards him, hand on the dagger sheathed in his belt.

"Was there a battle?" he asked. "The commotion was loud enough to wake the dead!"

"No battle." Finn jerked his chin to the wreckage behind him. "Just a chandelier."

"Dionysus's balls!" Callum cried. Slowly, he edged his way over, nudging the debris with his hoof. "She's not under there, is she?"

"You think I'm daft?" Finn chuckled. "A dead human brings other humans."

"Humans are crawling all over this place these days, so what difference would it make?" Callum chuffed. "First all those men with their boxes and furniture, now her."

"And I scared them all away. So, I'll take your praise startiiiiing..." He cupped a hand around his ear. "Now."

"These are the female's belongings, aren't they?"

"I...assume so?"

Callum's chest rumbled with a low growl. "Hells, she'll return from them, mark my words."

Finn's ears drooped, a pout puckering his mouth. "Getting acclamation from you is like pulling ticks off a deer."

"She'll return for them. Mark my words."

"And if she does, I scare her away again. Simple!" Finn slung an arm around Callum's shoulders, giving him a playful punch. "Come now, brother. Let's hear you sing my accolades. In the key of G please." Callum still refused to smile. A knot tightened in Finn's chest, his merriment dropping. "Did you take your potion, today?"

"Of course, I did. I never miss a day. I am fine, Finn. I swear to our God." Callum pinched the bridge of his nose. "But this sudden influx of humans makes me uneasy."

He wrung his huge hands, the crease between his thick brows deepening. Finn's tail flicked the air, his own unease rising. He slapped on a grin, trotting to the stack of boxes by the fireplace.

"I know what will make you feel better." He scooped up one of the boxes, plopping it down in Callum's path. "Who knows what shinies reside in that box? I know how you love your baubles."

Callum gave him a flat look. "Thieving? At a time like this?"

"At a time like what?" Finn replied. "And it's not thieving. It's preemptive salvage."

"You are sure she is not a witch?" Callum asked. His wide shoulders curled, turning from fierce warrior to timid mouse. "What if she has dark magic in those boxes?"

Finn cupped Callum's face, forcing his brother to meet his eyes. "She's not a witch. If she was, she would have hexed me. Yet here I am, limbs intact and flesh still on my bones."

"We lost so much. *I* lost so much," He clutched Finn's arm in a death grip, claws digging in. "I can't lose you too. Not to another coven... not to the Hunger."

"The Hunger is destroyed. And the coven is gone." He took the back of Callum's neck, tapping their horns together. "And I'm here."

Finally, Callum's lips curled, and a chuckle shook his barrel chest. "Lucky me. Trapped with your ugly mug for the rest of my days."

"Indeed. I wish I were you!" He gestured towards the boxes. "Now let's collect our bounty."

Callum's tail cracked like a whip. After a beat he smiled, then tore open the box, ransacking it with gusto. Finn's dread unfurled as his big brother hummed brightly, enjoying his hunt.

He turned for his own treasure trove but met a worn-out chair, its overstuffed cushions covered in faded roses. The faint scent of lavender and sage wafted from the fabric. Such a simple yet seductive scent. He leaned in with a deep inhale, eyes almost rolling back into his skull, then plopped himself down into its overwhelming softness.

"This chair is mine!" he declared, rubbing his back against it to imprint that beautiful aroma all over his flesh.

"Be my guest. I found her jewelry," Callum replied, his horns now covered in thin gold chains and sparkling bracelets. He canted his head. "So... this female?"

"What about her?" Finn asked, still burrowing himself into his prize. He scoured his cheek against the armrest. Oh yes, this was nice.

"Was she pleasing to the eye?"

Finn sat up, tossing some of his hair from his eyes. "You think I was looking at such things?"

"I know you little brother. You were *definitely* looking at such things," Callum snickered.

Finn jumped out of the chair, the brush of his tail bristling. "She was pleasing enough."

More like devastating. He had grown hard with just one look at her. The female was all supple curves from her breasts, to her backside, to her round belly, like the nixies he had laid with once upon a time. Bright copper curls were piled on top of her head in a messy bun, and laugh lines bracketed a full pink mouth.

But she was not so young that naivete still glowed on her cheeks. There was a twinkle in her blue eyes that spoke of experience. A well led life. He bit back the groan at the remembrance of her bare thigh when her skirt fluttered mid run. If she wasn't intruding, he'd consider a seduction, not a chase.

"Pleasing enough?" Callum laughed again. "Then explain why you're rubbing yourself against her chair like a cat in heat."

"It's a comfortable chair!" He marched away from it—and that heavenly smell—keeping his head high. "Do you know how long it has been since I sat in a chair such as that? Ages!"

"Then you won't mind if I..."

Callum's rump hit the cushions and Finn bared his fangs. No. That was his chair. *His* chair with *his* favorite scent that *his* female sat her beautiful, rounded backside in. His!

My female?

He froze, that dread returning. Callum drummed his claws on the armrest with a smirk. "Were you going to say something, little brother?"

"No." Finn flicked a hand at him. "Sit there all you like." *Even though its mine!* "I don't give a damn who sits in it." *Mine, dammit!* "I couldn't care less." *Get your filthy ass out of my chair, Callum!*

Fine, if Callum was going to commandeer his chair, he was going to hijack his treasures. He stuck his tongue out at his now cackling brother, then tore open a box. Instead of more baubles there was a large book. Its pages were yellowed and worn. Embossed on its supple leather cover was a circle filled with a maze surrounding a single star.

The wheel of Hecate.

A witch's symbol.

Ice filled his veins. He peeled backed the cover with shaking hands and skimmed the handwritten notes. No, not notes. Spells. *You're touching a witch's spell book!*

Finn recoiled, pulling away as if it would eat him alive. But how could that female be a witch? He had sensed their kind before, felt their power in battle. Nothing of the sort came from her. She was just a harmless little human. She had to be for Callum's sake.

For both their sakes.

"What have you got there?" Callum asked.

Finn kicked the box aside. "Just more ordinary human items."

Callum arched a brow, lips puckered. "What is vexing you?"

"Nothing!" he replied. "I'm merely starving is all."

"Again?" Callum laughed. "Always an empty stomach, you."

"And you should cook my dinner as my reward for scaring off that human." *Witch. You scared off a witch!*

"Fine," Callum said heading back to the kitchen. "We still have some rabbit downstairs. Build a fire and I'll cook us up a stew."

As soon as he was gone, Finn retrieved the tome from its box and dashed through the house. Breathlessly, he hurried out the back door and onto the deck. Just below sat a pond, its deep water overgrown with weeds. His hooves crunched over dead pine needles, the rushing sound of blood in his ears as he neared the railing. With a grunt he tossed the book. It gave a messy splash, bobbling before it sunk into the dark. He wiped his brow, giving one last look to the ripples left behind, a lump the size of a mountain resting in his throat.

"Just a human. Just some silly human," Finn muttered.

She *was* just a silly human. One that was fascinated with magic but had none of her own. Harmless and easy to scare. There was nothing to worry about. And yet that lump of fear remained, that voice still whispering...

Witch.

Chapter 3

*S*he was clad only in sunlight amongst the trees, one hand outstretched, beckoning him. Ribbons of fire lifted off her shoulders as the wind caught her glorious mane. Finn's heart thundered. He was eager to caress her, feel the heat of her soft skin. Power tingled as they touched, and he shot hard as steel. He laid her down in the grass and untied his loincloth, nestling himself between her thighs.

Her lips were upon his, sweet and hungry. His hips bucked, his arms wrapping around her. She smelled of lavender and sage and he needed that scent on his flesh, wanted that glorious creature surrounding him.

"Ivy," Finn moaned.

Her name was Ivy. What a suitable name. Just like the lush green vines that ensnared his homelands, she tangled herself around his very soul. Instincts as old as time whispered "Mine" as he thrust into her core, loving how her short nails dug into his back. His name sighed from her swollen

*lips. He would do anything for this female; catch the moon,
conquer the world, give in to her every desire.*

*"By the Goddess, Ivy." His voice was tight as he thrust
again.*

So hot. So wet.

So mine.

*He bared his fangs, seed rising to the quick. He needed to
come inside her, claim her as his own. He'd never be separated from his Ivy. His beautiful, clever...*

...Witch.

*The air grew cold and stale. Leaves withered from their
branches as the sun vanished. A chill ran up his spine as a
low guttural growl echoed around them. Something was
wrong, so very wrong. Eyes red as blood peered out from the
trees. Dark tentacles oozed from the dying trees, slithering
across the dirt.*

*Finn hissed into the darkness, flaring his claws. He
shoved Ivy away, shouting "Run!" but his hand passed
through her as if she weren't there at all. A disgusting powdery film coated him up to his elbow. His arm had gone right
through her.*

"Finn?" Ivy whimpered.

*Her color faded, blue eyes clouding over to a dull, mottled
grey. A deafening roar shook the world and her body shattered, ash raining down on him.*

*The tentacles lashed out with lightning speed, ripping the
scream from his throat. Needle like barbs burrowed into
flesh and bone, igniting a bonfire of agony. Death. It stole
upon him, taking him breath by breath. The forest grew*

silent, and the Hunger fed on his essence until there was only darkness.

"Finn!"

Finn's head whipped against the back of his nest. He swatted at whatever shook him, eyes opening to a kaleidoscope of browns and grays before Callum snapped into focus.

"Finn, wake up!" he cried.

"I'm awake! I'm awake! You're rattling my skull!"

He stilled Callum's arm before his horns flew off his head, a long sigh releasing between his fangs. He was drenched in sweat, and his stomach was brimming with acid, but he was safe.

Callum released him, sitting back on his haunches. "Usually I let you sleep through your nightmares but this one had you screaming. You kept calling "Ivy, Ivy." He arched a brow. "What do you need Ivy for?"

Great, he had cried the female's name in his sleep. Finn ran a hand over his horns. "Let's hunt some breakfast. I'm famished."

"No, you're not. You're never hungry in the morning. Haven't been since you were a fawn." Callum folded his arms across the wide expanse of his chest, his stern glare pinning Finn in place. "You have been vexed for days. What's wrong?"

Finn snorted. "I am not vexed."

Callum gestured to the gooseflesh on his arms. "You are full of shit. Out with it, little brother. I'll eventually figure it out so you might as well talk."

Finn's lips parted but his words stalled as Callum went to the rickety shelf beside the stairs. He plucked out a bottle amongst many, uncorking it and draining its contents down his throat. His potion. That was the only thing that kept him from falling into his phantasms of the past.

Dread coiled in Finn's belly. Gods and Goddesses if he told his brother that a witch was in their midst, not even that potion would keep him from his frenzies.

The sound of a door opening came from above, halting their argument. Soft footfalls crossed over them. Callum's breath grew clipped, and he grabbed Finn's arm, staring at the ceiling.

"It's not a poltergeist!" a familiar female's voice said. There was a pause before she spoke again. "You're so sure? You're a bazillion miles away in San Francisco. You can't feel shit."

Ivy has returned. No, that wasn't her name. That name was from a ridiculous dream driven solely by his long-neglected loins.

Finn held his breath, her conversation barely registering in his twitching ears. Soon her footsteps faded as she crossed into another room and both let out a long sigh.

"It's that damned human again," Finn grumbled.

Witch. She's a witch.

"A stubborn one," Callum replied. He puffed up like a bear, marching to the stairs. "Perhaps it's my turn to handle this."

Finn grabbed his swishing tail, jerking him to a stop. "No, no! It should be me!" He cleared his throat, hoping to banish his desperation. "I already know her tricks. I'll shoo her away."

Callum smirked, thumping his chest. "You just want to see her pretty face again, don't you? Maybe I wouldn't mind seeing it as well."

"Just let me handle this!"

"I have loins too, Finn."

"Cal!"

Callum yanked his tail free. "Fine, go on then. Gain a memory to touch yourself at night to."

"Shut up!" He stuck his tongue out at Callum just as he dimmed his form.

"I saw that," Callum said.

"Good! I wanted you to!"

Finn headed up the stairs, unsheathing his dagger. Witch or not, that female was leaving their territory for good.

Half of Ivy's boxes were opened and rummaged through. The invisible jerk had sticky fingers. She was about to storm through the house, find said jerk, and punch the shit out of them. But the memory of the falling chandelier slowed her rage. Instead of declaring war, she picked up the remains of her life.

Her jewelry box was empty, her books had been tossed everywhere, and every blanket she had packed had been taken. Pain radiated from her clenched jaw, her temper flaring again. Another glance at the shattered chandelier reminded her to keep her cool.

"They're just things. Only things." She slammed her fist into her thigh. "But they're *my* things, dammit!"

Fuck it all, this was too much for her already frazzled nerves. She had to go calm down, just sit in her car, take a few deep breaths, and regroup.

Ivy shoved the front door open, her hand passing over deep grooves. With a hmm, she pulled her hand away, examining what she had touched.

Runes. Not just runes, protection wards. They were carved in a swirling line around the door, more lining its frame.

"What the hell?"

It was like a game of Where's Waldo, wards popping up everywhere, the rafters, along the windowsills, and across the threshold. Powerful wards long dead after decades of neglect.

"How did I miss this?" she whispered.

Probably because the last time she was here she was too busy running for her life to notice them.

The sharp chime of her cellphone rang from her purse and she yanked it from the inside pocket. Rowan's name flashed across the screen. Her brother must have felt her distress.

Ivy hit the answer button, Rowan asking, "Is everything okay?" before she could say hello.

His bright warm voice lifted her spirits an inch. One look at the broken antlers and it plummeted once again. "I'm in a mood."

"Yeah, I thought so. Is it the new cabin?"

"New and cabin are two words I wouldn't use to describe it."

"That bad, huh?" Rowan clicked his tongue. A sign of his worry.

"This is what I get for buying the cheapest house I could find sight unseen."

"Does it have a pulse? Any life at all?"

Ivy pressed a hand to a wall, closing her eyes. No spark vibrated her palm. Every home had a life force that once upon a time she could harness. But this place was only cold wood and silence.

In a matter of time, you'll be just like this house.

"Nope," she said, hiding the tremble in her voice.

"Well shit," Rowan sighed. "Are you sure? Maybe you should try again."

"I may have no powers, but I can still feel a house's pulse. This thing is dead as a doornail. And there's something else." She chewed on the inside of her cheek. "Remember those stories when we were kids? About that warlock in the forest who used to summon all sorts of creepy crawlies and spirits?"

"That was just some crappy story to keep kids out of the woods."

"Well there are wards carved all over this place. Old as hell but strong ones. It was a magical dwelling once. What if this house was his?"

"Warlocks barely exist these days. It must have belonged to a witch or a coven."

Her teeth sunk deeper into her cheek. "One that maybe...oh, I dunno... summoned something?"

"Okay, now you're freaking me out. Explain yourself."

Ivy regaled him with her harrowing tale. After she finished with, "And that's when it slammed the door on me" There was a rustle, as if Rowan was sitting up ramrod straight.

"Ives, you're lucky that thing didn't crush you! Is it a poltergeist?"

Ivy read the runes carved in front of the threshold and frowned. "This place is warded against them."

"But you said they're old. A poltergeist must have snuck in. There's no other logical explanation."

"It's not. It's..." She shivered. "It's something stronger."

Rowan clicked his tongue again. "I think that's your anxiety talking there."

"I know my anxiety gets out of hand, but it doesn't make me delusional, Rowan!" She bit back her venom. "...Sorry. I didn't mean to snap. I just..."

Deep cold terror swelled inside her, whispering its honeyed lies. *You can't do it you can't do it you can't do it.*

"Ives?" Rowan's voice was a million miles away as she fell into her pit.

"I can't do this," she whimpered.

"Yes, you can," Rowan soothed. "You are still that badass girl who yelled curse words at the spirits we used to exorcise."

"That was before my powers were stolen!"

"Your trauma doesn't define you."

Ivy leaned her head against the window, staring out at the clouds, wishing she could float away with them. "I'm so damn scared, Ro. I'm scared of the fade. What if I can't bring this house back?"

"If anyone has a chance against the fade, it's you." She could hear his smile. "But remember what I always tell you?"

Ivy sniffled. "I can do hard things."

"Exactly."

Her fear melted into embarrassment, churning in her belly like lava. She wiped her eyes. "I should look around. Try and figure out what this thing is."

"Want me to stay on the line?" Rowan asked.

She wanted to give him a brave no, but in a tiny voice she snivelled, "Yes."

"Okay then. Let's go. Got your kit on you?"

She pulled a small wooden box from her purse, lifting its lid. She couldn't remember the last time she'd touched her exorcist tools but taking it along felt like Rowan was by her side. Salt, sage, some moon water, and candles were all still there.

"Yeah. I brought it just in case."

It was returned to her purse as she continued her exploration, phone pressed to her ear.

Slivers of daylight streaked through the window boards, highlighting the thick dust in the air. More overturned boxes made her blood boil and she clung to her fury. Anger was easier to deal with than fear.

"So how old is this place?" Rowan asked.

"The realtor said it was built sometime in the early twenties." Ivy kicked broken antlers from her path, making her way to the kitchen.

"Is it even wired for electricity?"

"Yeah, thank Brigid. It was apparently fitted a few years ago to try and get it to sell. But nothing is up and running right now."

"Hmm, old and no electricity. A ripe playground for a poltergeist."

"It's not a poltergeist, Rowan. Do you *want* to annoy me today?"

The kitchen was big enough to host a staff, and at one time it probably had. There were endless cupboards lining the walls, a large woodburning stove, and a place for a refrigerator. A small door was nestled beside the pantry. That must have led to a basement. In no mood to search a dark, dank, spooky room, she turned on her heels heading back to the living room.

"Any sign of the poltergeist?" Rowan asked.

"It's not a poltergeist!"

"I can feel it in my bones that it is."

Ivy smirked. "You're so sure? You're a bazillion miles away in San Francisco. You can't feel shit."

"Then it's my instincts talking. Nothing beyond spirits, poltergeists, and an occasional pixie has been seen on that mountain since we were kids. Hell, I can cross the veil and tell it to get lost if you want."

"You'll be wasting your time because it's not-"

The ceiling creaked, almost peeling Ivy out of her skin. She expected that menacing blur on the stairs, but there was nothing. She cursed, about to continue when she spotted a trail cutting through the dust coating the floor.

"Hold on," she told Rowan.

Ivy knelt, shining the light of her phone screen down upon the prints, heart in her throat. Heavy cloven hoof prints circled her boxes, shaped like a deer but the size of a friggin' horse. There weren't four sets of them, only two. Whatever that thing was, it was walking upright. She pressed her phone back to her ear.

"Ro, what do you know about demons?"

"Demons?!" Rowan shouted. "What exactly are you looking at?!"

A tell-tale clack-clack-clack whispered in the distance. The hair on the back of her neck rose.

"Shit!" Ivy hissed. "I'll call you back."

"After telling me you might have a demon in the house?! Are you crazy?!"

The clacking moved from the kitchen and through the dining room, growing louder with each passing second. Ivy lowered her voice to a whisper, "I got to go!"

"Ives, Wait! Don't-"

She hung up, shoving her phone into her back pocket. A flicker of movement passed the doorway to the dining room. She ran towards the wall of boxes, ducking down low, a good place to wait and...

What the hell was she planning to do? Yell at the demon to get out? She bit back her groan. Yes, that was exactly what she was planning.

You are *an idiot in a horror movie, Ives!*

The large blur moved into the living room, flickering with vague features; a shoulder here, a leg there, and horns jutting from what was probably its head. Ivy held her breath as it passed her, a swish of movement trailing behind it. Something bristly flicked her cheek, course like horsehair. It had a tail. At least she hoped it was a tail.

What else could it be? Its hairy dick? Ugh, don't think that!

She scrubbed her face as the blur headed towards the stairs. A shrill electronic chime screeched from her back pocket.

Dammit, Rowan! Ivy scrambled for her cell, but boxes rained down upon her in a tidal wave of knick-knacks. She rolled out of the way, and belly crawled to the door, only to run into something solid and unseen. A deep growl rattled in her ears, the blur towering over her, its breath fogging the air.

Ivy gave a weak giggle. "I warned you I'd be back."

Chapter 4

It snorted, almost as if laughing. Well that was somewhat encouraging. But when it lurched towards her, Ivy held out a hand for defense. That seemed to stop it.

"Wait, wait, wait! Let's talk, okay! Like just...talk?"

There was a soft, insistent clicking, as if it were tapping its hoof. Either it wanted to hear her out or it was looking for the softest parts of her body to tear into.

"Look, I'm still moving in." She quickly added, "But I'm willing to share the space."

It laughed for sure this time, a low contemptuous sound that drove deep into her belly. Her fear went forgotten and her anger returned. Yes, anger good. Anger helpful! She shoved herself to her feet. The thing fell silent, its glare unseen but burning.

"I'm not leaving!" Ivy patted her purse. "I have the keys to every door and I'm stubborn as hell! You keep throwing me out and I'll keep coming back!"

She was swept off her feet by strong arms, hoisted over something solid. She punched her fists against it, screaming, "Put me down asshole!"

A stinging slap hit her backside like a whip. The fucker spanked her! With its tail!

The thing carried her deeper into the house, further and further away from escape. Its grip was an iron bar around her waist, unbreakable, unrelenting.

Ivy's stomach turned to water. It was dragging her into some gore covered kill room so it can slit her throat and drink her blood.

"Don't kill me!" Ivy screeched. "Please don't kill me!"

A door blew open with a crash, as if kicked. Light stung her eyes, a wooden deck appearing beneath her. They neared a railing. Her heart stopped. It was going to throw her over into...

Into what? Sharp rocks? A pit full of snakes? An endless void where its monster pals would feast on her bone marrow?

It tore her purse from her shoulder. The world spun as she was lifted high and hurled over the railing. Ice cold water swallowed her scream, dragging her down.

Ivy pumped her arms, propelling herself up, choking and sputtering as she broke the surface. She tossed her hair from her eyes, looking up to the deck to see the blur storm away, her leather bag in its clutches. A thundering door slam announced it had gone back into the house.

She crawled up the shore, leaving a trail of water on the dirt behind her. A crisp breeze ripped through her wet clothes, chilling her to the bone. She shivered, body freezing but anger burning red hot.

Anger, gooooood.

Water gushed from her boots as she stomped her way around the house, dirt and leaves collecting on the cuffs of her jeans. She stormed up the porch steps and to the front door.

Locked.

Ivy banged her fist on the door. "Open up!"

No reply, naturally.

"Give me my purse back you piece of shit! My meds are in there!"

Her chest tightened as soon as the words left her mouth. Her medications,— both her Lexapro and Ata-rax—ones she needed every day, were being held hostage by an invisible dickbag. Frustrated tears pushed at the back of her eyes. She bit back the emotion with a sharp curse. *No rage tears, Ives! Get your meds back!*

The piercing shrill chime of her cell phone rang once again. She quickly took it from her pocket, checking it over for damage. Thank the Gods the phone guy talked her into buying that expensive, waterproof case. She hit the answer button, shouting, "The fucker stole my purse!"

Rowan's tirade ended before it began. "Wait...what?"

"The poltergeist! Demon! Whatever! It took my purse, tossed me into a pond, and locked me out!"

"By Hecate, are you okay?!"

"I'm all wet, Rowan! I'm soaked and its cold and that *thing* has my car keys, my meds, my wallet! Everything!"

"Okay, okay. Let's just try and think calmly here."

"Fuck calm! I'm done being calm! Calm never gets me anywhere!"

"Ivy, look-"

"I have to get back into the house!"

"That thing just threw you out and you want to go back in there?"

"I'm getting my damn purse back."

Rational thought had left the building. She went to her SUV and yanked out her emergency toolbox.

"Ivy, think for a second." Rowan's calm voice needled her. "You said it might be a demon. What if it is? If you go back in there it will either kill you or take your soul."

"I'm dying anyways. I got nothing to lose!"

"Do *not* talk like that!"

"Why not? It's true!"

"At least call Auntie Rosie and Lia and have them help!"

"They're only going to try and talk me out of this!" She pressed her head against her SUV. After a long breath, she steadied her voice. "I have to do this, Rowan. It's my life on the line. My life."

Rowan fell silent. After a beat, he softly replied, "Just be careful."

She yanked out her hammer. "I will. I promise."

Boarded windows lined the house's first story. With a swift game of eeny-meeny-miney-mo she picked one and pried a board free with the hammer's claw. Icy water dripped down her back and into the seat of her pants, but she burned. She was going to ride this maddening high, ride it until she dragged that demon/poltergeist thingy out by its invisible ear.

One board fell, then two, exposing a window coated with grime and cobwebs. She jammed the claw under its lip, pressing down on the handle like a lever.

"Stay angry!" she chanted. "Stay angry, stay angry, stay angry!"

The frame crackled and squealed, the pane jerking up. A puff of stale air hit her in the face. She shoved her shoulder under the window, pushing until she had an opening wide enough to squeeze through.

"Stay angry!"

Water squeezed from her coat, puddling below her as she wiggled her generous bosom and equally as generous behind inside. With a grunt, she hit the floor with a squishy thump. A cloud of dust rose, clinging to her damp face.

She had landed in what she assumed was the dining room, its ancient wallpaper peeling in strips. A huge table was all that was left, its chairs tucked underneath, all shielded by a filthy dust cover. The gentle tinkle of glass overhead signaled that another chandelier was waiting for her. Her anger faltered a second, but she sucked in a breath and headed down the hall hammer at the ready.

"Stay angry and bash its face in."

There was a soft clack of hooves, slow and pensive, as if pacing. Then they stopped, followed by some indistinct muttering. Ivy stilled, pressing her back against the wall. Now. She had to act now while it was distracted.

She ran into the living room, hammer held high. "I want my damn purse ba-!"

Her boots squeaked as she skidded to a halt, caught in a hypnotic mismatched gaze, one eye a deep cobalt, the other a bright sunny amber. That wasn't a demon. And it definitely wasn't a poltergeist. Hell, it wasn't even a human. Her weapon fell to her side as she gawked.

The satyr's deer-like ears flattened against his head, his long bull-like tail flicking. Grooved horns sprouted through his shaggy, caramel hair, curving over his head at a sharp angle. He looked just as shocked as she was.

"You came back?" His voice was as dark and smooth as chocolate.

He tucked her purse behind his back, as if that would absolve him of his crime.

"Uuuuh..." was her eloquent reply.

He had the face of a God, with high cheekbones, an aquiline nose, and a strong jaw dusted with scruff. And dear Gods, those lips. Ivy would have bet that perfect mouth had kissed, licked, and sucked its way through many a century.

"Uuuuuhhhh..." she repeated, her stare traveling down his chiseled bare chest to thick thighs.

Short velvety fur covered his calves. No feet. Just big, black hooves. A satyr in California. In Big Bear. When the hell did this happen?

And when did satyrs get so hot? Hooves shouldn't be this hot! Horns shouldn't be this hot! Why is he so hot?! This isn't fair!

Up went the hammer again, her grip shakier this time. "Give me back my purse." she squeaked.

Chapter 5

S he came back. That couldn't be possible. The female was terrified when he had thrown her into the pond. And yet there she was, soaking wet, leaves tangled in her bun, and blazing like a vengeful forest queen. Finn was in awe of her tenaciousness.

"Hand it over, goat boy!" she demanded.

Lavender and sage overpowered the pond water stench. It was the same bewitching aroma from her chair...from his dream. The need to touch her made him shuffle closer.

"Now!" she barked.

She is not yours! She's a witch! You're holding the proof right there! Her bag held a wooden box filled with witchy items. Items for his destruction, no doubt.

Finn hissed, his fangs elongating. The witch paled, seeming to forget what to do. He grabbed her arm, twisting it behind her back and the hammer fell. She stomped on his hooves, her heavy boots more of an annoyance than agony. So, he yanked her arm back harder, shoving her to her knees. "Returned to steal what's left of my essence, did you?"

"What?!" she cried. "What the hell are you talking about?!"

"You're scouting for your coven!"

"What coven? I don't have a coven, asshole! You're in *my* house and-" Another twist and she squeaked in pain. "I have no idea what you're talking about! Can't we just negotiate?"

Finn bent over her, murmuring against her ear. "Tell me why you're here or I take your arm."

When he nodded to the dagger on his belt, the witch's eyes went wide. "Okay, okay! I'm here because I bought the house! That's all! I didn't even know you were here!"

He jabbed a knee into her back, shoving her down. "And if you did, you'd hex me, wouldn't you?"

"I can't hex anyone because I'm powerless!" Her words were sloppy as her face squished against the floor. "I have no magic!"

"Powerless?" His grip relented slightly.

"Trust me, that is the last thing I want to admit but this fucking hurts and I can't breathe with my face jammed into the floor!" She groaned. "Your patron God is Dionysus, right? I swear to him I have no powers!"

Finn stared at the prone female, his tail twitching wildly. A witch with no powers. That was like a bird with no wings. She was utterly defenseless, or so she said. It could be a trick, but he still sensed no magic upon her. He released his hold.

The witch scrambled away on her rump, bumping into her wall of boxes, and cradling her arm to her chest. "I'm safe. I'm grounded. I can do hard things," she whispered, shutting her eyes tight.

Damnation, her fear dug under his skin with icy claws. He wanted to pull her into his arms, hold her until her breath slowed and her murmurs faded.

No, this is not your dream. Focus, Finn! "I don't have the patience to spill blood today Witchling, so calm yourself."

Her shoulders slumped, breath returning to normal. A scowl twisted her face. "How did you get here? Aren't your kind confined to the Mediterranean?"

Clearly, it didn't take long for her to find her backbone again. "I ask the questions, Witchling. You say you're completely powerless?"

Her glare was as sharp as a blade. "You think I'd put up with your bullshit if I wasn't?"

Finn ran a hand over his horns and snorted. "So you're hiding your shame from your kind."

"No." She raised her chin. "I'm here to get my powers back."

"Impossible."

"Wrong."

Dammit, why was her insolence so adorable? "When magic is taken it's gone. Forever."

"Well, I found a way to get it back."

"I know what I talk about little Witchling. I'm of the fae."

"Wrong again." She jabbed a finger at him. "Satyrs are earth dwelling fair folk, not high fae."

"Don't argue semantics!" Finn chuffed. Of course, he had to find the one witch that was well studied.

She pinched her brow. "What if we came to a truce? Live here together in peace. I won't bother you if you don't-"

Finn cut her off with a sharp laugh. "I don't make deals with witches. Especially arrogant little Witchlings who are too smart for their own good."

"Stop calling me Witchling! I'm a forty-two-year-old woman, not a child!"

His upper lip curled from his fangs and he sang, "Wiiiitchliiiiiing."

She wiped her eyes and Finn's laughter died. Was she crying? Witches didn't cry... Did they? Her sniffle confirmed that yes, witches cried. Much to his irritation, he didn't like it.

Despite the tears, fire was in her expression. "Listen goat-boy!" She slapped her hands onto her hips, pond water squishing from her pockets. "My name is on the deed! I sunk every last penny into buying this place!"

Finn rolled his eyes. "If you keep shouting like a banshee, you'll be sinking to the bottom of the pond again."

"I invoke the ownership of this magical dwelling!" Her voice echoed through the walls, loud enough to shatter glass.

The doors blew open. Boxes tumbled, and the remaining chandeliers swung as a mighty gale swept through the house. A crack of thunder shook the boards from the windows, blinding sunlight pouring into the room.

"What in the seven hells!?" Finn shouted.

Golden light spun about the witch in a tornado of chaos. She was pulled into the air, skin pebbled, nipples hard under her sweater. She arched in pure rapture, moaning, writhing, turning Finn as hard as steel. He had to take her, claim her, keep her as his own.

The wind stopped and she collapsed in a heap. Finn started for her then stopped, unsure if touching her was the best idea, especially now that he was tenting his loincloth. Quickly, he folded his hands in front of his groin as she sat up.

"Sweet Brigid," she giggled. "There *is* still life in this house!"

"Explain yourself!" Finn bellowed. "Explain what just happened!"

The witch climbed to her feet, wiping her dirt stained cheeks clean. "I invoked my ownership of this house! Suck on that!"

"What in Dionysus's balls does that even mean?!"

"I reminded this dwelling that I signed its deed. And it agreed." A smug smile peeled across her face. "You can't throw me out now. Sorry goat-boy. You got yourself a new roommate."

His tail whipped the air. "Take it back! Reverse this spell now!"

"Even if I wanted to—which I don't—I can't. The house has spoken."

"Enough of this!" He grabbed her by the collar, roughly marching her towards the door. "You will leave my territory right-gaaahhh!"

Magic hooked deep into his gut. It flung him across the room and into the toppled boxes with a crash.

"Woah! Okay, this is my first invocation of ownership and I didn't think the house would do *that*." She giggled, the freckles on her apple cheeks turning pink. "But that was friggin' hilarious."

The radiance of her mirth made her twice as vexing. Finn stood, yanking his loincloth in place before bowing his chest. "Fine, you won this battle. But the war has only begun."

She held out her hand, wiggling her fingers. "Just give me my purse."

Finn pulled it from his shoulder and with an angry snort he tossed it to her. The witch quickly rummaged through it, then sighed in relief before hugging it to her chest.

"What is your name?" he asked.

She smirked. "I'm not giving any of the fair folk my name. I'm powerless, not stupid."

"Would you prefer I continue calling you Witchling, then? Or I can think of worse insults while you reside here."

The witch eyed him a moment, then reluctantly murmured. "My first name is Ivy. But that's all you're getting."

Ivy. Her name really was Ivy. Just like in his dream. By Dionysus's balls this was not a good omen.

"Finn!" Callum charged in. "Why is she still here? And why are you talking to her?"

"Oh shit, there's two of you?!" Ivy backed away in horror.

"Callum, go back to the basement!" Finn demanded.

"I will do no such thing!" Callum pulled his dagger free. "How hard is it to scare away a puny human?!"

Ivy scurried away, holding out her purse as if it were a shield.

"Cal, no!" Finn warned.

Callum ignored him, advancing on the witch. "If your cock won't let you throw her out then I'll remove her myself!"

"Cal! Stop! She's-!"

Callum soared over Finn's head, slamming into the fireplace. Soot rained down from its flue on impact.

"... protected by the house," Finn finished meekly.

Ivy peeked out from her purse whispering a frantic, "Thank you!" to the ceiling.

Callum's eyes crossed and uncrossed before shaking his senses back. All color drained from his face. "W-witch? She's a witch?! Dionysus's balls, a witch is in our home!"

Finn ran to him, hauling him up and holding tight. Callum was either going to run and hide or throw himself at Ivy yet again. He did neither, only covered his head muttering "No no no no no."

Finn stroked his hair, murmuring a soft *shh* into his flattened ears. No potion was a match for seeing his nemesis in person.

Ivy wrung her hands, as she watched the exchange. "Is...he okay?"

"Get out!" Finn roared.

The witch ran, slamming the door behind her. The air was thick with Callum's whimpers, his head buried in his huge hands.

Finn pet his back. "Easy Cal. She's gone."

But he knew she wouldn't be gone forever. There was a desperation in her, a determinacy he had to battle to truly get rid of her.

"You should have killed her." Callum growled.

"She invoked ownership of this house. And we can't harm her."

"So, what do we do?! Wait for her to remove herself?!"

The idea struck so hard it almost knocked Finn over. He couldn't harm her, but he could make every day a living nightmare until she ran screaming. "Yes, but we won't wait. We'll... persuade." He hooked an arm around Callum's shoulder. "Let's get you another potion, and I'll explain."

Chapter 6

Pain.

Emptiness.

It peeled its insides, building a vast pit inside its gut. Eyes opened to tall blades of grass and the rough bark of tree trunks. How long had it been in slumber? A day? A month? An entire century? It didn't matter. The hollowness was unbearable.

Fill the void. Consume. Devour.

Branches above creaked. With a whomp, a massive figure landed, encased in swirling shadow. Its bat like wings flapped, raising a small dust storm before they folded against its back.

"Awake already?" It had a deep, masculine voice.

Yes, a male. It remembered him being male. In response it grunted.

The male knelt before it, holding out his hand, an apple resting in his giant palm. The shiny red skin was beautiful, enticing. Drool dribbled from its lips. It snatched the fruit, devouring it in seconds. But that wasn't nearly enough to fill its roaring belly, dammit.

"You look more like yourself today," he said.

It wiped its mouth, puzzled by his words. *I wasn't always this?* It examined itself. Slender arms crisscrossed with lines of black, grey, and putrid green. Fingers with jagged, dirt crusted nails. Human limbs.

The hunger returned, shaking the thoughts away. It doubled over, grasping its belly. *Feed! You must feed!* It pulled itself along its belly. Yes, it must feed. Hunt. Fill the empty pit that demanded its due.

The grass beneath its touch withered, life absorbing into its void. The pain was sated, bliss making it moan. Yes, that was what it needed. Not food but essence. Power.

"Still hungry?" the male asked. Golden eyes peered at it from churning trails of smoke. "Let me bring you something. A nice hare or perhaps-"

He leapt back as it swiped with newly sprouted talons. Green spittle dotted the earth as it hissed. He didn't understand. It wasn't meat it craved.

Its ribs cracked, bones tearing through its flesh. Thick ichor poured down its sides, hot and sticky as wiggling tentacles squirmed their way free. Its teeth sharpened to points, shredding its screaming mouth.

The male grabbed its shoulders. "Fight it! Don't give in!"

No. It was tired of fighting. Fighting was futile. There was nothing but hopelessness, loneliness. There was nothing but hunger.

The earth turned to dust as it writhed, its flesh thickening to leather. Eyes opened all over its body, hunting every angle for prey.

Devour! Consume!

With a howl its back snapped, spines bursting from each vertebra. Swelling. Growing. Starving.

Fill your void!

Yes. Take it all. All life. All power. Everything. It's the only thing that would fill the void. It pulled free of the male's grasp, tentacles greedy for leaves, roots, and insects. It sucked them dry, leaving behind greyed husks.

More, more, more!

The male bellowed but it paid him no mind, galloping into the forest. Sunlight spilt through the trees as they thinned towards a dirt path. And at the end of that path stood a dilapidated house. Its shingles were cracked from weather, its paint chipped and peeling. It smelled of age, dust and...

Life.

There were beings in that dwelling, ones that held more essence than anything that male could offer. A breeze whispered through the trees, carrying the faint scent of sage and lavender. It lifted its snout, the familiar scent tickling its mind with faint emotions.

Love. Joy. Heartbreak.

Charcoal on paper.

Drawing faces of loved ones.

Embracing arms giving security.

Safe.

I had been safe once. I had been...loved.

It wanted that house more than ever now, not for substance but to catch that beautiful emotion. Tentacles slithered onto the dirt road.

Love! I want to be loved again! I want it!

A painful jolt sizzled its nerves. It yelped, pulling all its limbs away from the road, cringing in the shadows of the trees. Another waft of lavender and sage ignited its wrath.

No! That house is mine! I need to be in that house!

Taloned feet slammed down before it, wings of shadow spreading to block its view. That damned male returned.

It hissed, baring its new sharpened teeth. Tentacles snapped, its hundreds of eyes glaring daggers. But that didn't scare the male away. He squared his massive shoulders, golden eyes narrowing as he hissed right back.

"Do not go near there. That was a powerful warlock's house once. It's warded from the likes of you. You think you're strong enough to get inside? Trust me. You're not."

Hunger howled to suck the life out of him. He was big, his essence throbbing with power. He would be rich, delicious. It lunged but the male leapt into the trees, branches bowing from his enormous bulk.

"Now you think you can take me as well?" he tisked. "Oh kitten, you're smarter than that."

The heat of anger flooded its body, sluicing the hunger away.

"Fuck you!" It shouted, voice raspy as a dust storm.

The twisting dark whisps around the male's face curled into what could be a smile. He crouched on the branch, his wings fluttering. "Ah. There's my bitch kitten, claws and all. Much better than whatever *this* is." He hopped back down, holding out his hand. "Come back with me."

It stared at his offering. It would be so easy to grab those fingers and take until his shadows faded away. Until no life pulsed through his veins.

No, it couldn't take this one. There was a promise made. A kindness done. One it couldn't remember. Dammit, why couldn't it remember?

"Please," he whispered, gently. "Come back with me."

There was no resisting his touch. It needed that almost as much as whatever was in that house. Flesh rippled, tentacles retreating inside its body. It shrank back to size, slipping its small hand into his. Warmth. Compassion.

Friends. We're friends.

The male let out a sigh of relief. Silently he led it back into the trees. The earth died wherever it stepped, filling the emptiness just enough to keep the pain away but the hunger still screamed. *Devour. Consume... Kill.* It glanced back to the house, running its tongue across its lips.

Its friend was right, it was too weak to take on the likes of that house. But only for now. It would rebuild its strength, grow large enough to overpower those wards. Then the house, and all who dwelled inside of it, would be in its belly.

Life. Essence. Love. All mine.

Chapter 7

I vy rubbed her temples, staring at the basement door. The electrical box was down there, the key to her main dilemma. She popped another slice of cheese into her mouth, chewing like her life depended on it. Thank the Gods her cheese stash was well stocked. It was the only thing beyond her medication that was keeping her sane.

Three very long days had passed with no lights, no heat, and her belly bubbling with acid. She had decided enough was enough. The phone call was made, and the electrician would arrive any minute.

The third electrician.

Electrician number one had run out as fast as his feet could carry him, screaming that he'd never work on her house for as long as he lived. Electrician number two had "mysteriously" ended up dumped in the pond. That's when she'd realized her unwanted roommates had been living in the basement.

Now there she was, standing in front of the basement door like a dope. For a second, she debated walking away and returning to the charcuterie plate she was making. But cheese and prosciutto—as tasty as they were— weren't going to solve her problem.

Ivy lifted a hand to knock but stopped when she heard soft murmurings below. Her much needed rage rose. The satyrs were plotting more shit, no doubt. Instead of knocking, she banged her fist.

"I can hear you down there! Open up!"

The voices stopped. Ivy rocked in her boots, waiting. When the voices resumed their conversation, Ivy took the skeleton key from her pocket, unlocking the door. "Ready or not, here I come!"

She flicked on her cellphone's flashlight, making her way down the stairs. Long shadows stretched across the walls, cast by branches hanging from the ceiling. Bits of glass, bottle caps, and feathers decorated their limbs. A mini makeshift forest. Not what she had expected.

"Oh no! No no no!" A satyr shouted. "You do not come into our chamber!"

It was aggravating how she could so easily recognize that beautiful voice. That was the sexy one shouting at her. Finn, his brother called him. Such a cute name for such a dickbag.

Ivy flashed her light towards him. "I told you I was coming down- Fuck!"

Finn came at her, his eyes reflecting like a cat's in her beam. She jumped back, something heavy hanging from the ceiling hitting her shoulders. It oofed and she turned her light, catching another set of reflecting eyes peering out from a hammock.

"Finn. It's touching me," Callum growled.

His mismatched gaze narrowed on her; one eye amber, the other cobalt, just like Finn's. But that was where the resemblance ended.

Callum was all roped muscle and sinew, covered in scars. His curved horns, chipped from battle, jutted from a wild mane of dark hair, the sides braided tightly to his scalp. Every inch of him screamed do not fuck with me and Ivy was planning on listening.

Callum swiped at her, but Finn snatched her arm, pulling her to safety. With a sharp "Woah!" she landed face-first into his chest.

Her fingers curled into Finn's biceps and she steadied herself. Dear Brigid, he smelt so good, like rain-soaked moss and winter. The sudden need to shove her face in the crook of his neck almost took her. She wanted to bathe in his calming aroma, wear it on her skin, let it envelop her completely.

Finn cleared his throat. "Enjoying yourself?"

The spell was broken, and Ivy hopped away. At least he couldn't see her blush in the dark. Or could he? Did satyrs have night vision?

Finn folded his arms, his mouth twisting into a smug smirk. "You look a little flushed. Are you warm?"

Crap, satyrs had night vision.

"I *told* you I was coming in." She rubbed her cheeks hoping her scowl hid the color that was now spreading down her neck.

"Beautiful timing, Witchling. We were just cleaning and sharpening our armaments."

Finn gestured to a lopsided shelf, where weapons were stacked haphazardly. Wooden handled daggers, two bronze short swords, and sturdy bows beside full quivers, were polished and oiled, ready for use. Those blades looked sharp. Very, very, sharp.

Ivy's stomach bottomed out. *It's just a show. He's trying to intimidate you.* She stomped her foot, pretending her anxiety were beneath it. "We need to talk."

Finn waved a hand, still wearing that infuriating grin. "No need for praise. I was happy to help you move in."

By helping he meant throwing her things into his favorite dumping ground, the pond. Two lamps, three chairs, and her microwave had sunk to its bottom, already. Yesterday, Ivy had dived into the freezing water to rescue her laptop. Alas, the victim was D.O.A.

Fire burned in her gut, but she took a deep breath. Yelling at him did absolutely nothing. "There's another electrician coming today, and he needs to work down here." When Finn clapped his hands like a kid in a candy store she groaned. "I know what you're thinking! Don't touch him!"

He pressed a hand to his chest with a dramatic gasp. "Me? I would never! Callum would you ever?"

"Never would I ever," Callum replied, daggers in his stare.

Ivy threw up her hands with a frustrated "Arrrg!" her phone's light flashing all over the room. The satyrs stilled, staring at her fingertips as if sparks would start flying. Slowly, she lowered them, palms out in a gesture of peace. "I just want to operate on good will here."

The two relaxed, but not much. They exchanged glances, Finn nodding while Callum hunkered down in his hammock with a pout. Oh no, that wasn't suspicious at all.

Ivy shook her head. "Whatever," she grumbled, starting for the stairs.

Finn blocked her path, a devilish gleam in his eyes. "You are being a very naughty Witchling, coming into my territory like this."

His tongue flicked across his lower lip. Oh man, was it... pointed? And just like that, her mind whirled with all the things he could do with that wicked tongue.

He caged her against the wall with his arms, their chests brushing. Even through her thick sweater she felt his heat. Her belly fluttered and her nipples shot hard as her mind went right back to that pointed tongue.

His tail swept over her thigh before wrapping around it. "Would a spanking be in order?"

The brush snapped against her in demonstration, stinging her flesh through her jeans. Ivy gasped, her core clenching. Dammit, it was just like last night's dream. Her on her hands and knees and him spreading her wide, pounding between her thighs while his tail lashed her ass until it was red and throbbing. Sweat dotted her forehead, heat spiking every vein.

Time out, Ives!

She ducked under his arm, tripping over her feet and turning her thoughts to baseball instead of his naked body. Satyrs were built for seduction. Sex was one of their primary functions. She knew this! But damn, she was not prepared for him to come at her both barrels.

Finn's cruel laugh shattered her desire. "Aw, the powerless little Witchling is flustered!"

She covered her bright red face. "Shut up, or else."

But he kept on laughing. "If you had your magic, I might be intimidated by your blustering. But you're helpless. It's sad, really."

Callum joined his mirth, their chortles a chorus of humiliation. Smug assholes. Acting like she was a pitiful wounded animal. Ivy threw herself at Finn, grabbed his wrists, and flung his hands around her neck.

"Hey house! He's trying to kill me again!" she cried.

Finn was thrown across the basement, landing with a tremendous crash. He rocked like a turtle on his back, groaning.

"Don't challenge me, Goat-boy." She shot Callum a glare, sending him cowering into his hammock.

"You want a war don't you, Witchling?" Finn snarled, through elongating fangs.

A loud knock echoed down the stairs. The electrician was early. Ivy waved Finn off. "Get out of here for a few hours or I'll have it throw you again!"

She ran up the stairs, leaving the declaration of warfare behind. Things were going to get worse after that encounter. She could see it in Finn's glare. Just what she needed, more chaos.

"You couldn't keep your temper down for even a minute, could you Ives?" she muttered to herself. "You just had to provoke him."

He was asking for it. She couldn't disagree. The way he laughed at her, how he sneered that she was helpless. She got enough of that from her own kind, she didn't need it from an arrogant basement dwelling man-goat.

On the third knock Ivy opened the front door, plastering a smile on her face. "Hi, there. You're here... early?"

The ruddy faced electrician nodded, hauling up his belt, then his tool kit. "I pride myself on punctuality, ma'am." He stepped inside and whistled low. "You got yourself an oldie but a goodie here, don't you? Bet you got your hands full, eh?"

You have no idea. She chuckled weakly. "Yeah, it's been a challenge."

"I bet." The electrician rubbed his chin. "Heard you've been having trouble getting work done here. Any... weird stuff happening?"

Well, word sure did travel fast in the electrician world.

She shook her head. "Nah. Nothing weird here." *Except for two satyrs squatting in my basement. You know, the usual.* "I'll show you where the box is."

She led him to the kitchen, the basement door sitting wide open. A lump splashed in her gut as the clacking of hooves echoed down the hall. The electrician turned towards the sound, but Ivy slid in his line of vision, coughing loud to cover the ruckus.

"Okay then. I'll just get started." He headed for the stairs, but Ivy grabbed his sleeve, yanking him to a stop. "Uh...ma'am?"

"It's pretty dark down there. And the previous owners left a mess." She stuck her head through the doorway, searching the darkness for traps. "Maybe I should clean up first."

"No need to be embarrassed. Can't be any worse than other places I've worked." He peeled her hand away with a reassuring smile. "You won't believe some of the stuff people pile up in their basement. Trash. Tons of magazines... dead bodies. You got dead bodies down there?"

"What?!" Oh shit, she never considered what Finn and Callum had kept hidden down there. A manic giggle trilled from her as she twirled a fly away strand of hair. "Dead bodies? Psht. What? Crazy! Heh...dead bodies."

The electrician laughed with her, thank the Gods. "Just seeing if you were listening. All right, I'll head on down. I should get this place up and running in a couple hours."

He clicked on his flashlight, swinging its beam around the basement. It looked all clear of bodies. Ivy deflated, relief finally setting in. "Great. Thanks for this. I've been without lights for..."

Finn, fully visible, peeked down the hall. The bastard was waggling his eyebrows. She waved him away, mouthing "No no no!" but he only grinned, mouthing back "Yes yes yes!" Wild hand gestures and grunts followed, Ivy desperate to shoo him away. The electrician cleared his throat. When she faced him, he was staring at her as if she were covered in lizards.

"You sure you're okay, ma'am?"

On went another fake smile. "Oh yeah! Everything is great! Uh, why don't I head down with you? In case you need something."

He started his venture down, undaunted. "I'm fine on my own thanks."

Ivy glared down the hall, finding Finn watching the entire scene. He wiggled his fingers together before throwing them in the air, mouthing "Surprise!"

Shit! She zoomed after the electrician, boots stomping on the hollow steps. With a surprised mumble, he flashed his light into her face, the bright beam searing her eyeballs.

"Ma'am, there's no need to follow me down. I got this."

Ivy twisted her fingers together, the flashlight's beam feeling like an interrogation. "Oh! Well...uh... I'm curious

how this all works is all. You know. Electricity and...
switches. Stuff... that is...electric."

Ugh, improv was never a skill she'd learned. She
should had taken theater in high school instead of art.

The electrician's mouth thinned. "Uh huh?"

"Yeah, sure!" She looked behind her, expecting to see
Finn hovering in the threshold. So far, no satyr attack.
"Maybe you can show me...uh... how it all works? You
look like a strong intelligent guy who knows his craft."

The electrician pinched his brow, staring up to the
heavens. "Lady, I'm married."

"Okay so I'll..." His words sunk in. "Wait, what?"

With a stern glare he held up a hand, showing off his
wedding band. "I've been happily married for twenty
years. I know lonely women like professionals, but there
are other places for those types of fantasies."

Ivy's jaw dropped. "You think I want to...I... what?"

"Look, it's not like you're not attractive. But I take my
vows seriously."

Finn's soft chuckle rolled from above. *That son of a...*
"Just go downstairs with me!" she cried.

"Hey! No means no!"

"I don't want to bang you! I just need to watch you!"

The electrician narrowed his eyes. "Why? You think
I'm going to steal your crap?"

"No! Gods! Just..." She sucked in a breath, her face on
fire. "You know what? I'm sorry. This was a stupid mis-
understanding. I'll leave you alone. Promise."

The electrician shot her a suspicious glower, watching her his entire trip down. As soon as he was out of site, Ivy barreled down the hall shouting. "Where are you assholes?!"

She found them in the dining room, Callum leaning against one of the tall windows and Finn perched upon the table.

"Little Witchling, you have to work on your seduction skills." Finn tapped his hoof on the tabletop, scuffing the shine she'd worked so hard to restore. "So clumsy."

Ivy marched up to him, shoving a finger under his nose. "What did you do to the basement? Set traps? Or some elaborate scare?"

He pushed away the offending finger. "I did absolutely nothing."

"You're such a liar!"

"And you are rather paranoid. Perhaps you need some rest?" His tail thumped the table as he straightened. "Yes. A good idea. You go rest, Cal and I will watch out for your guest."

"Just answer my question, Finn!"

"I told you I did absolutely nothing," His mouth twisted in a fiendish grin, revealing his fangs. "Or did I?"

"Oh, sweet Brigid give me strength." She turned to Callum, clasping her hands, and striding to him. "Can *you* at least give me a straight answer? Please?"

The enormous male went rigid as stone. He pressed his back against the wall, hissing as his ears flattened. His eyes flashed red.

Red.

Red eyes.

Oh Gods, red eyes! Hundreds of them had glowed in the darkness that horrible night. The memories hit her in a rush. The sounds of Aster's screams. Her hand slipping away, no matter how tight she had clutched it. Gone. Aster was gone.

Ivy's throat tightened as her sister's terrified face flashed in her mind. She wasn't strong enough to save her, was too scared. Too weak...

"You don't talk to him, witch!" Finn leapt off the table. Shit, did his eyes flash red too?

Aster's screams were deafening, rolling inside her skull. Ivy shoved her hands over her ears. *Stop! Please, please, please, stop!*

Finn herded her into a corner, slapping a hand against the wall to block her escape. He leaned in, their noses brushing. "You stay away from my brother." His voice was deadly. "You don't gesture at him. You don't even look at him. Do you understand?"

His eyes returned to the amber and cobalt she remembered. She had never been happier to see those eyes before than now.

Ivy swallowed, her mouth dry as the Sahara. "No talking to Callum."

Finn's mouth pursed, his fury fading. He studied her for a breath, then stepped away, his tail twitching. "Good little Witchling. Now off with you. Best you go guard that human."

Ivy ran, trying to shove her heart back into her ribcage. Once she returned to the kitchen, she pulled up a chair beside the basement door, her half-created charcuterie plate in her lap. Slice after slice of gouda was shoved between her lips as she stood vigil, trying to forget the horrible memory of her long gone baby sister.

It was sunset when the electrician finished. He ran as soon as he was paid, grumbling something about boundaries. Ivy was not only embarrassed, but so full of cheese she was sure she was going to puke. At least the electricity was on.

She headed up the stairs, phone pressed against her ear, regaling Rowan with her harrowing tale but leaving out her breakdown. She didn't want to give those red eyes any more real estate in her head. But they still lurked there, waiting for her to sleep, no doubt.

"So, you stood guard at the door the entire time?" Rowan asked.

"Yup," Ivy sighed. She waved a hand, clearing the dust the ancient heating system burped up.

"And the electrician thought you were hitting on him the entire time." Rowan giggled. When she groaned, it rolled into a raucous chuckle.

"Go on. Laugh it up. It's just another day for me at The Chateau de Caca."

"You got to admit, it is kind of funny."

"Why is it funny?" A floorboard creaked and Ivy bristled, expecting Finn. But there was no satyr or satyr shaped blur lurking. Paranoia was going to be her default state by the end of the month.

"It's funny because despite it all, you keep challenging one of the fair folk. It's like that exorcism when we were eighteen. The cabin over in Moonridge, remember?"

Ivy smiled even if she didn't want to. "The grumpy old ghost that kept throwing things and moaning..." She waved her hands in the air. "Geeeeet oooooout!"

"Yup, that's the one." Rowan's words were lost in his laugher. "And you said—and I quote—I will fuck you in the ear with a cactus if you throw another plate! I thought Auntie Rosemary was going to have a stroke when she heard that."

Ivy's giggle sputtered out in a mess. "It worked, didn't it? He stopped."

"Ivy Bennett. The only witch to strike fear in the heart of ghosts."

Her mirth faded. That Ivy was from a long time ago. When her biggest worry was if she could borrow Dahlia's car. When she had met every problem head on, despite her anxiety. *When I had my powers.*

She dragged herself into her bedroom, untying her hair from its bun. The long tangles fell down her back, as she slumped against the wall. *You can't do this. You're too old. Too broken. If you couldn't save Aster, you can't save yourself.*

Rowan cleared his throat. "So um, have you done homework on satyrs? Read up on their traits so you can deal with them?"

He'd sensed her emotion and changed the subject. She'd give her left foot if she could feel his again. Of all the things her powers had granted, the connection with her twin was the one she missed the most.

"Yeah." Ivy said. According to every book I read they're super territorial, great fighters, and even better lovers. Every picture has their cocks out. Just jutting from their hips like some sort of bizarre lawn dart accident."

"So, territorial cock monsters are in the basement."

"I am truly living the dream." She bit her lip. "I wish you were here, Ro."

"I know." Rowan cleared his throat. "I wish I were there too. And assignment or not, I'll be right by your side on Samhain, lending my power."

Ivy nodded, forcing a smile into her voice. "Sure thing. I should get some sleep. Talk to you later?"

"Always. Night Ives."

She hit the end call button then rose with a groan flicking the switch beside the door. The hanging fixture lit up, its shimmering crystals brightening her mood.

"Hooray, electricity." She gave a half assed fist pump. "Stay positive, Ives. You got this far. You can get further Just get some rest."

Despite its size, her bedroom was cozy. Unlike most of the house, she had taken time setting it up, making it her sanctuary. A queen bed donned her fluffiest embroidered comforter. Thick faux fur rugs and pillows were spread in front of the hearth for some fireside reading, and plenty of family photos hung everywhere. The smiling faces of Rowan, Aster, Mom, Dad, and her aunts boosted her mood. And best of all, a private bathroom all to herself. As long as she had this safe place to retire to, things would be all right.

She shut the door, turning the lock in case Finn decided to pay her a late-night visit, then kicked off her boots, her shirt following. A hot soak in the claw foot bathtub she had scrubbed the holy hell out of sounded like paradise.

Ice cold water soaked her socks, a widening puddle seeping from under the bathroom door. "Oh no. No no no." She splashed through the spreading lake, throwing the bathroom door open.

The blue tile floor was completely submerged. A gaping hole sat beside the clawfoot bathtub, hissing up a geyser. That was where the toilet sat. Or, used to sit.

Ivy screamed. She barreled down the stairs, socks squishing a wet path as she beelined to the front door. She had to shut the water main off before the entire second floor was flooded.

"Having troubles?" Finn was seated in her floral print chair, hands behind his head and legs crossed, waggling his hoof where it dangled. "Careful. Your feet are wet."

Ivy slid, catching herself before falling on her rump. "You suck!"

"Indeed, I do. Most seem to love that about me." His mouth curled into a wicked smile as he took in her leopard print bra.

A drop of water plopped onto her head. Then another. Ivy craned her head to the damp patch slowly spreading across the ceiling. "Ugh! I don't have time for this!"

She ran out the front door. Her toes turned to ice in the autumn air, followed by her half-bared torso. Maybe she should have gone back to get her sweater and boots. *No time! Get the water turned off!*

She rounded the house, tripping her way towards the pond. The water main was under the deck. Unfortunately, so was every damn rock, burr and sharp thorn in Big Bear. After groping in the dark, and a lot of cursing, her hands closed over the valve.

She gritted her teeth, chanting. "Righty tighty, lefty loosey!" as she turned the wheel.

Sweat coated the nape of her neck, dripping down her bare back. The valve stopped, the hiss of the water main silent. She shivered, leaning against the house as she picked the debris from her feet. At least the water was off. Now she had to figure out where Finn had hidden the toilet.

A soft glug-glug-glug whispered from the pond. Ivy's already aching stomach churned, bile creeping up her throat. "Don't look. You're only going to get madder if you look." But she didn't listen to herself.

There it was, solid white porcelain jutting from the black water, like a lonely iceberg. The toilet sank like the Titanic. All that was missing was Celine Dion's sad voice crooning over the air gurgling from its open seat.

Ivy fell into a sit, a thorn jabbing her ass as she landed. She banged the back of her head against the house struggling to yank the barb from her right butt cheek.

"Keep it together, Ives. Keep your shit together! Get your floor dry first. Then throttle Finn."

But the throttling part seemed far more satisfying. A final bubble rose from the pond as if mocking her. After flipping it her middle finger, she trudged back to the house.

Ivy was about to climb the porch steps when all the hair on the back of her neck rose. A chill swept over her bare shoulders, sinking right to her bones. Eyes were upon her once again. But not a curious gaze like Finn's. No, this one was empty. Cruel. She couldn't stop herself from peeking over her shoulder.

Red Eyes. Sweet Brigid help her, there were red eyes, hundreds of them, staring from the shadowy branches. A scream pushed against the edge of her teeth. but when she blinked, they were gone.

The trees swayed as the wind blew, revealing the empty dirt path into the forest. She scrubbed her cheeks. Shit, she was hallucinating. *Is hallucinating a symptom of the fade?*

She looked to her hands, half expecting to see through them. They seemed solid. After giving her fingers a confirmation wiggle, her heart started beating again. *Not fading yet. You're still good. You still have time. Right now just clean up the water.*

Ivy grabbed the doorknob, mentally counting all the towels she owned. It probably wouldn't be enough to sop up the mess, and she'd have to go into town to...

The door was locked.

"Fuck! You piece of crap!" She didn't wait for a reply, and rounded the house, once again in search of an open window to shimmy through.

"I hate satyrs!" she screeched. "And I hate you most of all, Finn!"

Chapter 8

The sun was warm upon Finn's cheeks, the sweet sound of bird song filling his ears. A breeze sang through the branches, carrying the rich scent of pine and earth. Autumn had already started its chill but there was still some heat left. A perfect day for a hunt. And by Dionysus, he was going to take it in.

Callum passed, giving him a nudge with his bow. "Are you coming, or would you rather stand there soaking up the sun like a delicate flower?"

Finn couldn't fight the grin. "Am I not allowed to enjoy the day?"

Callum chuckled. "Ah, so you *are* a delicate flower. Shall I weave you a crown of daisies?"

"If I recall, it was you who enjoyed wearing flowers in their hair."

"Flowers attracted good bed mates."

"And you needed an attractant, unlike me, who could lure them in with just a wink." Finn demonstrated, which only made his brother sigh.

"Here we go again. Can't go a moment without you boasting about your cock. Are we in such a fine mood today because of your victory?"

He preened like a peacock. Early that morning, Ivy had climbed into her vehicle and driven away. And she hadn't returned. Of course, all her things remained but that didn't matter. Finn's scheme had worked. She was gone.

But not from your mind. She might have left but his dreams remained. His second was more vivid than the first, her moans, her wet kisses, and the grip of her thick thighs around his hips. He had woken before he was satisfied and almost felt frustrated by her departure. Almost.

"Yes, that has put me in a very fine mood," he said. "Now, hunt me a celebratory feast. Venison if you please."

"You'll get a rabbit and you'll catch it yourself." Callum slapped his forehead. "Oh wait. I forgot, you're a shit shot. Never fear. I'll make sure you don't starve."

"A shit shot?" Finn poked him with the tip of his bow. "I am not a shit shot."

The placating smile was one only an elder brother could give. "Yes. Yes you are."

Finn rolled his eyes but laughed none the less. It was as if time had turned back to easier days. When their herd was plentiful and thriving. Carefree days of hunting, carousing, and laughter. When the most he had to worry about was what tree he planned to lounge under to watch the nixies bathe.

He followed close on Callum's trail, bow slung over his shoulder and quiver bumping his hip with each step. "You'll be singing my praises when I sniff us out a rabbit.

"I am singing it now brother. You resisted a witch's charms and have driven her out."

Barely resisted. Even now, lavender and sage haunted his nostrils. The dream returned in full force. Her copper hair unfurled and shimmering in the sunlight. Her channel tight around his shaft. Her whispers of "My Finn," as she came. Great, he was tenting his loincloth yet again. *Get out of my head, Witchling!* He scrubbed his nose across his arm with an angry grunt. He never should have fallen asleep in her chair last night.

"Did a bug fly up your nose?" Callum asked.

Finn sniffed then tucked his hands behind his back. "Huh? Oh, yes. A big one. With...lots of legs."

"What on earth are you occupied with, Finn?" Callum demanded.

Finn froze under his stern glower. He shuffled his hooves, cupping his hand in front of his groin. "Nothing! Just had some...puzzling dreams."

"Dreams?"

"Yes."

Callum looked at what he was shielding then smirked. He twirled his hand, coaxing more details out of him.

Finn cleared his throat. "Um, ones that involve-"

"Wait." Callum whispered, sniffing the air.

Never had he been so happy to be interrupted. Finn looked to the sky, mouthing a thank you to Dionysus.

Callum pointed to the bushes ahead. A rabbit hopped across their path. It scurried towards a patch of clover to nibble on, unaware of the two predators stalking it.

Callum patted Finn's arm. "This one is all yours, mighty hunter." The air shimmered around him and he disappeared.

Finn followed suit. He pulled his bow free, leaning against a tree to nock an arrow. Something drifted from above, sprinkling him in a fine dust.

"What in the Seven Hells?" He held out his palm to catch the substance.

Ash. Falling from the sky. There was no smell of smoke or fire, only earth and evergreen... and a stench he hadn't smelt in a very long time.

His gut twisted as he looked up to the tree's warped bare branches. They stank of death. Its life had been drained away, now only a disintegrating husk. Icy fingers of dread tightened around his throat, his bow almost tumbling from his fingers. Trees didn't just crumble to dust.

They had when the Hunger stalked these woods. No. The Hunger was dead. The warlock had destroyed it and he watched it die.

"Brother?" Callum whispered.

Finn gasped, reappearing with a pop. The rabbit continued to feast as if they weren't even there.

"Are you well?" Callum asked, voice still quiet to not scare their pray.

Finn gave the tree a long look. The ash had stopped falling. He took a wide step away from it, forcing a smile. But his pantomime didn't stop his pulse from racing.

Nothing more than a dead tree. You've seen plenty before. That's not ash on your shoulders. It's merely dirt that blew from its branches.

He pulled back his arrow, setting the rabbit in his sights. It was not the time for worry. It was time to lose himself in the hunt. Yet that tree loomed in the corner of his eye, a dark spectre. *It's just a dead tree. The Hunger is gone.*

He could still hear the screams of his herd as dark tentacles ensnared them. Their color draining, their faces twisted in horror as they were rendered to dust. With each life the Hunger took it grew larger. Hunting every satyr until all that remained were Callum and Finn.

Focus!

The silver haired witch's smug smirk as she carved pieces off Callum and fed them to her pet. How he had howled for mercy. And Finn couldn't do a damned thing while tied to that altar. Helpless as a fawn mewling for his mother. His hands shook and he gripped his bowstring tighter.

Stop thinking of it!

The bowstring snapped, slashing across his hand. "Fuck!". Finn dropped his bow and shoved his stinging fingers into his mouth. The rabbit took off, disappearing deep into the trees.

"That's it. You're going back home." Callum reappeared, scooping up the discarded weapon with an annoyed grunt. "Your head isn't in this hunt."

"I'm fine!"

"You may be fine, but your bow isn't. I'll catch us dinner tonight."

Finn snatched Callum by the tail, yanking him back. He couldn't go into the woods alone. There were things there that could ignite his rages. The remains of the altars they had almost died upon, trees that had never healed. *The Hunger.* "No! What if you stumble upon that place!"

The scars on Callum's face popped as he paled. His throat bobbed and he shook his head. "That place was not near our home. The smells were different, and the air was thin. Our territory is safe."

"But what if-?"

"Finnbar An Croí Láidir! Go fix your bow and your head!"

When his hooves started towards the house of their own accord, his pride shattered. Finn hissed at the use of his full name, powerless to resist the command.

He grabbed the nearest tree before he was whisked back home. "And if you have one of your rages and I'm not there to talk you through it?! Will you be so cavalier then?!"

Callum traced a scar's path from his brow and down to his jaw, eyes hard. "I took my potions this morning! I am not a fawn, Finn! I was a warrior once! Or have you forgotten!?"

Finn flinched, regretting every word that left his stupid mouth. "Cal...I'm sorry..." He nodded towards the dead tree. "The sight of it set me off. That is all. It reminded me of..."

Lines deepened across Callum's brow as he studied the tree, fingers tightening around his bow. For a moment, Finn hoped he would break it. That way they could both return home. Where it was safe, where he knew what to expect.

"It's only a dead tree, Finn. Just a victim of the last fire that crept through here." Callum blew out a strained puff of air, taking him by the shoulders. "The Hunger is dead. The warlock killed it."

Finn would have praised Callum on that declaration if it sounded like it was for him. Alas, it was one of Callum's many mantras to keep him from falling into the abyss.

"It has been ages since I've wanted to hunt on my own. Let me have this, Finn. Please." Slowly, Callum peeled Finn's death grip from the bark, placing his bow into his palm.

Finn's traitorous hooves began their trek back to the house. "Dirty play using my full name, Cal!"

"You're too dogged for otherwise." Callum waved him off. "I'll see you when I return. I'll be safe, I swear it."

"You better!" Damn his brother for commanding him home. And damn himself for making his brother feel powerless.

The top of the house peeked over the trees. Finn growled at the relief the sight brought. He should have been hunting with his brother, enjoying this day of peace. Instead, he had fallen into his own lunacy. His were never as bad as Callum's but they lurked in the corners of his thoughts. He usually let them pass through him like a summer storm but ever since that witch arrived, his mind had turned to chaos.

Ivy.

Ugh, she was invasive as her namesake.

Fuck the hunt and fuck her. He would raid the last of the witch's provisions out of spite. Finn's belly growled in approval, taking away the sting on his pride. Yes. He'd eat all those cheeses she had tucked away since those were her favorite. Then he'd drink her few bottles of wine. Hells, if he got drunk enough, he'd take great delight pissing on her bed as well.

The sight of her big red vehicle sitting in front of the house sucker punched all the hunger pangs from his gut. Finn stormed up the porch steps ready to fling the front door open and roar. The door wouldn't budge. He pulled at the knob but to no avail. It was locked. He dug through his pouch for his skeleton key. When he got his claws on that insufferable...

"Having trouble?" Ivy asked. "Because it looks like you're having trouble."

She was leaning against the railing, the golden glow of afternoon pouring over the luscious curves of her beautiful body. Freckles were spattered across her cheeks. He had never noticed them before. *And stop noticing them now!*

"You left this morning!" he snarled.

Ivy nodded. "Yeah. To get some fans and talk to a plumber."

"And now you're back!?"

Her defiant glare was almost admirable. "I don't know how many times I have to tell you. I'm not leaving."

Finn turned back to the door, to insert his key. "You are a foolish Witchling to think..." The keyhole was gone, replaced with a tiny jagged slit. "What is this?!"

Ivy batted her eyes. "I changed the locks."

"What do you mean you changed the locks?"

She spoke slow, as if to a child. "Well, I took the old lock out and put in a new one. There's a tutorial on YouTube."

"You...tube?" It must be one of her witchy tomes. He'd have to ransack her makeshift library and destroy it if it gave her such knowledge. "Give me the key. Now."

"Nope. I'm calling a parley." She gestured to the porch swing. "I'll give you a key after you sit and hear me out."

"A parley? Ha!" He rested a hand on his dagger. "Being so bold while we're not under your protector's roof?"

"Actually, we're on the porch." She opened her arms in welcome. "Go on. Try something. Let's see how it goes."

Finn glanced to the house. It was already thrumming with power, as if in wait. *Fuck!*

"Finn, I only want to negotiate. Nothing more," Ivy said. "The fair folk like to make bargains, right? I'm open to bargains."

Let's make a bargain, that silver haired witch had crooned to their chieftain. She had sounded so innocent at the time, so kind. And her coven had looked so benign.

"No bargains," he barked.

"Why are you making this so difficult? I'm willing to work with you! Can't you just hear what I have to say?"

"No! No matter how sweetly you present it, I will not be a plaything to a witch's darkness!"

"Darkness?" Ivy's lips tightened into a thin line and she took a cautious step towards him. "Finn, did witches hurt you?"

Her stare dug right to his core, demanding to see the scars he didn't wear on his body. He was naked under her gaze. Vulnerable. Helpless. And she sounded as if she truly gave a damn. The truth sat on the tip of his tongue, demanding release. That was more terrifying than the memories. He held out a trembling hand. "Give me the key!"

She shook her head. "Not until we negotiate."

"Give me the damned key, witch!"

Ivy wrung her hands as if considering it. After a moment she replied with a firm, "No."

Crimson rimmed the edges of his vision. His fingers tingled for his dagger. Damn the house and her ownership. He needed to slake the fury that was building inside him. He needed to spill blood. *But not hers. Never hers.*

Finn cursed, hand moving from his belt. Regardless of how infuriating she was, Ivy was innocent. And powerless. If he killed her, he'd be just as bad as the coven. And yet his anger grew, burning a path up his spine and into his brain.

He kicked the door open, the new lock splintering. Ivy pressed herself against the railing. Her breath was ragged, fear sharpening her features. The regret he felt at scaring her only incensed him more. "Looks like I don't need your key."

Ivy lifted her chin, her defiance returning. "So, you're going to have a tantrum? That's how we're solving this?"

"The only thing solving this is your permanent departure." He swept a low, mocking bow. "Good day, Witchling."

"Okay fine! Be pig-headed!" She circled her head with a finger. "But get used to this face!"

"Eat shit, witch!"

"Fuck you and your goat-legs!"

Finn stomped inside, throwing his bow against the fireplace. *She had no right!* He ran to the kitchen, chest constricted and his heart a fist. His legs shook, unable to take him down the basement steps.

He grabbed the lip of the counter before he collapsed, warmth dribbling down his cheeks. Tears. Tears for

Callum. Tears for the herd he couldn't save. Finn's throat tightened. *She had no right to ask such things.*

He had almost spoke of what happened that night, almost indulged her with his shame. Never. That confession would die with him and Callum alone.

Footsteps dashed into the house, heading up the stairs, clipped and clumsy. Finn ran his arm across his wet face, regaining himself. Dionysus only knew where that damn witch was off to now. To cause him more grief no doubt. Well, if she thought she was going to get the last word in, she was sadly mistaken.

He followed her path, curses ready on his lips. A slam came from down the wide hallway. She had gone to her bedchamber. Good. There was no place to run if she had shut herself up there. He reached for the knob then stalled as her boots clomped back and forth, in a manic parade.

"I can do hard things! I can do hard things!" she chanted.

A strange incantation. Maybe she wasn't as helpless as she claimed. After all, he had caught her carving runes and murmuring spells around the house. Conceivably, she had ways of sparking her magic. Perhaps she was doing that right now.

He cracked the door, watching Ivy reach for one of the small containers on the table beside her bed. With shaking hands, she flicked off the lid, pouring out a tiny white pellet and throwing it into her mouth.

Ivy winced when she swallowed, then fell back onto her bed with a sigh. "Please work fast, Atarax."

Potions. That was the source of her power. He fixed onto those amber colored jars, a devious smile creeping over him. Those potions helped her keep her strength.

They had to go.

And she would follow.

Chapter 9

Ivy poked at the fire in the living room, head droop-ing. She called this one "Gigantor" since she could sleep in it with room to spare.

A fireplace was the heart of a home and crucial to her ritual so, she had spent the remainder of her day cleans-ing, warding, blessing, and lighting each hearth. All six of them.

By the time she finished, it was well past midnight, and she was caked in soot. She wiggled her fingers, sing-ing "Cinderelly Cinderelly, night and day is Cinderelly..." then chuckled to herself.

She hadn't seen Finn for the rest of the day, which was a small perk. All right, changing the locks on him was a stupid idea, driven purely by spite. But she was sincere on the negotiations. Him going all berserker mode wasn't expected. Thank Brigid he stayed away from the plumber. Finn was probably too butt hurt to cause any-more mischief after their talk.

*That wasn't just a bruised ego, Ives. You saw his face
when you asked about his past.* It was only a split second
but there was no mistaking his despair. His horror. That
had shaken Ivy more than his temper. An angry satyr she
could handle and understand but the deep wound exposed in that moment was a whole other matter. Witches
had hurt him. Just like they had hurt her. *And if anyone
understands how evil a witch could be, it's you.*

Screaming "Fuck you and your goat legs" at a trauma-
tized male wasn't her best moment. What she should
have done was remain calm and continue to negotiate.
Maybe offer Finn something he couldn't refuse.

Like sex? It wasn't the first time she considered playing what's under the satyr's loincloth. Finn was hot as
hell and had an animalistic lure that she was drawn to like
a moth to a bug zapper. Not to mention she hadn't had a
good lay in over a year. But regardless of the cobwebs on
her vagina, she refused to imagine how big his dick was.
He's a satyr. It's probably huge.

Her core clenched. Sweet Brigid, if she had another
dream about him tonight, sleep would lose all priority to
finding which box she had packed her vibrator in. Something about this house made her way too horny. Not in
general, but for Finn in particular. *Couldn't you have erotic
dreams about Gerard Butler, instead?*

Exhaustion clung to her eyelids, her limbs like sand-
bags. She trudged up the stairs to her room desperate to
leave this embarrassing day behind her. She flicked on
the light as she entered, the merry crackle of the fire

soothing her frayed nerves. The two huge box fans she had picked up were roaring away, having dried most of the flood, but that damp musk still stuck in the air, thick and stale. She ignored it, stripping off her ash stained clothes, giving herself a quick wash in the sink, and pulling on her fluffiest pajamas.

Tomorrow she'd reopen negotiations, this time with logic instead of trickery. Now, sleep was calling. She pulled back her comforter, eager to lay her head on her brand-new pillow and let that brand-new mattress cradle her into dream land. Her one big splurge during this shit-show of a year. She burrowed in, a long sigh releasing the tension in her shoulders.

A high-pitched whistle cut through the air. The trilling rattled the walls with sour notes, trailed by the stomping of hooves. Ivy's skin crawled with each toot and whistle.

Was that a damn pan flute?

Another squeal sent needles right into her ear drums.

Yup. It was.

And to think she was feeling horny for him only a few seconds ago. This concert was what she deserved for being suckered in by his pretty face and sad eyes.

"Asshole!" Ivy shouted from under her mountain of blankets.

A sharp bang made the door bow. She screamed, expecting an aggressive break in, but the shrill crooning resumed, moving back and forth outside her room.

"That's it. I'm going to kill him. Just wrap my hands around his throat and squeeze." She grabbed her robe from the foot of her bed, sliding her arms through the sleeves before knotting her long hair on top of her head.

She threw open her door, to Finn skipping up and down the hall like some nightmarish version of Fantasia. Whatever angst he experienced earlier was gone, replaced with an arrogant grin and shrieking flute. His skin looked silver in the moonlight, ethereal and ghostly. When he shot her a wink, his eyes reflected with shimmers of blue and gold. The sight would have been eerie if it wasn't so damn ridiculous.

"Really?" Ivy asked. "You're really doing this?"

Finn stopped in mid frolic to sweep a low bow. "Practicing one's craft is never a waste." Spittle flew from his lips as he blew over his flute, his eyes squished tight in concentration. Skip skip, tweet! Skip skip, toot toot!

"I have ear plugs!"

"Then my musical escapades shouldn't be an issue,"

Skip skip tweet tootie toot toot toot!

Ivy rubbed her head as it started to throb. "I'm serious! This is a waste of time!"

Finn stopped to bat his eyes. "So why the complaints?" He puffed out a particularly sour note right in her face, blowing back her hair.

Ivy stomped to her room, retrieving her ear plugs from her nightstand. She returned, blocking Finn's path to make a show of putting them in.

"See? I can't hear you! You can't bother me now!"

The brush of his tail flicked her chin as he passed. Ivy swatted it, sputtering as the bristles tickled her lips.

Through the orange foam expanding in her ears, he sang, "I told you, this was war!"

"I didn't want this war!"

"You should have thought of that before you decided to stay!"

Skip skip, toot toot, squeeeeeal!

"I'm not leaving!" she screeched. "Spite is my motivator! Spite puts me in motion! I eat spite for breakfast!"

His tail flicked her cheek as he danced by her for the hundredth time. "Then why are you crying like a child?"

Ivy wiped a hand across her damp cheek. "Fuck!" She was rage crying. Her face heated and she ran back to her room, slamming the door behind her. He saw her cry, saw her weak. Now he'd never give up.

The concert raged on, scraping out each tear until the collar of her pajamas was drenched, and her eyes burned.

"I can do hard things. I can do hard things." *He's going to win, you know. He's ancient, stubborn, and strong. And what are you? A powerless witch with no resources.*

Ivy threw open the drawer to her nightstand, going for her bottle of Atarax.

There you go. Reaching for your meds. Your fucking crutch.

"They're not a crutch!"

It had taken her years to admit she had an anxiety disorder and even more to get the courage to get medicated. Her kind constantly told her that such things were strictly for weak humans.

Fuck those haters. She knew what worked. Witchcraft and science could coexist. Her medication was proof.

And now they were missing.

Ivy yanked the drawer from the nightstand, dumping it upside down. Everything tumbled to the floor in a pile, pencils, notepads, various odds and ends. But no pill bottles. She ran to the bathroom, throwing open the medicine cabinet, tearing through the packed shelves.

Nothing.

One daily medication plus a rescue drug had disappeared into thin air. A sob detonated from her lips and she slapped the sink. "Where are they?!"

A vinegary note blew past her earplugs, tearing her open with its barbed claws. Finn. That bastard had stolen her medication. They were probably dissolving at the bottom of the pond at that very moment.

Ivy clutched the cool porcelain, convulsing as anxiety buried her in its avalanche. "Get angry! Get angry! Please get angry!"

But she couldn't. Not while bleak reality was staring her in the face. The fade was coming for her. There was no stopping it thanks to that satyr dancing in her hallway. Acid filled her mouth and soon she was heaving the contents of her stomach into the sink until she was hollow. Medications returned her to her baseline. They allowed her to live, allowed her fight. But her last line of defence was gone.

Her legs gave out, hands pressed tight over her ears. "I'm going to fade away alone in this fucking house! Oh Gods oh Gods oh Gods no no no no no!"

She cried like a baby on the godsdamned bathroom floor. The fear was never going to go away. Not until she was cold in her grave.

"No! This will pass. It will pass. It always passes! Oh Gods please let this pass!" she wept through the screaming flute. "Ground yourself! What do you see, Ives? The sink. That's one. The shower head, that's two..."

After naming everything inside her bathroom, her panic attack did indeed pass. The steely grey of morning light trickled across the tiles when she finally gained the strength to sit up.

With a groan, she snatched a towel off its rail to dry her face, pulling her earplugs free to listen for Finn. Silence greeted her. Her heart slowed and she shoved herself upright, knees still quivering.

"Finn?" she called. Dammit, why was she calling for him? It's not like he'd have the decency to answer. She ventured to the hall, finding it empty. That wasn't enough to calm her. She tiptoed down the stairs, listening for any sign but all was silent.

She took a deep breath, dragging herself towards the kitchen, and his subterranean territory. Leaving well enough alone would have been the smart choice but her mind wasn't going to rest until she confirmed Finn was asleep. Then she could lock her bedroom door and try to get a little rest before starting another day in Hell.

No one was in the kitchen. But the cabinets were open, each one completely emptied. She blinked heading inside.

"What the...?"

Her toes brushed something cold and jagged. Shards of broken ceramic and glass littered the floor, arranged like a moat in front of the doorway. The familiar pattern of red and orange leaves covered several jagged pieces. Her plates. Her bowls. Every teacup and glass she owned. They had all been destroyed. Ivy's wrath returned. Powerful. Comforting. Glorious.

"You want a war, Finn? You'll get your damned war."

The door crashed open, the din of pots and pans clanging together in a horrendous rhythm. Finn bolted up, blankets tangled around his horns. The dull thump and shout announced that Callum had fallen from his hammock.

"What in fucking seven hells?!"

"Rise and shine boys! The daylight is a burning!" Ivy shouted, followed by a rapid-fire bang-bang-bang. She stood on his threshold, spoon in one hand, and pot in the other, singing, "Oooooh! If I'm not sleeping, neither are you! If I'm not sleeping neither are yoooooooooou! La la la la!" She rattled the spoon inside the pot with a flourish.

Callum's ears flattened against his skull. "What is she doing?! Is she casting a hex?!"

"This is my wake-up soooooooong! I haaaaaate you booooooooth!" Ivy crooned at the top of her lungs.

Finn spared a glance up the steps, scowling as she danced a little jig across the doorway. "...Singing would be my guess."

"You stole my meeeeeeeeds!!" Ivy warbled. "And now I'm piiiiiiiissed!"

Meds? What in the name of Dionysus were meds? "I don't know what you're talking about!" Finn shouted. "Now stop this foolishness and get out!"

"Why?" Ivy said in her normal voice. "You said this was war! Well, I'm warring, asshat!" She lifted her pot, giving it a sharp thwack and sang, "And I hold a gruuuuuuuuudge!"

Callum pressed his back to the wall, a craze gaze set on the doorway. "Make her stop." A shroud of madness fell over him.

"Cal, just breathe." He inwardly cursed as he raised his voice over Ivy's din. "Breathe and I'll fetch you a potion."

He dashed to the shelf, rummaging through the bottles to find the right tonic, one that would put Callum into a dreamless sleep. Empty bottle after empty bottle found his hands. There had to be a fresh one. He had just brewed some yesterday.

"You said she was gone Finn!" Callum shoved his hands over his ears. "But here she is, hexing us!"

"It's not a hex. She's only singing." He couldn't hide the tremor in his voice. "Dammit, where did you move your potions?!"

Ivy sang another round, thwacking away at her pot and stomping her feet. Callum howled, dragging his claws over his face. "She sounds like them! The singing! They sang so loud! Gods above, they're going to skin me alive again!"

The basement shook as Callum threw himself against the bricks, horns scraping, skin tearing, frantic to dig himself to freedom. "I can't stay here! I can't! I can't! Make her stop! Please!"

"Callum! No!" Finally, Finn uncovered a full bottle.

Callum wailed, thrashing and biting, his tail striking Finn like a whip. Red welts rose under the beating, raw and stinging, still Finn pulled his brother to his nest shoving him into the pile of blankets. "Easy Cal. Easy. You're safe. She's just making noise. Nothing more." He uncorked the potion with his teeth. "Drink. And promise me you won't do yourself any harm."

His fight drained away as Finn offered him the bottle. It was guzzled in a breath then Callum burrowed into Finn's nest, throwing a blanket over his head. His petrified whimpers were like knives.

Finn tucked a blanket around Callum, teeth gnashing. This is what that coven had reduced his fierce hearted brother to. This was the curse of their evil. Another klang-klang-klang passed the doorway, Ivy shouting, 'You give up yet, goat boy!?"

The roar he released was deafening. Callum grabbed his hand, but he pulled away, marching to the foot of the stairs. "I'm finishing this, Witchling!" he thundered.

Chapter 10

A roar rolled up the stairs, deep, guttural, and filled with a fury that Ivy never heard the likes of before.

"I'm finishing this, Witchling!"

Hard slow clacks traveled up the stairs. Finn's shadow filled the door, two glowing red orbs glaring at her from the darkness.

Red eyes.

Her spoon fell from her fingers. She couldn't feel her skin, couldn't breathe as Finn emerged from the basement, fangs glistening, and razor-sharp claws flared. Panic took the driver's seat, tearing all rational thought to shreds.

"You frightened my brother!" he bellowed.

She screamed, shattered dinnerware crunching under her feet as she ran. Agony shot up her legs, blood making her toes warm and sticky. Logic told her to stop before she hurt herself further, but fear forced her to keep moving. She dashed down the hall, lungs tight with another scream. She had to get out, get as far away from this demon as she could. Get away from those horrible red eyes.

"Get back here, witch!"

Ivy looked over her shoulder to see him right on her tail. The wind rushed from her lungs as the dining room table slammed into her middle. sickly green spots danced under her eyelids her face slapping against the smooth wood.

Finn was upon her, pinning her to the table with his hips and seizing her wrists in one fist. She tucked her face against her shoulder, but he grabbed her chin. "Face me witch!"

"No no no no no! I just...I...Oh Gods, please don't!" She squeezed her eyes even tighter. "Your eyes!"

"What about them!?"

"Your eyes are red! Please don't make me look at them!"

Finn's hold on her wrists loosened. He didn't claw her. Didn't bite or strike. "They're...they're gone now."

She held her breath, daring a peek. No red eyes, only cobalt blue and amber. More tears streamed down her face in a relief that only lasted for a second. "You're going to kill me now, aren't you?"

He released her, dragging his hands through his hair. "You know I can't harm you, Witchling. Not while this house is on your side."

"Oh...yeah." Logic finally returned. She swallowed, her cheeks flushing. "Then what was your plan?"

"I was too furious to come up with one. I suppose I just had intentions to scare you."

"Well..." A sad laugh escaped. "A-plus on that one, goat boy."

He snorted, the corners of his mouth rising. "Indeed."

Holy crap they were talking with no threats. Finn backed away, then looked down to her feet and winced. "You cut yourself, horribly."

Her toes were covered in dark crimson. The pain returned and fight or flight took over once again. "What did I do to myself?"

He held up his hands as if to calm her. "Witchling, you're in a panic."

She was, but she wasn't listening as her anxiety took over yet again. "I'm going to bleed out alone in this fucking house and no one will find my body! I'm a Gods dammed idiot! Why did I run!? Why am I so fucking stupid?!

"Ivy." He used her name. Not witch or Witchling but Ivy, said in a steady, comforting voice. She shut her mouth daring to meet his gaze. No fury. No hatred. Only sweet concern. "I'm going to touch you," he continued. "May I touch you?"

Ivy nodded before the answer even touched her brain. Finn's hands slipped under her backside and he scooped her up, plopping her down on the table in a sit. With gentle hands he brushed her sweat drenched hair from her face. She wanted to lean into his touch, press her cheek into his palm and close her eyes until the world was forgotten.

"Breathe with me." Finn made a show of taking a long breath, his broad chest expanding, then deflating.

Ivy mimicked him, precious oxygen filling her needy lungs. Another breath and the black that haloed her vision faded. Another and her belly unclenched.

"You're not going to bleed to death," he said. "And you won't be alone. I'm here."

"Says the satyr who wants to kill me."

The tiniest of smile quirked his lips. "Ah, there's that bothersome Witchling. I wondered where she went."

She sniffled. "Get bent."

"Only after another breath. With me now."

Inhale.

Exhale.

He was touching her. She usually couldn't stand anyone touching her when she spiraled but Finn was pure comfort. Gentle and tender, as if he had done all this before. Her senses returned; the hard table under her, the dusty scent of the old heater running, the crackling of the fire. Ivy slid her hand over her chest, feeling each breath as it traced through her lungs.

"Are you grounded yet?" Finn asked.

She took one more deep breath for good measure. "I'm... better."

"Good," he replied. "May I look at your feet?"

"...Yes."

Finn set his jaw then knelt, taking her foot into his hands. "It looks far worse than it is."

Ivy tensed, letting out a little hiss as her skin turned to fire "Sure as hell doesn't feel like it,"

"It will feel better after I pull the glass out."

"You're going to what?! Shouldn't we call an ambulance?!"

"A what?"

"A...um...healer! I need a healer!"

"I know the healing arts. I can do this."

"Why should I trust you?"

Finn unsheathed his dagger, sliding it over the table until it rested beside her hip. "Take it. If I do anything adverse, stab me."

A short manic giggle shook her. "Are you serious?"

"Will it give you peace of mind?"

"...Yes."

He jerked his chin to the dagger. "Then I am."

Slowly, she curled her fingers around its wooden handle. It was still warm from resting against his body.

Finn sat on his knees, tail swishing in uneasy circles. Other than that, he was perfectly still, watching with sharp eyes as dark as the night sky and bright as the summer sun. She could get lost in a gaze like that. Fall in with a smile and never return.

Ivy hugged the dagger to her chest. "Okay then."

He rose, cupping her cheek, the tip of his thumb grazing her jaw. "I'm going to fetch my healer's pack. Don't run away. You'll only do yourself more harm."

He turned to leave but she grabbed his wrist. "Why are you doing this? Why are you helping me?"

He ran a fang over his lower lip. "I don't like seeing others suffering. And clearly you are... In more ways than one." Then he disappeared down the hall.

Ivy sighed. She could chance it and limp out to her car, but he was right, it would only make things worse. So, she stayed put like a good patient, the dagger pressed against her heart.

Finn returned with a leather pouch, emptying its contents. Strips of linen, a small towel, a wooden canister, and a glass vial filled with a glowing green liquid. She watched as he lined up his items, nose scrunched, and lips pursed in studious concentration.

"What is that?" She pointed to the potion.

"That is to clean your wounds." He uncorked it and held it under her nose. "And to numb the pain."

Ivy inhaled the herbal earthiness, clean and fresh as the land itself. "Tea tree and oak bark," she said, taking another whiff. "Maybe some calendula?"

"And some fae magic you can't find on this plane. You know your healing herbs."

"I'm a cottage witch. It comes with the territory."

"Ah. So that is what you are."

Ivy tensed, waiting for the insult to come. Everyone knew that cottage witches were the weakest of her kind, even the fae. But he didn't quip, only picked up his towel and wet it with the potion. The cloth flickered bright green then faded before he dabbed it across her sole.

Ivy squealed as fire shot through her nerves. "Oh shit mother fucker piss! Should it hurt this much? Crap, what if it doesn't work?! Shit!"

His hand was on her cheek again, slowing her pulse. "It will sting while I apply it. But it will work. I'll be quick."

She nodded, wishing he would keep his hand right there while he worked. Her own personal sedative. Another wave of pain made her howl. "Bitch bastard fuck that stings so much!"

"You do have quite a mouth on you, don't you?" Finn replied.

"You lose all decorum when you hit forty, goat boy," Another buzz of torture shook her nerves. "Oh, jumping Jeebus on a pogo-stick!" Finn's low chuckle made her smirk. "So, this is funny?"

"I'm merely impressed with your creative swearing," he replied. "It's far better than your singing."

A tiny chuckle escaped. "Like you're one to talk. Did you hear yourself play that flute?"

"I assure you my horrible playing was on purpose." Gently, Finn took her other foot, cleaning that one down as well.

Ivy squirmed. "I call bullshit on that."

A crooked grin lit his face. "Witchling, I could seduce you with only my music if I so wished."

Oh wow, that smile. She was sure he could seduce her with just that. Another shock jolted her back to reality, and she yelped.

"Almost done," he assured her.

Sweat dotted her forehead as every muscle knotted. "I can do hard things. I can do hard things. I can do hard things."

"You...you say that often. Is it a spell?"

"No." Ivy clenched her fists. "It's a mantra. I say it to calm myself down when I'm...um...like this. Usually I take my meds but-"

"Meds?" he asked, still focused on his work.

"Medication. I take pills because I uh..." Gods, how do you explain an anxiety disorder to a satyr? Short and sweet was probably the best way. "My pills keep me from panicking all the time. My everyday pill is called Lexapro. And Atarax is my rescue one. I mean its really an antihistamine, but Xanax put me on a coma so my doctor prescribed this instead to calm me down and... Fuck why am I babbling about this?"

A scowl crossed his lips, forehead wrinkling. "That's what those little white tablets do?"

"Yes. And I'm sure they're enjoying their little swim in the pond out back."

The lack of reply only confirmed her suspicions. Ivy scrubbed her face, praying to Brigid that another spiral wasn't coming.

"Callum takes potions for the same thing," he muttered.

"Wait, your brother has an anxiety- Ow! Fuck fuck fuck!" She slapped the table with every swear. "Ass cheeks, fucksticks, dick-butt!"

"I'm almost done," Finn soothed.

Cool relief made her toes go numb. She slumped wiping the sweat from her brow. "Finally. Thank Brigid."

Finn plopped the blood-stained towel onto the table. "No more pain?"

Ivy wiggled her toes. No pain. Hell, she barely felt her own skin. "None. I'm impressed."

Finn grinned again and if she were standing, her knees would've given out. "I brew it myself. Most items can be found on these lands. It used to be more potent when..." He trailed off, sadness brushing his face. Then he shrugged, picking up her foot yet again. "I'm going to pull the glass out now. You shouldn't feel a thing."

The pressure of his claws dug into the ball of her foot, but as promised, no pain came. Bit by bit he removed each shard, placing them beside her. Soon a small pile formed, making Ivy's stomach churn. Damn, she really messed herself up.

"I have a question for you, Witchling," Finn said.

Ivy wet her lips, expecting him to ask about striking a bargain. Of course, he would. He had her in his power. A fair folk had done her a solid and would expect a favor in return. Probably her leaving in exchange for his healing services. Dammit, she was so stupid to let him help her.

He tapped his lower lip in mock contemplation. "What in blazes is a dick-butt?"

Ivy stared then slapped a hand over her face before her laugh splattered all over him. "I... have no damn idea."

Through her fingers Finn smiled, his chuckle sweet as he joined her mirth. She'd bet dollars to donuts he had a magnificent laugh if he ever let it fly.

"Well, Witchling, I believe I removed all the shards." He took the wooden canister, popping it open to another wonderful scent.

"Rosemary and sage?" Ivy inhaled the heavenly balm. "Gods, I love those smells. Second only to lavender."

His jaw ticked as he dipped his fingers into the white balm, slathering it over her skin. "It's a healing salve."

Every inch of her unraveled as he kneaded her arch. "And a foot rub? Sweet Goddess what did I do to deserve this?"

Finn didn't answer. His hands ran up the length of her calf, working each muscle with a slow, languid touch. His gaze was hot, longing, demanding she strip off her clothes and lay back on the table for him. Heat swelled between her legs and she slammed her thighs shut before she made good on that silent request.

"Apparently I could seduce you with just a touch," he said, his cocky arrogance returning.

"Oh, shut up."

"Just as well. You're unwilling and I'm finished." He backed away, running his hand over his horns. "They should be healed by morning."

Ivy gestured to the bright blue sky outside. "It is morning."

"Ah, so it is." He rose, turning swiftly as he made his escape. "Then farewell, Witchling."

A line of intricate knotwork traced down his spine, shining gold as his back rippled. How could she have never noticed that before? It was gorgeous.

"Finn?" She wanted to ask him what those marks meant but his magnificent shoulders tightened. "Thanks, for patching me up," she finished.

His chin lifted. "Can you walk?"

"Maybe?" She slid off the table to stand. "I mean I can't feel anything from the ankle down and-whoa!"

Her feet slipped out from under her. Finn swept her up into his arms before she hit bottom. "Clearly, you cannot."

He clacked out of the dining room, with her in a princess carry. He was so warm, so solid and sure, taking her up the stairs as if she weighed nothing at all. When was the last time some dude held her like this? Never, that was when. No boyfriend in the past ever bothered to try. Yeah, this was going to be vibrator fantasy fodder when she found the damn thing.

"Your chamber is at the end?" he asked.

She nodded dumbly and he marched forward, bumping open the door with his hip. He placed her on the edge of her bed then turned, his tail thrashing.

"Get some rest," he said gruffly.

"I didn't mean to scare your brother," she blurted.

He stopped, hand on the door frame.

"I...I was...am...pissed and I lost it, so I struck back," she continued. "I have a little bit of a temper I try to reign in and... I haven't slept in days and then you stole my meds but... It wasn't meant for him. Ugh... I know these are all excuses so... Tell him I'm sorry."

Finn strode towards the bed. Ivy scooted away, her breath catching. Was he pissed? Aroused? She could deal with aroused.

Ivy, can you not be horny for five seconds?!

He stopped a hand span away, then reached into his leather pouch. With a rattle, he placed two pill bottles on her nightstand. Her medication.

"You didn't throw them in the pond?" she gasped.

"I didn't know what they would do if I did," he admitted. "And now that I know what they are for, I think you should have them back." He left, closing the door behind him with a soft click.

Ivy gawked at the place he once stood, head spinning. That couldn't have just happened. Finn despised her, despised all witches from the sound of it. So why did he help her? Why did the house let him touch her? Hell, why did *she* let him touch her? With a groan, she flopped onto her back, pulling her pillow over her face to block out the bright morning sun.

Negotiate, a soft voice whispered, raspy and sweet as if coming from another world.

Ivy sat up. "What?"

Only the crackling fire answering her. Great, now she was hearing things on top of-

Now is the time.

She reached over her headboard to press a hand against the wall. "Was that you? Did...did you just talk?!"

The wall vibrated, beneath her palm. Life. It was there, struggling across the veil to communicate. *He is willing to negotiate. His mind is open.*

"What can I do to bring you fully back? I'll do it now! Anything!"

Talk to the satyr. Negotiate. Get him on your side. Perform your ritual on Samhain.

"Samhain? Because the veil will be thin? You'll be able to pass through?"

That is the start.

The magic that tingled her fingers vanished, leaving the wall cold. Ivy's heart pounded. Her power, her life, it could all be returned. She stood a chance.

Only if I negotiate with Finn. Well, if there was any time to swallow her pride, it was now. The house was right. Strike while he was still feeling kindness towards her.

Ivy stood, wobbling on her still numb feet. She shuffled across the floor, dragging herself down the hall and after what felt like forever, made it to the stairs.

Stairs.

Walking down a long staircase, while sporting two numb feet. "Oooh boy."

She stepped, then snatched the banister before cartwheeling the rest of the way down. Okay, this was going to be a challenge. She sat down at the edge of the stairs, then at a creeping pace, scooted herself step by step on her rump.

"I can do hard things. I can do hard things," she muttered the entire way down.

Chapter 11

Callum had fallen asleep, the potion bottle still clutched tight. The coolness of relief spread over Finn as he watched his chest rise and fall with slow breaths.

He wished that bottomless resentment towards Ivy would return so he can go back to hating her, but it didn't. There was only her terror as she begged him not to kill her. Her shivers and screams, her complete panic. Her pain. *She suffers like Callum.*

Finn climbed the basement stairs. He needed to think, regroup, and gather his fury. Ivy was a witch and witches had killed his entire heard. *But she apologized. She didn't want to hurt him.*

Witches didn't apologize. They took what they wanted and damned the rest. But she was sorry. The gleam in her eyes spoke of her sincerity. He snarled at himself. The last thing he wanted was to feel compassion towards her and yet there it was.

Finn dragged himself into the old floral chair, staring at the fire crackling away. The last time he remembered seeing the hearth lit was ages ago. When that warlock resided here. He created a roaring inferno that pumped magic through the walls. It had died the day the coven broke through its wards and looted everything inside.

A pang of guilt struck. *I never thanked the pretentious prick for his sacrifice.* Without that man's help, he and Callum would be dead. The entire mountain would be dead.

Finn grit his teeth, rubbing against the chair in hopes of absorbing Ivy's wonderful smell. It enveloped him like a hug, and he pressed his nose against the armrest for an indulgent whiff. Comfort. Peace. At least for the moment. His tail twitched and he rolled his back against the worn fabric like a cat. This chair was pure heaven. He would steal it from her as soon as possible.

Unless you let her stay. Then you can keep the chair. And keep her. Not the worst idea. Ivy was a mouth-watering creature with a body as supple as the most voluptuous nymph, eyes as blue as the summer sky, and hair like fire. And her scent. By Dionysus her scent was sweet nectar.

Finn bit back his moan. What was he thinking? He couldn't keep her. She was a thorn in his side, and a terror to Callum.

There was a sharp oof and his ears perked. Finn fled his chair, following the echoing grunts to the stairs. Ivy was contorted in a strange squat. She slid to the edge of each step on her behind before landing on the next with a thump.

"I can do...hard...things," she grunted, after each slap of her derrière.

"What in the seven hells are you doing?" he asked.

She froze, mid scoot, eyes wide. "Oh. You're just... right there... watching me drag my ass down the steps... Lovely."

He hurried to her before she crab-walked her way further down. "I thought I told you to get some rest."

"Since when did I ever listen?" She managed to flop down one more step before he scooped her up into his arms. "Woah!" she shouted, flinging her arms around his neck.

There was her wonderful aroma again, more potent than it was on her chair. Finn sunk a fang into his tongue. So warm and soft. So damn tempting. His shaft twitched. Quickly, he deposited her on the couch. "Are you so keen to undo all the work I've done?"

Ivy folded her arms tight. "We need to talk about a truce."

"Dionysus's balls, this again?"

"Yes, this again. The house said I needed to talk to you. So here I am."

"The house... talked?"

Finn took a large step away from Ivy. The warlock had once said the house knew many tricks. And if it was regaining its life, he didn't want to discover any beyond getting thrown about.

"Please. Just hear me out," Ivy said. "No tricks, I promise. And if you don't like what I have to offer-"

"Then you'll continue being irritating?"

Ivy frowned. "I was going to say I'll leave you alone but if you keep pushing me, I'll be *more* than irritating."

"Fine. Say your peace"

Her face lit with hope, sending a tiny thrill down his spine. "Have a seat." She gestured to the coveted chair.

If he sat, he'd be tempted to roll in it once again. "I uh... rather stand."

Ivy cocked her head. "You sure?"

"Yes."

"Because you're eyeing that chair like it's made of gold."

"Standing is fine!"

Ivy gave him an impish grin. "Okay, but its suuuuper comfy."

With an exaggerated roll of his eyes, he dragged himself over. "I'll appease you. But only because I am very magnanimous."

He plopped down with a satisfied exhalation, falling under the chair's spell once again. Gods and Goddesses, he could die happy here. Ivy's giggle made him bristle. She clamped a hand over her mouth, her sapphire eyes twinkling.

"Did you curse this chair?!" he demanded.

Her smile dropped. "No!"

"Then why are you laughing?!"

"Because you looked like a bear trying to scratch his back and it was funny!"

"I did *not* look funny! I don't look funny! I look majestic! You hexed this chair, didn't you?"

"What part of I have no power do you not get?" She stood. "Look, if you're so certain I cursed the damn thing, I'll sit in it and- Aah!"

Her feet slipped out from under her and in a flash, Finn caught her. He could hear her heart flutter, could feel her nipples hardening through her flimsy night clothes. She was so close, her mouth only a whisper away from his.

"You can't walk, Witchling," he said, his voice husky.

Ivy swallowed, her fingers digging into his lower back. "I'm trying to make a point."

"Then make it sitting down."

He refused to let her go. How would she react if he kissed her? Just took her mouth without a thought. She'd probably slap him but it would be worth it.

The question went unanswered as Ivy untangled herself from his hold, setting back on the couch. The tell-tale blush said all he wanted to know, and the corner of his mouth twitched into a tiny grin.

"Give me until Samhain to do my ritual," she said, patting her messy bun into place. "As soon as I have my powers back, I leave."

"Samhain is quite a bit away."

"It's just a month. You can put up with me for at least a month, right? I get my powers, and you get your house back fully alive and well. I'll even keep the electricity running when I'm gone."

Finn rubbed his chin. If Ivy did bring the house back and was good on her word, its magic would be theirs. This place was once a fortress of power and enchantment under the warlock's care. Granted, a cottage witch's magic wasn't as strong, but was still magic. And magic was a good ally.

Eagerness could be seen as weakness, Finn. Take your time with her and maybe she'll sweeten the deal. "That's all you're offering? After I've been so reasonable about you being here."

"Reasonable? You stole my toilet!"

"I left you a perfectly fine hole to use."

"And you dropped a chandelier on my head!"

"I dropped it beside your head. You were well out of range when I untied that rope. See? I've been completely reasonable."

The way she puffed out frustrated little breaths, how her round cheeks pinkened. Adorable. He hadn't had this much fun in ages.

Ivy groaned. "Fine. You can have the chair too."

Finn blinked. "I...can?"

"Keep it. Cherish it. Dance naked around it. I'll be chair-less for the rest of my life and pine for it all my days. Now do we have a deal?"

Well, well, she really *was* willing to give him what he desired. How far could he push this little game? Finn settled across from her, draping his arms across the couch's back. Her gaze instantly fell on his bare chest, pupils dilating.

Yes, how far can *I take it?* "What else?" he purred.

"Um..." Ivy rubbed her eyes, as if trying to sober up. "You can have all the rooms across the hall from mine. Free reign down here too."

His tail stretched across the cushions, its brush sweeping over her thigh. "What else?"

Ivy scooted away. "We're not having sex," she said flatly.

"So, you were thinking it."

"Finn!"

"You wanted to negotiate."

His tail flicked across her thigh again. If only she wasn't wearing those sleeping trousers. He would have loved to discover how her bare skin reacted to his touch. Oh yes, this was a fun game indeed.

"Clearly I'm getting nowhere with you. This was a stupid idea." She rose once again.

"Where do you think you're going? You still can't walk yet!" Finn grabbed the back of her sleep shirt yanking her to the couch. Her arms wind-milled, and she tumbled on top of him with a grunt, her legs sliding around his hips. Her sex was as hot as a forge. Hot and pressing against his now swelling shaft.

"Can you stop yanking me around like that?" Ivy snapped. "Or at least warn me when..." She trailed off, shooting him a glare. "Are you seriously getting hard right now?"

Finn shrugged. "Well, what do you expect when you offer me sex."

"I did *not* offer you sex!"

"Finn!" Callum bellowed. "What in the Seven Hells are you doing!?"

The two froze, locking stunned gazes before turning them towards the fuming satyr. As usual, his brother's timing was miserable.

Finn offered a sheepish smile. "Negotiations?"

Ivy scrambled away only to fall flat onto her rump. That didn't stop her from scooting across the floor. She huddled behind her eye sore of a chair, peering over its top.

"Is this your pathetic idea of finishing this?" Callum sneered.

Finn hurried towards his brother, hands up. "Cal, we are negotiating terms of her stay. It would only be temporary, of course."

"You want her to stay?" He clutched his horns with a growl. "Of course, you do! You're fucking her!"

"We're not fucking!" Ivy shouted.

"There is a lot she can offer us," Finn continued.

Callum glared at Ivy, murder in his eyes. "Like what?"

Finn stepped in the path of his glare to shield her. "Well, she *is* giving me the chair."

Callum gaped at him. "You're an idiot."

"Cal, she's powerless. She would have killed us both already if she wasn't." He looked back to Ivy. "Right? Just obliterated us?"

"No!" Ivy cried. "I'm not some crazy murderer!"

Finn jerked his thumb towards the witch. "See?"

Callum shoved Finn aside. "If you're not ending her, I am."

"I'm sorry! I didn't mean to scare you!" Ivy scooted away as fast as she could, but the speed of her rump was no match for Callum's hooves.

Finn shoved Callum back. "I will not let you harm her!" As soon as the words left his mouth, he blanched. Ivy gaped, appearing as stunned as he.

The two never fought beyond some playful ribbing. And yet Callum looked ready to tear him apart. "Don't test me, little brother. I'm stronger than you."

Finn bowed his chest regardless. "And I'm willing to test that theory."

Callum's eyes flashed red, his fangs elongating.

"Ivy Siobhan Bennett!" Her voice roared with a deafening resonance.

Warmth swelled inside Finn, buzzing with the faint echo of her full name, anchoring itself inside him. Then it faded, leaving only a slight heaviness on his heart. Ownership. Chains that only he could break. Callum skidded to a halt., hand pressed over his chest. By Dionysus, he had felt the same sensation.

"My full name is Ivy Siobhan Bennett," she said, voice steady despite her trembling. "And now it's yours. Both of you. If I do you any harm, you can punish me however you want."

Finn went slack jawed. She had given him her full name. He could do anything with that power; enslave her, enchant her, make her his for all eternity. That didn't feel as satisfying as he thought it would.

"You're insane," he whispered.

Ivy banged her forehead against the floor. "Yeah, we're finally in agreement on something, Finn."

Callum shook his head. "Why would you do that, witch?"

Ivy pulled herself onto unsteady feet. "Because I need to be here. I need my powers back. And if this is what it takes to get your trust, then I'll do it."

"You are either the bravest witch in this world, or the stupidest," he murmured.

"I'm thinking more of the latter," Ivy sighed.

The softest of laughs bubbled up Finn's throat, her courage filling him with a strange pride. "I believe more of the former." He looked back to Callum with a smirk. "Is that good enough for you? Can we take murder off the agenda?"

Callum backed away, hatred spilling from his glare. "Don't think I won't use your name if you make one wrong move!"

Ivy tightened her mouth, giving a curt nod. She appeared to be holding back her words. Obscene words, no doubt. The thought of the tiny female drowning his mountain of a brother in a tidal wave of swears made that laugh rise again. "All right then. Negotiations are done. The witch stays until Samhain."

"Samhain?!" Callum cried. "That's forever a way!"

"Only a month." Finn shrugged. "...However long that is."

"Thirty-one days," Ivy added.

"There. Only thirty-one days. A blink of an eye." He nudged Callum down the hall. "Now leave us be so we can finish negotiations."

"You mean so you can finish fucking," Callum snapped.

"We are not fucking!" Ivy wailed.

Callum grabbed Finn's arm, his claws digging into his skin. "As long as that witch is under this roof, I will not be."

He tossed Finn aside, leaving his arm aching and his belly knotted. The basement door slammed. Well, at least he saved the witch. But at what cost?

Ivy was hobbling back to her chair. Gods above, he was going to spend the rest of his days wrangling stubborn asses, wasn't he?

Once again, he picked her up, enjoying her shocked squeal then placed her gently into the chair. "Witchling, stop trying to walk."

Her cheeks flushed. "Remember when you asked for permission to touch me? Can we stay on that route?"

"You didn't have to give him your name," Finn said. "You could have lived under the protection of the house."

Ivy leaned back in her chair with a sigh. "I know but I'm tired of this bullshit. So, I'm giving him my dagger... Like you did for me."

Finn blinked, tail lashing in a wild S. "So, it's settled then. We have a truce."

"Yes. A truce until Samhain. Then I'm gone."

"Good." He jerked a thumb over his shoulder. "Now get out of the chair. It's mine now."

Ivy gave his leg a hardy thwack of her foot, a little smile teasing her mouth. "You put me here."

"Ah. So, I did. Well, enjoy your final moments then. I best go grovel for Callum's forgiveness and when I return, only my backside will grace those cushions."

He turned to leave but stopped as Ivy cried. "Wait!" She raised her eyes to the ceiling, that blush returning. "I uh...can't walk to my room."

Finn grinned. "Oh yes. That."

"You don't have to carry me. Just- Whoa! Crap!" Ivy screeched, as he picked her up, chair and all. He held her over his head like a prize, tromping up the stairs and snickering at the barrage of curses she threw at him.

"What?" he said. "You didn't give me permission to touch you, yet. I'm compromising!"

Chapter 12

The door swung open before Ivy could even touch the knob, sweeping in a theatrical gust of air, a swirl of leaves, and her Auntie Dahlia. She was a grand woman of eighty who dressed like the lovechild of Morticia Adams and Bettie Paige and took up space like a bulldozer.

"Oh Ivy!" She clasped her hands, delight twinkling in her dark eyes. "Simply divine! High ceilings and an old-world charm! ...Still a bit dirty though."

Ivy replied with a strained smile.

She had stood firm an entire week before finally capitulating to her aunts' visit, which was impressive all things considered. The texts, calls, and in person passive aggressive nudges had been daily. When they had announced they were coming the next morning, Ivy was a one-woman army, clearing every cobweb and sweeping every floor before they steamrollered in.

Finn had kept his side of the bargain and stayed out of her way. Yet he was always about, an invisible lurking blur, hovering curiously. It should have creeped her out, but his presence had been reassuring, especially in the evenings when the wind rattled the windows and shadows crept across the floor. Who would have thought that jerk would be a comfort?

Dahlia's wide brim hat bumped Ivy's cheek as she passed, her bright red stiletto heels almost as loud as Finn's hooves. She held up a gloved finger, closing her eyes with a melodramatic hum.

"I feel the life here," she said. "It's faint, but it's here. You do have your work cut out for you, Darling. But look at you, getting all these hearths cleansed and lit. I'll be honest, my cards implied you couldn't pull this off." She smiled warmly. "Well, there's a good chance that they could be wrong this time."

Ivy's pride twisted. *Don't let it sting. It was meant to be a compliment.* "Uh, thanks."

Dahlia patted the thick binder under her arm. "I brought wallpaper samples! All antique of course. We want to keep the old fashion aesthetics of this place, not modern it up like a group of tasteless philistines."

"Auntie Dahlia, I already told you, I'm not staying. I'm just going to do my ritual and leave."

Dahlia's lips twisted into a skeptical frown. "Oh yes. That deal thingy you made with the satyr. Of course, Darling. Of course. Now then, decorating."

A low growl rumbled from behind Ivy, the sound of hooves scraping across the floor. Finn's blur saddled beside her, radiating tension.

"You said there would be no covens," he whispered.

"Two witches don't make a coven," Ivy muttered out of the side of her mouth.

Dahlia dropped her binder on the coffee table, oblivious to their conversation. "Now, in here I was thinking greens and dark wood. Keep that hunter's lodge vibe. Perhaps one of those chandeliers with antlers! Oh...oh wait. No. You have an aversion to those since one almost crushed you."

Ivy bristled at Finn's quiet snicker. "Don't you dare laugh."

Dahlia settled herself on the couch, smoothing her pencil skirt. "Sit, Darling. We have so much to look through."

"Auntie Dahlia, there's no point. I'm just going to clean up and get the heart of the house beating again. Then I'm gone."

"And what better way to get its magical blood pumping than..." Dahlia threw her hands in the air as if about to start tap dancing. "A makeover!"

A crash followed by a cry of "Oh drat!" came from the front door. There was Auntie Rosemary all cozy sweaters, and earth tones. The epitome of the perfect green witch.

She frowned at the broken pot, dirt, and plant that now covered the floor. A dozen fully intact herbs were cradled in her arms.

"That was going to be part of the kitchen garden," she sighed, sweeping the mess aside with her worn leather boot, the skirt of her flowing green dress spattered with soil.

"I see three witches!" Finn hissed. "That's a coven!"

"It's not a coven!" Ivy growled between her teeth.

Rosemary smiled, laugh lines bracketing her wide mouth. "Oh, Ivy dear, it's so wonderful to finally see this place! ...but it is still a bit dirty, don't you think?"

Ivy hurried over, brushing her cracked ego under the carpet. "Auntie Rosemary, what is all this?"

"Any proper witch home needs its own garden." She shoved potted herb after potted herb into Ivy's arms. "There is a lovely space right in front of the porch that gets a healthy amount of sunlight. We can put it there."

"...Garden?"

"My rototiller is in the truck."

"Rototiller?!"

Rosemary went to Dahlia, giving her a kiss on the cheek before sitting down beside her. "What did she think of the wallpaper, love?"

"We haven't even gotten there yet," Dahlia groaned.

Ivy juggled the herbs as she stumbled after her aunt. "But I'm not staying. There's no reason to go to all this trouble."

"Darling, you need all the help you can get in your condition," Dahlia replied.

Ivy's teeth clamped down over the string of curse words sitting on deck. "It's not that I don't appreciate all this. I do. I really do. But I made a bargain."

"Oh, yes." Dahlia batted her eyes before cupping a hand beside her mouth, shouting, "Of course this house will belong to the satyrs after all this!" Her exaggerated wink hid nothing.

"Dear, he's of the fair folk," Rosemary added, patting her frizzy gray hair with a smile. "Their bargains aren't nearly as iron-clad as the high fae. There is always a loophole."

Not while two satyrs have my full name. There's a tidbit that her aunts didn't need to know. As usual, she forced on a smile and rolled over. "Okay fine. What loophole did you have in mind, then?"

"Well, have you offered him sex yet?" Dahlia asked.

And the pots almost crashed to the floor. "What?!"

There was a snort of approval from the invisible satyr.

"Sex, Darling," Dahlia said. "Satyrs love that sort of thing. That would have been my first approach. It usually *is* my first approach."

"Just like our first date!" Rosemary squealed.

Ivy's face heated. Sex was almost her first approach as well. Hell, during negotiations she had almost said, "Fine. Just fuck me. I'm game. Here or upstairs?" when the offer was first implied. But numb feet and recovering from a panic attack was a big-time mood breaker. "No, I didn't offer him sex."

"*I* offered and she declined," Finn added.

She could feel his smirk under that cloak of invisibility. Ivy would have slapped her forehead if her arms weren't full.

"Is that him?" Rosemary beamed, bouncing in her seat like an eager child. "Is he here now?! This is so exciting!"

"Come on, satyr. Let's have a look at you." Dahlia snapped her fingers. "My wife has always wanted to see one of your kind."

"He's not going to appear," Ivy replied. "He never does what he's asked to."

Finn appeared with a pop and she jumped, the pots tumbling from her arms. He caught them faster than she could blink, tossing them onto the coffee table. Each one landed with gentle precision.

"You only appeared because I said you wouldn't, didn't you?" Ivy sighed.

His mouth curved into a sly grin but faded at her aunts' titters. He edged away from the couch, his tail flicking with wild snaps.

"Look at him, Lia!" Rosemary clutched her wife's arm. "He's stunning!"

"I'm looking, Rosie! I'm looking!"

He took another step away, giving them a fierce glare. "I thought you said you weren't part of a coven."

"I'm not. These are my aunts," Ivy replied. "Just family visiting."

"And I'm sure he's a pussycat." Dahlia reached to pat his arm.

Finn recoiled. He bared his fangs, eyes darting around for escape. Ivy took his wrist before he ran. "Hey, hey. They're trustworthy, I swear it," she soothed. "And don't forget the safety net I gave you."

He glanced to her hand, mouth thinning. Much to her surprise, he didn't pull away. Ivy stepped between him and her aunts as he laced his fingers with hers. Her heart fluttered.

"Finn's got things to do," she said, casting a look back to him. "Right?"

His ears perked, face brightening at the offer of escape.

Rosemary clasped her hands under her chin. "Surely he can sit and talk for a moment."

"It's really important satyr things, Aunt Rosie. Like..."

Shit, what did satyrs do? Frolic? Play the flute? Right now, the only thing she could think of was fucking and that was not where her brain needed to be.

"Hunt." Finn peered out from behind Ivy. "I have to hunt."

Ivy jerked a thumb to him. "Yeah. That."

Rosemary let out a disappointed sigh. "Well. It was lovely meeting you."

Finn vanished before she even finished her sentence. The front door slammed shut and he was gone. Shit, witches really did spook him.

"Well, now that he's occupied, it's time for girl talk."
Dahlia grinned leaning her elbows on her thighs. "When
are you planning to have sex with him?"

"Auntie Dahlia, I'm not banging anyone!"

"Well, that's part of your problem, Darling."

"We have some books you can read specific to satyrs,"
Rosemary added.

Dahlia gave her wife a pointed look. "Because *someone*
was on the hunt for them on our honeymoon in Greece."

Rosemary snorted. "Oh, don't act like it was all my
idea." She looked to Ivy. "Satyrs are very well known for
their sexual prowess and I was hoping to make things
special that week."

"You two were going to have a threesome. With a satyr." Ivy said flatly. Well, this conversation was getting
out of control.

"One of those books contains an entire chapter on
how their horns are an erogenous zone," Rosemary
cooed. "Detailed instructions as well. I'll bring it to you."

Yup. Completely out of control. "No please. It's fine.
Really."

"We'll drop it off later tonight." Rosemary beamed.

Ivy's fake smile started hurting her face. But hey, it
kept her from screaming. "Okay, fine."

Rosemary stood, shaking out her skirt. "Well, herbs
don't plant themselves and day light is short these days.
I'll go get your garden started."

Ivy could only give a thumbs up as her aunt headed
out. She flopped on the couch, waiting to be attacked

with wallpaper samples. Instead, Dahlia clicked her tongue, heel tapping. "You're not getting enough sleep."

"No, I am. I'm getting plenty now that there's a truce."

"Then it's your condition."

Dammit, why did she have to refer to it as a condition? It sounded so terminal. *Because it is terminal, Ives.*

Dahlia pressed a hand against Ivy's forehead. "I knew that being out here on your own in the cold would only make things worse. Rowan is coming back to help with this insanity, right? At least one of you will have magic when things go south."

"I'm fine on my own. I can do this."

"It's not too late to come home, Darling." Dahlia swallowed, then gave her a watery smile. "We'll take care of you. Until the very end."

Ivy covered her eyes, not wanting to see her aunt's pity. "I'm seeing this through."

But you can't. They're right. Sweet Brigid, she wished she could stab that shitty little voice in her head.

"I'm sure you think you can," Dahlia said in a gentle tone. "But Darling, and this is said with love, you're a cottage witch. You aren't as strong as the rest of us. And what if this turns out like it did with Aster?"

Ivy stiffened, the simple mention of her name making her insides curdle. Dahlia's chatter faded into the background. Aster. Sweet, gentle Aster. She was supposed to protect her baby sister. But she had failed.

Aster was dead and Ivy would follow.

And it was all her fault.

Her sister's screams flooded her mind. The red eyes in the darkness. The black tendrils curling up Aster's body.

"Breathe, Witchling," Finn whispered in her ear. The rush of cool air filled her lungs as gentle fingers brushed her jaw. "Another," he commanded.

Ivy flattened her palm over her heart, sucking in another loud breath. Her pulse slowed.

"Ivy? Darling, are you all right?" Dahlia pressed the back of her hand against her cheek. "You're ice cold. Oh no. Are you having a-?"

"I just forgot to take my meds is all." She dashed to the stairs. "I'll be right back, okay?"

Dahlia eyed her. "Take your time, Darling. I'll go keep Rosie company while she digs. We can discuss wallpaper later."

Ivy nodded, dashing up the stairs. She burst into her room and fell into a sit on the end of her bed, counting her things to ground her. One, the thick fur rug in front of the fireplace. Two, the brass lamp on her nightstand. Three, the purple perfume bottle that sat on her vanity in the corner. Four-

Finn appeared, shutting the door as he strode to her.

Four. The gorgeous satyr who doesn't know how to knock. This made it two anxiety attacks he had witnessed.

"Well, your aunts are quite overbearing, aren't they?" He slapped his hands on his narrow hips. "I do admire their insistence toward our coupling, though." The mockery in his expression faded, his ears folding back as he knelt before her. "Are you having another episode, Witchling?"

"Just a small one. It's nothing."

"Perhaps you should take your medications like you said."

"I already took them this morning." Ivy wrapped her arms around her belly. "I lied to get away. I...I don't like it when they see me having an anxiety attack. It's better if I'm alone."

His tail flicked, then he began to rise. "I'll leave you be, then."

The idea of being left alone with her thoughts made sick bubble up her throat. Ivy snatched his tail, tugging him back. "You, I don't mind. You're actually good at talking me down."

The brush of his tail flipped about in her grasp then he nodded. "Then I'll stay."

She released him, letting him sit on the bed beside her. "Thanks for reminding me to breathe down there."

"When it comes to breathing, I'm a true master. Brilliant, really." He polished his claws against his chest. "Ask Cal."

His smile obliterated the last of her panic. "I haven't seen Callum lately. Is he okay?"

That beautiful smile vanished, and Ivy cursed her question. "He doesn't wish to be in the house while you're here, so he hides in the forest. He only returns when you sleep."

"Blessing in disguise. My aunts would drive him crazy. Hell, they drive *me* crazy." She grinned when he snorted a tiny laugh. "They...they make you uncomfortable, don't they?"

Finn shrugged, rubbing his palms together. "More than one witch troubles me."

"Why?" She asked. "Not that I'm expecting you to answer that."

"Good. Because I don't intend to," he snapped then ran his fingers through his hair, tone gentler when he added, "It's... not a situation I wish to breach."

"I get it," Ivy gave his arm a pat. "Sorry, I should have asked you before inviting them over."

A crease of confusion formed between his thick brows. "Ask?"

"It's *our* house, right? Well, until Samhain at least. I should respect my roommate."

"Oh." Finn blinked then lifted his chin with a haughty nod. "Yes, you should."

"Caveat." She wagged a finger at him. "That means you should respect me too."

He snorted. "I was about to imply that!" His expression relaxed as she giggled. "May I ask *you* a question now?"

"Sure."

"Who is Rowan?"

"You were listening in? I thought you left."

"My curiosity was stronger than my suspicion." He pulled open her nightstand drawer and peered in, as if demonstrating.

Ivy chuckled. "Rowan is my twin brother."

Finn's ears twitched. "You have a twin?"

"Oh yeah. Hell, he'd be here now but he's on assignment working with our law enforcement. Rowan is really talented. He can cross the veil between the living and the dead which makes him extremely useful helping murder victims. And he's a talented healer too. He's my rock."

"Is there a magical bond between you two?"

"Yup. Witch twins have strong ones. We can sense each others' emotions. Before I lost my powers, I always knew when Rowan was happy or upset." She sighed. "You never really know how alone you can feel until you're *really* alone."

"And Aster?"

The knot in her belly tightened at the name. She turned her gaze to her boots. "My baby sister. She... she died about a year ago."

"Oh..." Finn's tail flicked against the bed. "May I ask how?"

Ivy bit her lips shut. Everyone who had heard her story had recoiled in horror, only furthering her guilt. But ever since that night in the dining room she had felt safe with Finn, no matter how hard he blustered or bellowed. Maybe venting her sorrows to him would be therapeutic. It's not like she'd see him again after a month.

"Aster was the only one of us that left the mountain. I stayed to help my aunts with their shop. And while Rowan traveled for work, his home base had always been here. This was our home. But Aster wanted to see the world. So, she moved to San Diego and everything was fine for a while... Until she hooked up with this guy. And he invited her into a coven."

She held up a hand to Finn, afraid he'd protest. "Covens are mostly harmless. And usually they're the safest place a young witch on their own can be. But this one... The way she talked about them wasn't right. It was like they made decisions for her, forced her into a way of thinking. Hell, it was almost like Aster got sucked into a cult. I was worried, so I went to San Diego to check things out.

"I made up some lie that I was interested in joining too, that a cottage witch should branch out, blah blah... Aster was so excited when she took me to their meeting, like we were going to Disneyland. And they were so welcoming. It all seemed so...normal. Then like an idiot, I let my guard down. I blacked out and woke up tied to an altar."

Dammit, she didn't want to be emotional, didn't want to cry for the billionth time while she talked about this. But the memories slashed her apart. The cold stone against her back. How the rope that bound her wrists burned. The warm splash of blood as hands pulled her soul apart like taffy.

"All I could think while they tore my powers from me was, they all seemed so normal. So nice." Ivy wiped her eyes. "After they got what they wanted, they left me there. Guess they assumed I'd die sooner or later."

Finn's tail grazed her ankle, the warmth of his velvety fur fortifying her. Its brush stroked her calf, coaxing the rest of the story free.

"Aster freed me. She kept sobbing 'I'm sorry. I'm so sorry. I didn't know,' and I believe her. Aster didn't have a cruel bone in her whole damn body. She wasn't a taker, she was a nurturer. I could barely stand, hell, I could barely see. Everything hurt so much. But I ran. Just clung to Aster's hand and ran. The next thing I knew she was shoving me through an open window. I turned to pull her through but..." Horror overwhelmed her like a tsunami, taking her breath away. "Eyes. Hundreds and hundreds of red eyes opened in the darkness. Something grabbed her. A lot of somethings. I tried to save her, I really did! But I was too weak... And she was gone." She buried her face in her hands. "That's why I freaked out when you came after me that night. Your eyes turned red like...like those things."

"Ivy..." Finn's mouth quivered, and he cursed under his breath.

"Look, I don't want you to feel guilty. You didn't know my triggers and didn't do it on purpose."

"Yes, but I..." He took her hand, giving it a firm squeeze. "I know how vicious covens can be."

"Not all covens are bad, Finn," she sniffled. "But that one? That one can eat a shit sundae."

Finn gave her a sad chuckle. "A large bowl of it."

She snorted a messy giggle. "The biggest bowl we can find."

"You find the bowl. I will make arrangements with the animals to donate."

Ivy threw her head back, laughter splitting her mouth and clenching her stomach. More tears rolled down her face as Finn joined in.

"Thanks for the laugh. And thanks for listening. I guess you're not as big an ass as I thought you were."

"I'm not?" He tsked. "I'm losing my touch. I'll do better at infuriating you later."

She gave his shoulder a gentle smack then dried her eyes on her sleeve. "I should go check on my aunts, make sure they're not painting the walls plaid. Maybe we can... talk again later?"

"Perhaps. Yes." Finn leaned in, taking her face into his hands. "What happened with your sister was not your fault. Don't listen to your aunts. You're stronger than any witch before you for surviving that."

He strode out without another word, the clack of his hooves fading down the hall. Her lips parted with a gasp that never left her throat.

That strange, beautiful male made it so easy to talk. And damn her, she felt better for it. If she wasn't careful, she would do it all over again.

Chapter 13

Music—if you could even call it that—rattled Finn's door with pounding beats. He dropped his flute, shoving his palms against his ears. And here he thought moving out of the basement would be more peaceful.

"Stop that noise!" he shouted, banging his fist on the wall.

The melody blared on, buzzing through his teeth. Apparently, he'd have to shout his protest to her face. Well, laying eyes upon the voluptuous Witchling wasn't a bad thing.

Ever since hearing her tale a few days before, he had felt a kinship with her. They weren't so different, he and Ivy. She cared deeply for her siblings, had been hurt by a coven, and felt responsible for it all. His resentment had grown into respect, maybe even a little admiration. Gods above that made their time trapped together so much easier.

He followed his tender ears down the hall to her library. Ivy's voice sang along under the blaring din, something about someone's lover having to get with their friends to make it last forever. She was probably playing that music from what she had called a Bluetooth speaker. Why it was named that was a mystery. It had no teeth, let alone blue ones but it amplified sound to head splitting levels. Finn jammed his pinkie into his ear, giving it a twist.

"Witchling!" he yelled, banging on the library door. "Stop your racket!"

Ivy continued to sing, this time about zigaziging. He opened the door, ready to lodge his complaint but fell hypnotized.

She danced as if no one else resided in the house, eyes closed, her hips swirling in a wild figure eight. Her smile was like summer. Stray tendrils spilt from her bun, glittering like pure fire as she tossed her head.

He'd never seen her so unguarded and free. It was beautiful, seductive. Arousing. He bit back the groan, growing hard at the thought of her supple body clad only in the length of her beautiful hair. He needed to know how long that burning mane was. To her shoulders? Her waist?

Ivy spun, still singing, "Slam your body down and zigazig-" Her eyes popped open, meeting Finn's. "Aaaahhh!" She dropped the broom.

"Am I interrupting your... ritual?"

"You really need to learn how to knock!" She fished her tiny box from her pocket to frantically tap its surface. The music stopped, and Finn flared his ears, with a sigh of relief.

"I did, but you were so busy gyrating, you must not have heard me." He grinned. "Go on. Continue. I'm very entertained."

The smart smirk that graced her lips made his heart flutter. "Are you here for a reason or just to torment me?"

Finn pursed his mouth around his original protest. After that unabashed and enticing display, he'd let her play all the horrible music she wanted. "Just tormenting you. I'll let you get back to...whatever this is."

But he wanted to stay. Join her and revel like he had during the days of the Dionysia. Dance and drink and fuck. But just with her.

Only with her.

She beckoned him into the room with the crook of a finger. "Actually, wait a second. I got something for you."

His ears perked, a small thrill chasing up his spine. An offering. It had been some time since he had received one of those. A part of him was hoping that it would be her lips on his already throbbing cock. Alas, she didn't lower herself to her knees, only walked across the room for something leaning against the wall. She held it out to him.

"My bow?" He took it, turning it in his hands. The wood had been polished to a shine, a new string replacing the one he'd broken.

"Yeah. You left it on the floor the day I changed the locks and I noticed it was broken." Once again, her amazing smile took his breath. "Honestly, I was so pissed at you I almost threw it out. Instead, I took it to a sporting goods store and got it repaired. You should have seen the guy's face when I handed it to him. He kept calling it a work of art and offered to buy it off me."

Callum and he had carved those bows together. Polished them, strung them, kept them by their sides for ages. He had meant to fix it himself, but the chaos had distracted him.

"You fixed my bow," he murmured, unable to tear his eyes away from it.

"You know how hard it was to sneak it out of the house? You practically sleep with that thing."

"Why would you do this?"

Ivy rubbed the back of her neck. "It's a thank you. For the feet thing. And reminding me to breathe."

Mischievous, clever little Witchling. He couldn't fight the smile. "I'm...touched."

"I'm glad." She gave him a playful nudge. "Because I turned down a thousand bucks for you."

Finn had no idea what she would do with one thousand male deer, but warmth spread from his heart all the way to his fingertips, regardless.

"Thank you, Ivy Siobhan Bennett. Truly." He slung his bow over his shoulder. "I suppose I should remove the fire ants from your bed now."

"What?!"

"I'm joking."

She pressed her palm against his chest, shoving him to the hall. "Bye Finn."

"You don't think I deserve another reward for my cleverness?"

"Goodbye Finn."

"Not even a kiss?"

She shut the door on his face, her laughter pealing behind it. He cracked his knuckles, ready to re-enter and continue their sparring when Callum's growl stopped him short. "The way you cluck over her is disgusting."

Finn tilted his head back with a sigh. "I figured you'd still be gone."

"I was hoping to talk some logic into you but after this display..." Callum snorted the rest of his sentence, revulsion thickening the scars on his face.

Finn grabbed Callum's arm, tugging him to his room. "We're not discussing this where the witch can hear."

"Why not? Are you afraid I'll offend her?" Callum laughed bitterly. "Remember this when you're tied to another altar!"

"Even after getting her full name you still have no trust. For the love of the Goddess, she has no powers, Cal! She's harmless! And need I remind you she is protected by this house? I couldn't harm her even if I wanted to."

"That's the problem, Finn! You don't want to! You're constantly playing with her, talking to her, and lusting after her!"

"Of course I am! She's comely! And I'm a satyr! Satyrs fuck! If she presents her consent, I'm taking it! Perhaps if you found yourself a piece, you'd be less of a horse's ass!"

"It's your cock on trial here, not mine!"

"Your cock hasn't been on anything for almost a century!"

Callum looked ready to send a fist through the window. Instead he shut his eyes, leaning a forearm against the wall.

Finn's belly clenched. "She isn't like the others, Callum. I swear it."

He glared over his shoulder. "Orlaith had said the same of that coven. That they weren't like the others. She was convinced they were harmless and made a bargain. Do I have to remind you how that turned out?"

The heartbreak in Callum's eyes made him ache. There was no need for the reminder. Every day he thought of their chieftain's innocent words. Orlaith's optimism only led to their destruction.

Ivy's music resumed at a lower level, pulling him back to the world. If only Callum could see who she really was. Stubborn and fierce, but kind. Loyal. Strong.

"She's different," he insisted.

Callum sent his fist through the wall. "Don't make me force your hand in this!"

"Do it!" Finn faced him, fangs lengthening. "Use my full name! Force me to kill the witch if it's the only thing that will subdue your irrational fear!"

142

Callum's fight vanished, replaced with a callous frown. "You chose a witch over the herd that died by their hand. You chose her over me. I hope you can live with that, Finn." He marched from the room.

"Cal! Wait!" Finn dashed after him. "Where do you think you're going? The forest? Alone?!"

"Yes, the forest, alone!" Callum sneered. "That abandoned hunters shed we've used during storms will be enough shelter for me! And far away from her!"

"This is madness! Just stop! Listen to me!"

But he had disappeared, the sounds of his hooves clomping down the stairs. Finn clutched his horns, tears burning his eyes. Callum was gone. Yes, he'd be secure in that old shed but they hadn't been separated in ages. Suddenly, he felt more alone than he ever had in his long life.

"Everything okay?" Ivy asked, peeking out from the library.

He bit the inside of his cheek. He wanted to be furious with her again but couldn't find the strength. Not anymore. "Another row with Callum. Nothing new."

Ivy nodded in a fog of distraction. "I'll leave you alone then." She slipped into her bedroom, cursing under her breath. Something was vexing the witch. Perhaps the fight had worried her.

He turned back to the stairs, ready to hunt down Callum and beg for him to return. There had to be a way to fix this.

"Dammit!" Ivy snapped, followed by drawers slamming shut.

The sounds of her distress almost sent him running to her rescue. His tail lashed, and he tightened his jaw. It was time to leave well enough alone. Already he was growing too close to this witch, running to her aid would do nothing.

Her cursing turned to desperate whimpers. Finn raked his claws through his hair, the pull towards her undeniable. With no more hesitation, he went to her.

Worry lines were deep around Ivy's eyes, that familiar wild look washing over her. "Where is it?" she hissed, digging through a box.

"Did you misplace something?"

She slammed the box shut only to open another one. "My mom's spell book is missing. I know I packed it. I just assumed it went to the library." She looked at him, her big blue eyes hopeful. "You haven't seen it, have you? Its green and has the wheel of Hecate on its cover."

Oh yes, he'd seen it. Watched it sink to the bottom of the pond. Finn's stomach fell to his knees as he shrugged

Ivy frowned. "That book has all our family spells in it!"

He wrung his hands. "I'm sure your parents have those important spells memorized."

Ivy slumped. "My mom and dad died in a car accident twenty-five years ago."

Guilt walloped him right in the chest. And here he thought he couldn't feel any worse.

"That book has all my ritual notes. I need it if I'm going to bring this house back to life!" She paced her room, pinching the bridge of her nose. "Hell, it had drawings Aster did of our family! Dammit! Where the hell did I...?"

Her tirade stalled, color draining from her face. Finn dared a step towards her, his tail swishing in frantic circles. "What's the matter?"

Ivy's body flickered like a flame. Her skin vanished, exposing bare bones and a slow beating heart. She returned only to wink out again completely.

"Witchling!"

She reappeared, crashing to the floor. Finn dove for her, gathering her in his arms.

"Witchling! Can you hear me?" She was as limp as a dead fish, her breath shallow and ragged. He gave her a violent shake. "Ivy!"

Her eyes popped open. Finn's heart restarted and he took a thankful breath. He cupped her face, turning her head from side to side. Her color was returning, but not fast enough for his liking. What in the seven hells happened?"

Ivy pulled herself free, ignoring his question. He growled, reaching for her, but she dodged him, wobbling on her unsteady feet.

"I need that book, Finn!" She tripped to her closet, digging through it like a mad woman.

"You disappeared!"

"Please, help me find it! I am screwed without it!"

And for the thousandth time, Finn's heart twisted. He bowed his chest, chin high. He may have failed his brother, but he wouldn't fail her. "I know where it is."

He took off before she asked questions. His pulse pounded, the rush of blood loud in his ears. *Dionysus, please let that book be impervious to water!*

His loincloth was tossed aside as he burst onto the deck. *Get that book. Get that book!* With a deep breath, he climbed the railing, and dove into the freezing pond, praying that leather tome was still at its bottom.

Chapter 14

The fade. It had started. And once it began, there was no stopping it. Ivy thought she had more time, that she could make it to her ritual.

"Shit shit shit!" She pressed her hands over her eyes. "Calm down! The more you panic, the worse it gets!"

The moment she had feared had finally come. The last stages of her powerless life. The fade. Every time it struck, a little piece of her was sent across the veil. It was only a matter of time before she'd vanish completely.

She stared at her hands, expecting to see sinew and bone. They remained solid but that did nothing to slow the frenzy running laps in her belly. *First goes your powers. Then your very life.*

Fatigue seized her again and she grabbed the closet door before falling to her knees. "Calm down!"

She imagined Finn beside her, whispering "Breathe, Witchling" his tail entwined around her ankle. The cold prickle of fear dulled as she melted into his sweet low tones. *Finn is my anchor, my white noise. Think of him and let this pass.*

She took another long breath, clearing her mind. Finn believed in her. Called her strong. It was going to be okay. She'd make it to Samhain in time. She'd survive. Finn would bring her book to her, and things would be right on track.

Breathe, Witchling.

It was so easy to imagine his confident, soothing voice. Her strength returned, the tornado of worry whirling to a small breeze. Ivy cracked her eyes open, pressing her hands to her very solid torso. Yup. She was still there. And she was thinking rationally again.

"Holy shit! That worked!"

All she wanted now was to throw her arms around Finn and squeeze tight. Thank Brigid for that egotistical man goat.

*Look...*the house whispered.

Ivy perked. "You're back? Crap, I faded just now! Are you sure I can make it to Samhain? There has to be a way we can move the ritual sooner!"

Look, it repeated.

"Look at what? Did you find my book!?"

There was an exasperated sigh as it once again said *Look!*

Ivy turned in a frustrated circle. "What am I looking at?! You're being cryptic!"

The window rattled in response. She crept towards the dim light pulsing through its frame. Power vibrated under her fingertips as she touched the glass and peered out at the deck below.

The pond was a still as a mirror, disrupted only by the fallen leaves rippling its surface. "So, what am I looking at? And where are you getting this power from?"

Finn charged onto the deck, a grim frown creasing his mouth. He removed his belt and untied his loincloth, tossing both aside. Ivy's anxiety and her breath were whisked away as she drank in every inch of his naked body.

He was nothing but hard-chiselled muscle below his waist; powerful thighs, sculpted fur covered calves, and the most perfect ass she had ever seen. The caramel hair that covered his chest trailed down his belly, between sharp hip creases before gathering around his cock.

His huge cock.

A surge of magic shot through her fingers and into her brain. Desire. Lust. It flooded her, making her sex throb and flesh burn. In reality, Finn was on the deck below, but in her mind, he was with her. Against her. Inside her. Oh, Goddess yes, inside her.

Her head fell back, and she moaned, feeling him thrust deep into her core over and over, filling her with his heat, whispering, *My Ivy. My clever beautiful witch.* Yes, she was his witch. Completely his. And he was hers.

Ivy squeezed her thighs together, hands grazing her hardened nipples as another rush made her quiver. This reverie wasn't enough. She needed him. To join. To bond. And it needed to be now.

A loud splash woke her from her trance. Finn had leapt into the pond, swimming to the bottom. He disappeared into the dark water, Ivy still tingling from his imagined touch. It was all a hallucination. She was alone.

...And yet you're still kneading your own breasts. She pulled her hands away, slapping her cheeks to sober herself. A giggle echoed from the walls. The frigging house was giggling! Great, on top of it all, her house was a total pervert.

"What the fuck! This isn't the time for this! I'm fading, for Brigid's sake!"

The house's laughter faded, along with its power. Ivy threw up her hands with a pterodactyl screech. She wasn't here for some torrid love affair, she was here to not die.

"Take me seriously!"

No reply. Stupid pervert house.

Finn had crawled out of the pond, shaking from horns to tail like a wet dog. Water glittered off his every muscle and Ivy couldn't take her eyes off him. Pinching her nipples again seemed like a great idea. Another pterodactyl screech vibrated her throat.

Her noise must had been loud enough for him to hear. His ears swiveled toward the window, followed by his gaze. She was about to duck away when she spotted the large green tome under his arm. "Mom's spell book?"

It was in the pond? *Just like the microwave, three lamps, and the toilet! He threw mom's spell book in the pond!* Every sexual thought of him vanished, her vision turning red. She stormed from her room, her pterodactyl screech turning to a lion's roar.

Finn had climbed back over the railing when she reached the deck. He offered her the waterlogged spell book with a pleased grin. "Problem solved. Your ritual can begin."

"What was my mother's book doing in the pond!?" she cried.

He flicked a dismissive hand. "That's neither here nor there. The important part is that it's been found."

"You threw it in, didn't you? Just like all my other things!" She snatched the book from him, its leather cover squishing under her fingers. Her belly clenched at the wet sound.

"It wasn't a recent action. I threw it in days before the truce!"

"That doesn't make me any less pissed off, Finn!"

The cover groaned as she opened it, water trickling onto the deck. If those pages were washed out, she might as well start digging her grave now. *Please be okay! Please be readable!*

"See? You can open it!" Finn insisted. "No need for anger!"

"Shut up!"

Her heart rattled as she gingerly flipped through the pages. Runes she hoped she'd see were scrawled in the margins. Her mother's protection wards kept the spells and her ritual notes still readable. Thank Brigid her mom always had a contingency plan. The tight fist in her gut relaxed... Until she reached the unprotected section. The one her family used for memories.

Rowan's childhood poems had disappeared. The family tree her father had drawn was nothing more than a blur. And Aster's art. All her charcoal sketches; the horses, the face studies, and the beautiful family portrait she had drawn a year before her death. Gone. The last memories of her mother, father, and Aster were reduced to puddles at her feet.

Ivy hugged the book to her chest, water streaming from its swollen pages and down her jeans. Tears scalded her cheeks, her teeth grinding until she was sure they'd turn to dust.

"I didn't think you'd be sad, Witchling," Finn said.

"Sad? You think I'm sad?!" A volcano of fury rose, melting every compassionate feeling for the satyr away. "These are rage tears, Finn!"

He had the nerve to look puzzled. "At me? Why? I found your book. And the spells seem intact."

"But my family memories aren't!" She turned, stomping back into the house. "Don't ever touch my things again! And don't talk to me either!"

"Witchling! Don't be mad!" Finn called.

Oh no. She was going to be mad. She was going to be furious until the sun burned out and the earth grew cold. She was an idiot to trust him. A complete and utter idiot

Ivy climbed the stairs, throwing back her head and screaming, "Fuuuuuck!"

Chapter 15

The winged male was asleep in the trees. It heard his snores through the darkness of night, could see the droop of his wings hanging limp. It had waited for this moment, trying to be patient, trying to hold the aching pangs of hunger at bay. It crawled out of their den, inching around twigs and leaves. One slight sound would rouse him. He had keen ears, that gargoyle. That King of Shadows.

King of Shadows? Where did it hear that moniker before?

Guilt forced it to look back at the male, its only friend. He was kind. He cared for it. He was the only reason it still lived. Who would care for a monster like it? Another monster, of course. The King of Shadows understood, knew its torment. It whimpered, turning back. No, it couldn't abandon him. Perhaps one more night by his side would quench the void.

Emptiness tore at its guts. It twisted, begging the agony to stop. *Please stop the pain! Oh Gods above the pain!*

It growled, its affection for the male fading. The King of Shadows may have understood, but he was still going to let it starve. Whatever it had mistaken for kinship was power and control. If he had truly cared, he would never let it suffer like this. Well, the suffering had gone on long enough. No more. It had to slake its hunger.

It left the male behind, the faint glow of that house in the distance. Its belly clenched, demanding to be filled.

Essence. Power. Love. I want it all!

The need to storm its borders forced it forward but it stopped, remembering the horrible jolt of electricity that sizzled through its limbs. It was still too weak to fight those wards. It wasn't ready. Not yet. But it would be after it regained its strength.

Feed! Feed! Feed!

It needed food if it wanted to get into that house and it would get into that house. Crickets and birds fell silent while it stalked. They knew it was on the hunt and didn't want to be prey.

The brush rustled in the distance. It narrowed its eyes, moving on silent feet towards the noise. Leaves withered to ash as it parted the bushes with mottled hands. A grand stag stood in the clearing, antlers proud and fur sleek as velvet.

Life. Beautiful life. It flowed through the stag's veins in rivers of light. So delicious. So divine. A growl resonated from its gut.

Devour. Consume. Feed.

The stag's ears swiveled, head following. Fear was in his wide eyes and that was even more pleasurable than the mouth-watering scent of its essence.

Its sides split, slimy tentacles lashing out. The stag brayed as he was entangled, struggling for freedom. He gouged his antlers down to the bone, but it didn't care. No slight flesh could even compare to the pain of its void.

Tentacles squeezed, bones snapped, the fight making his essence all the sweeter. Glorious life filled its belly. The stag turned cold, his brown fur greying to ash. He fell from its grip, hitting the ground and evaporating to dust.

Power. Strength. Ecstasy. Finally, the hunger subsided. But it wasn't enough. It needed more. And it would take more, sneak away from the King of Shadows every night if it had to. The feeding would go on until its strength had returned, and the house was in its keeping.

Instead of investigating the rustling outside her bedroom door, Ivy rolled over. She pulled her comforter over her shoulder, burrowing deeper into her cocoon.

The crackling fire plus the mountain of blankets created the perfect nest, the only thing calming her ire after yesterday. And yet, anger still tickled the back of her skull.

How did Finn think what he had done was okay? The more she ruminated, the angrier she became. He should have said sorry, shouldn't have acted like she was being irrational. She pulled her blanket over her head in hopes of drifting back into dreamland.

Another rustle came, soft and insistent. A reluctant grunt rumbled her throat. "Go away."

It was Finn, she knew it. She hadn't seen him since last night but felt him under his invisibility spell, trailing her like a scolded puppy. Ivy had refused to say a word to him. Nope. Not a word. She was pissed and going to stay pissed.

The noise continued, scratching at her door like a cat. She pulled the blanket off her head, greeted by the slim slivers of the golden dawn. It was barely sunrise.

"I hear you," she called. "Finn, just leave me alone."

The rustling continued. Ivy sat up, twisting her long mane into a rope before knotting it on top of her head. She got out of bed and padded to the door, and into the hall, her fury simmering.

"Finn, I mean it! I don't want to talk to you so..."

A wild tangle of color laid at her feet; blues, reds, yellows, and oranges all bundled together with a worn piece of twine. Wildflowers. Not what she was expecting.

Ivy stared at the bouquet, giving them a poke with her toe, then carefully picked them up, their fresh scent delightful. *That arrogant man goat picked me flowers.*

She couldn't remember the last time anyone got her flowers, let alone picked them for her. Where the hell did he find them so late in the year? Her heart did a little flip, despite herself, her mouth curling into a tiny smile.

The door across the hall squeaked and an amber eye peered out from the crack. It shook Ivy from her dreamy swoon, and she scowled, mind going back to the spell book drying in front of the box fan in the bathroom. "Don't think a few flowers are going to make things better."

"Then why are you clutching them like that?" Finn asked.

She was hugging the beautiful spray to her chest. She threw the flowers to the floor, stepping over them and making her way to the kitchen. Coffee was definitely in order. Wine would come later. No, she would not be swayed by gifts. When Ivy got a grudge, she held that grudge. End of story.

The day began with cleaning, repairs, and no sign of Finn, other than the clacking of his hooves echoing in the halls. Ivy did her best to busy herself, but she couldn't forget the blurred pages that once held Aster's drawings.

Her sister was an artist in every sense of the word, and she wanted to leave her mark on the family's book. Since Ivy was the eldest sister, it was in her keeping but she was happy to let Aster sketch in its back pages to her heart's content. Dammit, she intended to add more protection wards to the pages but never got around to it.

That fist tightened in her chest once again as she climbed the stairs, broom clutched in her hands. She should have written those runes ages ago, should have protected the last bit of her sister.

Lets just kill Aster all over again, Ives.

The sound of a flute cut through the thick silence, a beautiful melody that danced through the air and tickled her ears. Each note brimmed with emotion; happiness one minute, sorrow the next, only to swell into overwhelming bliss. It seeped into her skin sweeping her guilt aside.

She followed the tune to Finn's room, her heart demanding more. She peered through the open door, surprised to see he had been decorating.

Branches were hung from the high ceiling, a garland of leaves and flowers festooned over the tall windows. He had no furniture beyond the old chair that she had promised him. The eye sore sat proudly in the middle of the room as if it were a throne.

Finn reclined on it upside down with his flute, hooves propped on the back rest and horns brushing the floor. Sunlight poured over every cut muscle of his bared torso, loincloth tucked to keep from falling, yet outlining the contours of his shaft. Yup, it was still huge, and he wasn't even hard.

She almost sank to her knees as his entrancing melody flowed between her legs, making her ache with its joy. He was right, he really could seduce her with just his music. Hell, he could be playing the kazoo and she'd drop her panties without a thought.

Finn's eye winked open, sneaking a peek at her. His tune stopped and he sat up, pulling the flute from his lips. "Are you willing to be rational now?"

And the mood was shattered. "No."

"Even after my concert? I wrote that song for you, after all." When she scoffed, he shrugged. "All right, I didn't write it for you. But you were on my mind while I played it. Regardless, it's time you stopped this anger and talk to me." He twisted his flute in his hands. "Like you did before. I liked that and it should continue."

"Go to Hell."

She slammed his door and walked away. The asshole didn't even know how to accept responsibility for his own actions. Finn's clacking hooves were tight on her heels.

"Witchling! Talk to me! Do you know how hard that song is to perform? I only break it out during the most sacred of festivals!" He sighed. "Fine then. I'll play a different song if that first doesn't please you."

There was a blast of his flute and Ivy groaned. "Finn, stop! Stop with the gifts and the songs and..."

More wildflowers sat in front of her room, twice as many than before. Lying beside the bouquet were three large pinecones, each with twine tied in a bow at their tip. Finn, spread his arms at the pile as if to say "Tah Dah!"

She threw up her arms. "Leave me alone!"

"Not until you talk to me!"

"I don't want to talk to you! I don't want anything to do with you! You've been a pain in my ass since I got here and apparently that's not changing anytime soon!"

A confused frown curved his lips. "What can I do to make you talk to me again?"

"How about an apology? That could be a start!"

"An apology?" He tilted his head, his tail twitching. "But your spells are readable. The important parts were salvaged. That's all that should matter."

"But all the family memories in the back are ruined! Those are just as important as the spells!" Judging by the puzzled look in his face, he wasn't getting it. She shook her head. "I'm not going to stand here and try an explain empathy to you, Finn. If you can't figure out why I'm pissed, then leave me alone."

She side stepped him, her rage pushing her feet down the stairs and out the door. She should have never confided in him, should never have told him about Aster's death.

The house's tinny voice demanded, *Stop.*

"No."

Stop and go back. Talk to him. Bond to him.

"No!" she slapped the porch swing, sending it soaring, "I'm not here for your amusement! This isn't a game! Why don't you understand that I'm dying!?"

"What do you mean, you're dying?" Finn stood in the doorway, eyes wide and face drawn.

She felt naked, skinned alive under his stare. The swell of panic closed her throat. *You're weak, He sees it now. And he'll watch you fail and die.*

She shoved her hands over her ears. Finn's brows knitted. He reached for her, but she jerked away. *Now he knows. He knows you killed Aster and now he knows you can't even save yourself.*

He looked at her just like her aunts, like every other witch in town had. With the pity you'd only reserve for an animal who stupidly hurt itself. A witch's dirty little secret. *You said it out loud to him. Now it's going to come true.*

She searched frantically for something, anything to ground her, the trees, the rocks, the porch swing. But the overwhelming panic was too much this time. She was too tired to fight it. Too frightened to be angry. The spiral finally swallowed her whole.

She ran, boots crunching along the gravel drive before hitting the soft dirt path. Finn called her name, but she ignored it, breath in short, manic gasps as she dodged through the trees, putting as much distance as she could between her and the house.

You're going to die. Die. Die. Die.

Her legs ached, sweat pouring as she continued to run. She couldn't breathe, couldn't speak, couldn't even focus enough to use her coping skills. The panic attack rolled on, never ending. *Oh, sweet Brigid please make it stop!*

A branch caught her ankle, sending her tripping into a tree. She hit the rough bark, scraping her palms as she caught herself. A sob exploded from her lips and she sank.

Breathe, Witchling, Finn crooned in her memory. His voice forced the air through her nostrils, despite her resentment.

"One. The big ass fir tree I just ran into," she muttered to herself. "Two. The dirt under my feet. Three. The sounds of the birds overhead."

Her heart settled and she fell into a sit, resting her back against the tree's trunk. Minutes rolled by, the sound of her exhales her only concern. Soon she regained control.

Well, this was a stupid situation she got herself into. She was forty fucking two years old and here she was, running away like an angsty teenager. Anxiety certainly brought out the best in her, didn't it?

"Go home, Ives. Take an Atarax. You're going to be okay."

She dusted her knees, rising with a groan. Towering trees surrounded her, her house far out of sight. Shit, she had no idea which direction she came from.

Ivy turned in a circle, trying to orientate herself when the snap of a branch made her sigh. "Finn, I'm sorry I ran. But can I get two seconds to pull myself-"

A low, guttural growl turned her blood to ice. Birds fled, their wings flapping wildly as they took to the sky. Ivy went cold. She spared a slow look over her shoulder.

A huge paw reached out from the brush, then another. Yellow eyes narrowed on her as a mountain lion stalked forward, its giant body coiled tight, ready to pounce. It bared its fangs and hissed.

Ivy staggered, her back hitting a tree. Her hand brushed deep gouges in the bark. Gouges made by its razor-sharp claws, a marking of its territory. And she had stumbled right into it.

She threw out a hand as if a spell would shoot from her fingertips. In the past, a quick flash of magic would send wildlife running. But not this time. Shit, what did they tell her about mountain lions when she was a kid? Remain calm. After the panic attack she just had, that wasn't a possibility. *Why did you have to be so stupid and run like that!?*

The lion's hackles rose. It bent into a crouch releasing a scream that shook her teeth. It was going to tear her apart for stepping right into its domain.

An arrow stuck in the dirt between them with a loud thwack. The lion leapt back then snarled, slapping the arrow with its enormous mitt.

Finn charged out from the trees, bow trained on the beast. "Leave her be."

Its horrible roar split the air.

"Her wandering into your territory was an accident, not an offence." Finn's voice was steady and sure, but murder was in his mismatched eyes.

Another scream, rage contorting the lion's features.

"No, the witch is not yours. She is mine." Finn bared his fangs. "And I decide her fate."

The lion pounced and Finn shot. But the arrow only grazed its cheek, raising its ire. It took the satyr down with an earth trembling crash, his bow flying from his grip. Finn pushed away its snapping jaws, scrambling for his dagger. Claws raked his chest, blood trickling down his sides.

Ivy tried to grab his bow, but it was too close to the lion's swinging claws. She picked up a rock and hurled it, striking the lion between its shoulders. With a snarl, it turned its angry sights upon her, leaving Finn behind. It leapt but was stopped mid-air as Finn grabbed it by the tail.

He flung the mountain lion to the ground, jumping on its back and wrapping his arm around its neck. It thrashed but Finn held strong, pressing his forearm into its throat.

"Yield!" he demanded.

The lion wailed in furious protest.

"You know what I am, beast. And what I am capable of. Yield and we will never encroach again." Finn tightened his grip, the veins on his arm standing. "Fight me, and you will die."

The mountain lion choked, eyes widening. Its paws fell limp and it relaxed into the dirt with a submissive purr. As promised, Finn released it, shoulders rising and falling with his heavy pants.

Ivy ran for Finn then stopped as the mountain lion stood. She remained frozen until it shook the dirt from its fur then slunk into the trees, tail between its legs. Once it was gone, her feet unstuck.

Finn met her halfway. He took her shoulders, his brutality draining. Nothing was left but pure fear. "Are you all right?!"

"Me?!" Ivy searched her pockets, happy to have found a handkerchief hiding in one of them. She pressed the cloth against his bloody chest. "I'm not the one bleeding out!"

Finn grunted. "It's just a scratch. I'll be healed by morning."

The white cloth was soaked in crimson in a matter of seconds. That was anything but a scratch. "We have to get you back home and cleaned up." She herded him away, but he took her arm, forcing her to face him.

"You didn't answer my question, Witchling. Are you all right?"

She pursed her lips then nodded. "Yeah. I'm fine. Just...shaken."

The answer seemed to satisfy him. He lifted his chin, eyes scrunching in pain. "Then let's go home."

Ivy fetched his bow and slung his arm over her shoulders, letting him rest his weight against her. When the peaked roof of the house came into sight, she slumped, relief taking its hold. Soon she had him sitting in her bathtub and was washing away the blood with the shower head.

Finn bit his lips as the water trickled down his wounds. His forehead wrinkled with strain. "Well, isn't this a change? Is it my turn to shout ridiculous curse words now?"

"Shout anything you like. You earned it." She dipped her fingers into Finn's wooden canister, scooping out his healing salve. "So... you can talk to animals, huh?"

He nodded, wincing as she smeared his now clean cuts with a generous handful. "I'm of the fair-folk, it's what we do. Though he was a rather cranky cat and not willing to listen."

She gestured to his chest. "No kidding."

The damn satyr had fought a mountain lion. For her. And only hours ago she had told him to go to hell.

"Thank you." Ivy stared at her work, unable to look him in the eyes. "And I'm sorry. I really shouldn't have stormed off like that."

"And I...uh... I wish to...perhaps..." Finn looked up at the ceiling, the brush of his tail snapping against the tub. "A moment please. I rarely apologise. Finding how it begins is difficult."

"You're apologising?" Ivy wiggled a finger in her ear, wondering if she heard him correctly, or if there was a wax build up.

"At the time, I thought my reasonings for tossing away your book were sound. If Cal had seen it, he would have fallen into his rages. I was trying to protect him. But that is only an excuse. I now realize how much those destroyed pages meant to you. It's like my bow. It's not only my tool; it's part of me." He took her chin, tipping it so their eyes met. "I'm sorry. Truly sorry. I hope with time you'll forgive me."

Warmth spread from her chest to her fingertips, tickling a smile to her lips. "Apology accepted."

Finn's brows shot up. "That's it? That's all I had to do?"

"Words are powerful, Finn. Thank you."

The side of his mouth lifted into a lopsided grin then he sank against the tub, expression sobering. "Are you truly dying?"

Her shoulders bunched, fingers shaking as she wiped them on a towel. "Yeah. I am."

She pushed herself from the bath, desperate to move from this uncomfortable subject but he caught her wrist. Their eyes met, Finn's face softening into grief.

"Why are you dying?" he asked, barely above a whisper.

"A witch's power is their driving force. Their soul, practically. And when it's gone, it's like pouring water over a fire. The wood may burn and smoke for a while but eventually, it dies. We call it the fade. And mine started yesterday."

Finn released her wrist, leaning forward, as if studying her for further signs of her aliment. "And how long do you have until you disappear completely?"

She shrugged. "Weeks? Days? Maybe a couple months? I don't know. I'm one of the lucky ones. I lasted an entire year after my powers were stolen. Usually the fade starts way before. That doesn't make me feel any better though."

"It seems your stubbornness worked in your favor, Witchling."

She snorted a little laugh. "Guess it's good for something."

"Indeed." His sweet, crooked smile returned. "And this ritual, it will bring your powers back?"

"In theory, yes. See, a cottage witch can bring dead homes like this back to life. And in exchange for life the house gives us power. If I can revive this place, it could refill me." She sighed. "But I need others to help power this ritual. I only have Rowan on my side."

"What about your aunts?"

"They think this ritual will hurt me worse than the fade. They won't support it, keep trying to talk me out of it. So, it's me and Rowan." She shook her head. "I just hope he's enough."

Finn rubbed his chin. "This home once belonged to a powerful warlock. Its magic was incredible when it was alive. Would that make up for the lack of support?"

Ivy sat up, wide eyed. "Wait, a warlock *did* own this place?"

"I met him, myself. Unfortunately, he was killed when..." He shook his head. "That matters not. What matters is that this was once a very powerful home. Will that help?"

The old tales were true. A warlock *had* lived here, had walked these grounds, hell, he'd probably built this house with his bare hands. No wonder it had the power to cross the veil and speak to her. *And now it's yours, Ives.*

Hope shot through every nerve, pushing laugher from her lips. "Yes! Holy shit, yes it would! With power like that in these walls? I really could pull this off!"

Ivy flung herself over the tub, wrapping her arms around Finn tight. When he grunted in pain, she pulled away, face heating.

He didn't seem upset by her sudden affection, only grinned, arms resting on her shoulders. "What do you need of me for this ritual?"

"Power," Ivy replied. "Lots and lots of power."

"Well, it so happens I am a being of magic. I have plenty to spare." He winked. "I'm at your disposal, Ivy Siobhan Bennet."

Chapter 16

*F*inn burst into her bedroom, a wild look in his beautiful mismatched eyes. He threw her onto her bed,
ripping Ivy's nightgown down the center. It was
tossed away, forgotten.

Heat pooled in her core. It longed to be filled with him,
his tongue, his cock. All of him. He crawled over her, his
body heavy, pulsing with heat. His lips trailed up her throat,
nipping, biting, marking her as his.

"My Ivy." His tail whipped across her ass, the sting making her arch. "My beautiful, clever Witchling."

Yes. This. More of this. All of this. He untied the knot
of his loincloth and her knees fell wide, cradling his hips, his
hard shaft grazing her sex. She leaned in to seal her mouth
against his, but he flicked his pointed tongue against her
nose. The slimy sensation stopped her cold.

"Uh, Finn?" she asked. "Why did you-"

Another lick ripped her from her dream.

Ivy shook off the last of her lust as she cracked her eyes open. A pair of beady eyes surrounded by black fur greeted her good morning.

"What the fuck?!"

The raccoon perched on her belly squeaked. It rolled off her and onto its back, its little paws flailing before it righted itself with an indignant chitter. Ivy pushed herself away as it approached, falling off her bed with a loud thud. The comforter and the raccoon were dragged along for the ride. Both screamed, the furry creature running circles over her tangled body, dodging her swinging limbs.

"Finn! Fuck fuck fuck! It's going to bite me!"

The door flew open and Finn charged in, dagger in hand. His ferocity dimmed as he surveyed the situation, blade returning to its sheath. "Ah, I see you've met Maximus."

"Maximus? Who the hell is...?" Ivy's back hit the nightstand as her furry visitor approached. "The raccoon?!"

"Yes." Finn gave a sweeping gesture towards it. "Meet your familiar."

Ivy gaped like a wide mouth bass. "My what?"

Maximus scrambled up her back and settled on her head. With a slow hand, she reached up, giving his rump a nudge. He slid down obediently, letting out a little whistle before trotting to her front and plopping himself down. His shiny black eyes beamed at her as he reached forward, pressing a black paw on her knee. Dear Brigid, that was cute.

"I don't have a familiar, Finn," she said.

A vainglorious grin spread wide across the satyr's face. "You do now!"

Finn bent, hands resting on his knees, as he clicked his tongue. Maximus scampered over, climbing on his shoulder to nuzzle his ear. Ivy's heart turned over with a thud. If that knee pat wasn't the most adorable thing she had ever seen, this definitely was.

"Maximus will be your eyes, ears, protection, and support for when you're in one of your panic attacks." Finn scratched Maximus under his chin. "I once tried to get one for Callum but he kept scaring them off. You're far more agreeable though and Maximus here volunteered the minute I asked. Said he'd be stellar at the job."

Ivy was sure her eyeballs were going to pop out of her sockets with the way she was staring. "So... you got me an emotional support raccoon?"

"No. A familiar." He covered Maximus's ears, speaking in a hushed tone. "He doesn't want to be called anything else." Then he uncovered his ears and gave him a pat on the head. "You do like him, yes? He'll be very disappointed if you turn him away."

Familiars weren't anything she was, well, familiar with. No one in her family had one except for her great-great-grandmother and that was of the usual black cat variety. What was she supposed to do with a raccoon?

Could raccoons even be familiars? *Shit, what do raccoons even eat?*

Maximus's tiny black nose wiggled, dark eyes widening to puppy dog proportions. Great, now she felt guilty over jilting a raccoon. She nodded with a tight-lipped smile. "Welcome to the house, Maximus."

Finn lit up like a roman candle and her heart turned over a second time, the thud even louder than before.

"You hear that, Maximus?" he crowed. "She has accepted you! Good work!"

Maximus's delighted chitter made her melt. He hopped off his shoulder, his bushy ringtail swishing. With a happy chirp he plopped into her lap, curling up. Then the purring started. Another paw was placed on her knee. Ivy was going to die from all this cute first thing in the morning.

Finn clapped his hands. "Come now, Maximus. Let me give you a tour of your new home."

The two left, and Ivy's laugh exploded. "He gave me a raccoon. A friggin' raccoon!"

A soft giggle joined her, ringing from the walls like delicate bells. She gave the house a smirk. "Uh huh. Laugh it up. It's going to be your floor he shits on."

The giggle grew louder.

"And don't deny that you're implanting dirty dreams in my head. I know what you are now. Half dead or not, you have the capability. What's your game?"

The silence didn't surprise her. Ivy shook her head. "I'm going to assume that your lack of answer is because you're too weak to give one, not because you're being coy like every damn magical thing in the world."

She yanked her robe from her footboard and headed to the bathroom for a shower. A shower and perhaps more fantasies involving Finn's kisses. Things were good today. Maybe they would be good tomorrow too. If Finn was around, she had hope. And that was an amazing feeling.

Maximus trotted eagerly behind Finn, chittering fast.

"The kitchen?" That's downstairs. And you'll have to ask *her* if you're allowed to eat her trash."

More chittering, Maximus peeking through cracked doors before moving to the stairs. He was a curious fellow, a perfect trait for a familiar. Or at least Finn assumed it was. Frankly, he had no idea what a familiar did, but knew witches had them. And Ivy distinctly lacked one. Well, what his Witchling lacked, Finn would provide. And the extra protection over her put his heart at ease.

Maximus nudged another door open with his snout, crawling through. "Ah ah! Careful in there! That's where the witch keeps her books! They are precious to her!"

If you could even call it a proper library. A few books were scattered on the floor, but the rest were still packed in boxes. Finn frowned. So many empty rooms. No furniture, no little touches of the witch's presence at all beyond lit fires and clean swept floors. A reminder that Ivy's stay was temporary.

Samhain was closer now, their bargain almost at an end. Dammit, he had grown so accustomed to her presence. His hand absently brushed the healed wounds on his chest. The ones she was kind enough to tend to only a few days before. She would never tend to him again if she leaves. *Or fades.*

His ears flattened. That's not how it would turn out. Ivy was clever, stubborn, and strong. And she had him. He'd move the heavens, hells, and the earth itself to make sure she survived. No one, not even death was going to take his Witchling before her time.

And what of Callum? He glanced out the hallway window to the trees. His brother was out there alone, and the cold seasons were coming fast. Did he have a blanket? By Dionysus, did he have his potions?

Finn had already tried hunting him down twice and was unsuccessful. Callum excelled at hiding ever since they were fawns. If he didn't want to be found he damn well would not be. Finn blew out a sigh. All he could do was wait until his brother's ire cooled. Then he'd find him, talk to him, and make him understand that he would not give up his Witchling.

He gestured to Maximus. "Come along. I'll show you the witch's kitchen. I'm sure you'll want to see her pantry. It's stocked with all sorts of delights."

Finn's mind ran in circles. Happiness. It was right there, ready to be grasped. Only two hurdles stood in his way. Two enormous hurdles. But he had survived this long, he would endure more, and this time come out victorious.

He made his way down the stairs, a grin tightening his cheeks. *You'll put things right, Finn. You'll get everything you desire. And it's about damn time.*

Chapter 17

I vy swished around the last teaspoon of moon water in the mason jar. The rest was in the puddle on the floor. If she hadn't lost her footing on her way down the stairs, she'd have enough to anoint every doorway and window. Well, at least the floor was cleansed. It was a start, but she was going to need more.

She placed the jar on the coffee table, looking at her fingers suspiciously. *Did you lose your footing? Or did the fade make your legs weak?* She held her breath, waiting for them to vanish. After five minutes of standing at the foot of the stairs, staring at her hand, she snorted.

"Not today, anxiety," she muttered.

There was no use crying over spilt moon water. She was in a good mood today, the best she'd felt in a year. Samhain was in two days and she truly felt she could pull off the ritual. Her emotions were not going to get the better of her. She'd just head down to her aunt's shop and pick up a jar. An easy fix.

Of course, that meant subjecting herself to their passive aggressive pressure. She stalled before grabbing her
keys. Their visit two weeks ago had been the last time
she'd seen Dahlia and Rosemary face to face. Her ego was
already hanging on by a thread, getting bombarded with
constant "are you sure about this?" questions wasn't going to help much.

"I'll be in and out in a minute. Two tops. You can do
hard things Ives. Just pick up the water and come home."

She snagged her coat off the hook by the door, then
her purse. "Finn? You around?"

Maximus gave a shrill mew of greeting as he skuttled
from the hall, his ringed tail poofed.

"Oh, hey Maximus. Have you seen Finn?" She wrinkled her brow. "Or do you have no idea what I'm saying?"

Maximus plopped his chubby behind down and
tugged on the leg of her jeans with a squeak. The gleam
in his shining eyes said he understood.

"Okay, good. You understand me."

He ran a little circle around her, chirping in conversation. He may have spoken human, but unfortunately, Ivy
didn't speak raccoon.

"Whoa, whoa. I don't know what you're saying here.
Are you hungry? Sleepy? Uh, you want me to...pick you
up?" When she bent down to grab him, Maximus's ears
flattened, and he chuffed. Quickly she retreated. "Okay,
okay, no picking you up. Got it."

He weaved between her legs, chastising her with irri-
tated squeaks. Sweet Brigid, it was like an episode of

Lassie. "Look, I have no idea what you're saying. And I never had a familiar. Bear with me, okay? Can you show me where Finn is?"

He hopped on all fours like he was spring loaded. Hopefully that was a yes. Whatever it was, it was adorable. She laughed, wanting to give him a hug but thought maybe she should give him a bath first.

Maximus started to the hall when the fur along his back bristled. He spun, hissing at the front door, his tail sticking straight up. Ivy blinked as he scratched his claws against it.

"What is it?" She clenched her fists, peeking outside a window. Leaves spun in wild dervishes as clouds rolled across the sun. It was an average autumn day out there. "I don't see anything, Max."

The dull thump of the porch swing hitting the side of the house made Ivy jump. A hollow moan drifted through the trees, agonized and starving. Every hair on the back of her neck stood straight. She nudged Maximus away from the door, peering out once again.

A long tentacle slithered across the dirt path, its leathery skin mottled with black, grey, and green blotches. It skimmed over every blade of grass and fallen leaf as if tasting each one.

Ivy rubbed her eyes. "What the hell?" She pressed closer to the window, squinting. It could have been a shadow, could have been a trick of the sunlight.

A loud thud almost sent her out of her skin. Ivy yelped, spinning to see Finn shoving a worn steamer chest into the room. "I have something for you!" he announced.

Ivy looked back out the window. There was nothing along the path, only the shadows of trees. Dammit, was hallucinating a symptom of the fade? *You're losing it, Ives.*

She rubbed her cheeks, shoving the strange sight out of her mind. "What's with the trunk?"

Maximus chirped and ran to Finn, scaling his length before draping himself across his broad shoulders. Finn didn't even flinch save for an ear flick when the raccoon gave it a nibble. He patted the trunk, dust flying everywhere. "You need more furniture. This house is far too empty."

"Yeah but I'm not staying-"

He waved off the rest of her sentence. "No, you need more. This is all I have but I'm happy to donate."

She smiled, his insistence washing away her earlier unease. "Thanks. That's really sweet."

"I know." He grinned, hands tucked behind his back.

"Well, while you move that, I have to head into town. I'm out of moon water."

"Ah, splendid! I'll tag along!" The raccoon on his shoulder let out an annoyed mew. "Oh, and so will Maximus."

"What? Finn, no."

"I think you mean Finn, yes!"

"I mean Finn, no! I'm going into the heart of town. Humans are everywhere." She gestured to his legs. "And you are part goat!"

"Easily disguised." Finn flung the steamer trunk open, more dust rising in an ominous cloud. He yanked out a pair of worn out jeans.

Ivy folded her arms, putting on her best stern expression. "And a shirt?"

Again, he reached into the trunk. Out came a baggy black sweater. "It's amazing what humans will leave outside."

"Okay, fine, so you stole clothes from campers." She swept a hand around his face. "But what about from the neck up?"

Finn flattened his ears against his skull, finger combing his shaggy caramel hair over them. Then with a snap of his fingers, the air around his horns wavered and they vanished. "My dimming ability can work in isolated areas as well." Another snap and they reappeared.

Ivy cleared her throat and nodded to his hooves.

He gave her a smug smile. "Ah, but wait!" With the flourish of a Las Vegas magician, out came a pair of ratty hiking boots.

Ivy's brow knitted. "How can you even keep those on? You have no feet!"

He opened his mouth then shut it, nose wrinkling as he examined the boots. "Good question."

"Finn, when was the last time you've been around humans?"

He pursed his lips, tapping his fingertips and muttering numbers under his breath. By the fourth pass on all ten fingers Ivy waved a hand for him to stop.

"You know I have to visit my aunts' shop for my supplies, right?"

He ran a fang across his lip, tangling his finger together. "I can endure."

"Really? Mister more than one witch troubles me? The answer is still, no."

He lifted his chin, expression saying he would not take no for an answer. "You almost came to harm once, Witchling. I will not tolerate another. I'm coming with you."

Ivy rubbed her palms together. He was worried about her. Her heart did a double backflip. "Okay, fine. But you do as I say, and you stay close."

"Excellent! I shall dress and then we shall be on our way!"

He unceremoniously dropped his loincloth. Ivy spun around, but it was too late. She had seen everything. Every single glorious inch. Again. Yeah, it was going to be another date with her vibrator tonight.

It was trial and error getting into those boots, Finn cursing the shape of human feet as they slid off his hooves. After the fifth time, he tried to convince Ivy that they weren't necessary, but she insisted that humans, did indeed, look down. Eventually they laced them tight enough to stay in place. Walking in them was an entirely different hurdle.

He tripped and stumbled, ping-ponging from the door, to the porch swing, then back to the door. Ivy grabbed him before he plummeted down the stairs. Twenty minutes later, they had gotten into her vehicle, Maximus running circles across the back seat. She pulled what she had called a seatbelt across him, and they headed down the road.

Finn bounced in his seat, both from bumps and from his excitement. The last time he had been close to humans was when they still had festivals to honor him and his God. Now here he was, heading into town with his Witchling. An adventure to share.

The dirt roads turned into paved roads, their ride smooth as silk. They rounded the lake, cabins dotting its shore, and boats bobbing in its waters. Humans spilt out onto the streets, laughing, shouting, hurrying about in their hats and scarves. Finn stared, hands pressed against the window.

"You look like a puppy," Ivy giggled.

"This is fascinating! Maximus, are you seeing this?" The happy chirp confirmed that yes, he was. Maximus pressed his muzzle against the glass, tongue lashing across it.

There was a click then a hum and the window rolled down from Finn's fingers. Crisp scent of pine filled his nostrils, combined with others; spices and cooking food, fresh water, and an acrid stench coming from the other vehicles.

Ivy smiled. "Thought maybe you'd want the window open."

Maximus leapt over Finn's seat and into his lap, sticking his head out the window. Finn followed suit. This is what he'd been missing. All this beauty, this excitement. It was all here while he hid under a crumbling old house. The world was growing, and it made his heart thunder.

"When did the population grow so large?" he shouted over the rush of the wind in his ears.

"You should see it during ski season. Tourists everywhere."

"What are tourists?"

"Visitors. They pay good for a winter vacation in Big Bear and kind of keep our economy going."

"So, tourists are good?" Finn settled back into his seat, letting Maximus cool his tongue in the wind.

"More or less." Ivy shrugged. "Some can be assholes, but most are good people."

"And they help you as well?"

"Definitely. My aunts own a shop downtown and they're always busy when the tourists come."

"Does this shop bring you money as well?"

"Yeah. I make oil blends and lotions to sell there. So, I make a decent amount."

Finn arched a brow. "...Decent amount?"

"Enough for me to get by. Granted, things are a little tight since most of my money and savings went to buying the house but I'm doing okay."

"But more money would make you happy?"

She shrugged again. "I wouldn't turn my nose up at it. I could always use it."

The vehicle slowed to a stop and humans paraded by, crossing from one side of the road to the other. Tourists. Tourists that brought money. Money that made Ivy happy. And he wanted his Witchling happy.

His head was back out the window. "You there! Human female!" He shouted at a woman still on the corner.

Her head jerked up and she almost fell over at the sight of him. "Uh, me?"

He beckoned her towards him. "Yes, you! I have a proposition!"

Ivy grabbed him by the collar, yanking him back. "Finn, no!"

"Finn, yes!" He braced himself on the sides of the window.

"I don't understand." Slowly, the female inched towards him.

He could see the intrigue in her eyes, the desire. All he had to do was lure her in. "Oh, but you will, my sweet." He gave her his most tempting grin and a blush stole across her cheeks.

"Get back in the car, Finn!" Ivy demanded. "Maximus! Help me out here!"

Maximus head butted his chest to push him away from the window, but Finn grabbed him by the scruff and dumped him into the back seat.

"You wish to spend your tourist money, my sweet flower? Well there's a witch shop somewhere in town filled with wonders."

The female leaned against the door, a flirty smile spreading across her full lips. "Wonders, eh? Like you?"

"Indeed, though maybe not as magnificent as I. We are on our way there now. And you should be too. Give them your money." He hiked a thumb over his shoulder. "Especially this one. It makes her- Ow!"

Somehow Ivy grabbed one of his invisible horns. He flew into her lap, Maximus hopping onto his shoulders to pin them down.

"Sorry! He's just very friendly!" Ivy called to the woman. "Uh, Welcome to Big Bear?" The vehicle lurched forward as she pressed her foot on one of the pedals.

"Wait!" The female cried.

They jerked to a stop with an ear-piercing screech. Finn broke free, leaning back out the window with a grin that would melt butter. "Yes, my perfect posey?"

The female twirled a lock of dark hair around her fingers. "So, where is this shop?"

Finn looked back at Ivy, gesturing for her to answer. Her stare flipped between the two before she replied with a dazed, "Witch Way on Pine Knot Avenue."

"Now there, was that so hard?" He chided then looked back to the female. "Witches tend to cackle so I'm sure you'll hear it before you see it- Ow! Witchling, stop elbowing me!"

The female sauntered back over, heavy lidded. "And what's *your* name?"

Finn tapped the tip of her nose. She giggled, cheeks flushing. "My name is of no importance. What is, is to give your money to-"

His send off was cut short as Ivy rolled up the window. She slammed her foot down on the pedal and they took off, Maximus rolling across the seats and to the floor with a yelp.

"What the hell was that about?" Ivy demanded.

He lifted his head with a proud smile. "You said you could use money. I was helping you get money."

Her mouth opened, then shut with a click of her teeth. "...I'm not sure if I should be annoyed or grateful now."

Moments later Ivy had halted her vehicle and turned off its engine. Finn was eager to walk amongst the meandering humans and even a tiny bit smug that none of them could tell he wasn't one of them.

"Sorry Max, but you're going to have to stay here," Ivy said, groaning as he let out a protesting hiss. She looked to Finn. "He's not going to stay put, is he?"

Finn clicked his tongue then turned to the pouting raccoon in the back. "You need to guard the witch's vehicle. There are thieves about."

Maximus's ears perked, a series of clicks and squeaks asked, *is that true?*

"Most certainly," Finn replied. "A familiar has to protect not only his witch, but their belongings as well."

With a battle chitter, Maximus dashed to the front seat, perching himself on Ivy's steering wheel. His tail shot straight, every inch of him ready to defend.

Ivy turned to Finn, mouthing "I can't believe that worked!"

Finn beamed under her adoring gaze. He was impressing his little Witchling left and right today. He opened the door, slid from his seat then took three steps before falling face first onto the pavement with a meaty smack. Dionysus's Balls, the ground was a lot harder here than at home.

"Finn! Are you okay!?" Ivy cried.

A chorus of gasps rose, the sound of footsteps rushing towards him. Arms snaked around his waist, hauling him upright. Finn stumbled into Ivy's soft, welcoming bosom, cheek throbbing.

Dozens of concerned faces surrounded them, murmuring as they watched. He lifted a hand in the air. "Never fear! I'm unharmed!"

The crowd dispersed, the few giggles poking his already bruised ego. A sharp shake of his head cleared his vision but did little to quell the pain of his cheek.

Ivy cupped his face. "You got a nasty scratch there." He hissed when she passed her thumb across his cheekbone. Her frown grew deeper. "You're sure you're alright walking in those boots?"

He pointed towards the crack running through the pavement. "That is the culprit. Not my agility." Ivy bit her lips together, her eyes crinkling with mirth. Finn huffed. "I'm perfectly graceful!"

"Fine. We'll go with that theory." She wrapped a secure arm around his waist, her closeness making his flesh tingle. "I'm sure we got something at the shop to put on that scratch. It's a short walk. Promise."

He leaned on her, catching the hint of her intoxicating scent. Lavender and sage. Beautiful. Seductive. He leaned closer, almost rubbing against her neck like he had her chair.

Ivy nudged him forward. "I'm not going to carry you."

"But I'm *so* weak from my fall." Finn pressed the back of his hand to his forehead with a dramatic moan. "Oh, so weak! Alas! I swoon again!"

He mock stumbled into her, draping his arms around her shoulders. Ivy caught his waist, throwing her head back with a laugh so loud, full, and joyous that it made his skin prickle into gooseflesh. He wanted to hear it again. And again, and again, and again. Wanted to make her smile. Wanted to touch her. Kiss her. *Keep her. Keep her for all time.*

After a quick, but trying walk, they made it to *Witch Way*, its gilded sign proudly perched on its roof, flourished with stars, moons, and arrows. Ivy pushed open the wood door, a merry bell announcing their arrival.

Finn stalled, peering into the shop. *You're going into the lion's den.* This was a witch's domain, one filled with secrets and alien sights that brought no comfort. And it was filled with witches. The Gods only knew how many were lurking around each table and shelf. Watching him. Waiting to discover what he was and take the last of his strength.

His tail longed to swish, wanting to relieve the tension knotting his insides. But it was wrapped around his middle under his sweater, the brush tapping frantic against his belly. He reached up, wiping the sweat that now coated his forehead. Dammit, his hands were shaking.

"Finn, you coming?"

His gaze snapped to Ivy. She was holding the door open, her eyes soft. "You can wait with Maximus if you want. I won't be long."

He frowned, puffing out his chest. "Absolutely not." And with that, he marched in, head held high.

The shop was like nothing he expected. No altars or scent of blood, but warmth and comfort, as if spelled to be. Herbs hung along iron rods across its ceiling, much like how he and Callum had adorned their own dwelling. Crystals sparkled on small tables covered in red velvet, shelves packed with jars and books, and brooms of every size mounted on the walls.

Soft music wafted through the atmosphere, along with a beautiful and all too familiar scent. Lavender, sage, smoke and, Goddess help him, sex. Ivy. It was all Ivy. "This place... smells of you."

Ivy stopped by a shelf and plucked out a bottle amongst many. "It's one of the blends I created. I wear it all the time. I wanted it to smell feminine but not use the usual bases a lot of perfumes do like rose or jasmine. So, I came up with this. If I may toot my own horn, it's a best seller."

She unscrewed the top and stuck the bottle under his nose. His eyes rolled back. Pure liquid lust. His cock stiffened and he stepped away before he started rutting against her leg like a damn dog.

A giggle caught his ears. A pink haired female tittered, her stare a sharp blade, seeing through his disguise. Magic radiated from her in a soft halo. A witch. She tilted her head, her lips twisting into a knowing smile.

More gazes fell upon him, sharp and curious, closing in. They were casual in their curiosity, coming closer as they browsed the wares. There were so many of them. Almost as many as that horrible night.

His throat thickened, the rush of blood drowning out Ivy's idle chatter. One grazed his shoulder, gasping. He stiffened, stepping closer to Ivy. His hand went for his dagger, but it wasn't strapped to his belt in these clothes. His tail slammed against his belly, sweat drenching his face. Suddenly the adventure to go to town was a horrible idea.

Chapter 18

Finn was ready to scream when Ivy squeezed his hand. "Brace yourself. Here they come."

A beaded curtain rattled and one of her aunts appeared with a grand flourish, clad from head to toe in leopard print. "Darling! What brings you here today?" Dahlia is what Ivy called her. She paused, a devious smile curling across her blood red lips, one that made Finn's belly roll. "Oh my, my, my. Look who tagged along! Rosie! Come look!"

Out barrelled the other aunt, Rosemary, clasping her hands under her chin. "It's him! This is so exciting! I just made lunch in the back. You should both join us."

"Don't get excited. I'm only here for moon water and I'm going back home," Ivy replied. "I have to anoint the windows, finish carving the runes, figure out how to charge-"

"And you can do that all that in your condition dear?" Rosemary asked.

Condition. The way it rolled from her tongue, like it was a cancer. Finn frowned at the aunts' tutting. How they could not see the fierce female he did was a mystery.

Ivy swallowed her sigh. "Yep. Doing fine so far."

"And no signs of..." Dahlia looked around then cupped a hand around her mouth whispering, "the fade?" far too loudly.

Tension thickened the air, all conversation around them ceasing. A few patrons inched away as if Ivy's fade was contagious. Others watched, their shaming gazes first falling on Ivy, then on him. Far too heavy on him for his liking.

The pink haired female began to edge her way towards him. Their eyes met, another smile curling her black painted lips. They always smiled before they struck, soothing their victim before the kill.

"Darling, you don't have the strength to do the things a normal witch can." Dahlia wrung her hands, continuing on as if they weren't surrounded by evil.

"Can I just get my jar of moon water and go?" Ivy said.

Rosemary sighed. "It's in the back, dear."

Ivy released Finn's arm. "I'll be right back. Promise," she told him.

His lifeline drifted behind the glass counter and into the back room. "Wait! Ivy!"

He reached for her, but the pink haired witch jumped in his path. She tilted her head seeming to enjoy his recoil. "You're not human, are you?"

He took a breath, raising his chin. No, he would not let this insolent witch frighten him. "I am perfectly human."

Her cackle made his skin shrink. "Such a liar."

She grabbed his chin, turning his face to hers. Memories of the silver haired witch froze him in terror. How she had examined him with devilish glee. Her magic seeping into his eye sockets, forcing him to watch Callum get torn to pieces.

"Oh, look at those eyes!" The pink haired witch shoved his upper lip away from his teeth. "And fangs! You are totally not human! Everyone! Come look at this!"

Bottles rattled to the floor as he threw himself out of her grip and against a table. He hissed, baring his fangs. "Stay away from me!"

The commotion only brought others. The pink haired witch continued towards him, undaunted. "You're one of the fair folk, aren't you?" Another cackle made him shudder. "Holy shit! I could use one of you!"

Witches surrounded him, gazes alight and voices rising. He couldn't breathe, couldn't even turn his eyes red with fury. There was no fury, only horror as they pulled at his clothes and tugged his hair, each one demanding a piece of him.

"Ladies! Stop this at once!" Dahlia shouted but they ignored her, clamoring for Finn.

So many hands. Just like the night Callum and he were taken to the forest. Hands, blades, blood, and screams.

Oh Gods, Callum's screams. His heart pounded, knees buckling as he clutched his middle. Nowhere to run or hide. It was all happening again.

A thick clutch of straw slapped the pink haired witch in the face. She screamed, tumbling over a table and onto her bottom. Ivy stepped in front of Finn, wielding a broom like a sword and blazing like a vengeful goddess.

"Back. Off." She swatted the witches away, sending then scurrying.

The pink haired witch tossed her hair from her eyes, jabbing an accusing finger. "You don't own him, lady!"

"No one does! Can't you see he doesn't want to be touched? Or are you power thirsty bitches too wrapped up in yourselves to read the damn room?"

The crowd murmured to themselves, shame deep in their voices. Soon they dispersed, some returning to browsing, others leaving. But the pink haired witch wasn't detoured. She climbed to her feet, sparks of magic swirling between her fingers. Finn stumbled to his hooves, ready to throw himself in front of Ivy but she nudged him back.

"I know who you are, Ivy Bennett," the pink haired witch sneered. "We all do. The witch who was stupid enough to get her powers stolen. You can't do shit to me! You can't-"

Another wack of the broom sent her flying ass over kettle. She hit a shelf, a tall stack of books tumbling over her. Her spell winked out, face paling as she stared at the redheaded goddess that loomed over her.

"I don't need my powers to beat the shit out of you." Ivy raised her broom, blue eyes burning. "Remember that when you're in the emergency room. I'm Ivy Bennet. I'm powerless. And I am terrifying!"

She sprung at the witch sending her screaming out the door. Ivy tossed her broom, taking Finn into her arms. "You okay?"

Her touch was unlike the others. Gentle, yielding, one that would never harm. He nodded, unable to find his words. Safe. He was safe with her, surrounded by her scent and strength.

"Ivy, dear. That..." Rosemary wrung her hands. "Are you tired? Do you need to sit down?" She looked to Dahlia who was still gaping, hand over her heart.

Ivy's sweet touch left him as she hung the broom back on the wall. "Before either of you start in on my *condition*, let's get something out in the air. I know you're both worried, but my ritual is happening with or without your approval."

"Darling, it's dangerous," Dahlia replied. "And you are in no shape mentally or physically-"

"I'm not my anxiety and I'm not my fade!"

"And we want you to have a peaceful, merciful death" Rosemary replied. "It's what you deserve."

Ivy stomped her foot, voice quivering. "Do you think mom and dad would want me just to lay down and die? Do you? Hell, even Finn believes in me and I've only known him for a few weeks!"

Finn could see the rage tears gathering in the corners of her eyes. He ran to her, wrapping his arms about her shoulders, shielding her like she had him. Her posture straightened, and she stood taller than before.

"You both raised me. You know having your support is what I need the most when things are bad," she continued. "I'm petrified of what's going to happen. And that's why I need you now more than ever."

Dahlia and Rosemary exchanged looks, the lines around their eyes tightening. Finn squeezed Ivy tight, willing his strength into her, an angry growl rolling from his throat. No one would make his Witchling cry. No one. She gave him a grateful nod, pressing her hand over his knuckles.

Dahlia stepped forward, a blush on her face. She took Ivy's hand. "Darling, I'm so sorry. Truly, deeply sorry."

"We only wanted you at peace," Rosemary added, pressing her palm to Ivy's cheek. "We're so sorry, Ivy dear."

Ivy untangled herself from Finn's grip, face softening. "I know, we're all still grieving Aster but, don't grieve *me* yet, okay? I'm still here. I'm still fighting."

Her aunts sniffled, pulling her into their arms as they cried. Rosemary snared Finn's hand, pulling him into their embrace as well. He stiffened, then eased as Ivy snaked her arm around him.

After a long moment, Dahlia fetched a jar of moon water, pressing it into Ivy's hands. "If you need anything. Anything at all-"

"Power to lend to her ritual on Samhain," Finn said. Ivy turned to him, lips parted in a surprised O. He nodded. "You need the power, don't you?"

Dahlia winced but Rosemary rushed forward, kissing Ivy on the cheek. "If that's what you need, we'll be there at your side. Right Lia?"

The apprehension faded from Dahlia and she offered a wan smile. "We'll be there on Samhain."

The happiness that lit Ivy's eyes was enough to power the ritual on its own. "Thank you. Thank you both."

She took his hand, leading him out the door. As soon as they were outside, Ivy kissed his cheek. "That's for standing beside me through all that." She smiled, looping her arm around his as they walked back to her vehicle in companiable silence.

Millions of pixies took flight inside his belly. A smile curled around his mouth. If all he did was stand there in the glow of Ivy's joy for the rest of his days, he would consider it a life well spent.

Chapter 19

Stay," Ivy commanded.

Finn sulked. "I won't fall again!"

"No, you won't because you're not leaving that seat until I come around and help you out." She snapped her fingers. "Max!"

Maximus hopped from the back seat and onto Finn's lap, digging his claws in and growling. Thank Brigid he was a familiar that took his job seriously.

"Stay!" she repeated.

Ivy left her SUV, looking to the sky as a distant clap of thunder echoed beyond the mountain. Dark clouds rolled in, the house silhouetted in the silver light of the oncoming storm.

Quickly she released Finn, leaning over him to unbuckle his seatbelt. Her cheek grazed his sweater, delicious heat radiating from him. She paused, taking a moment to bask in his closeness. He smelled so good, masculine and earthy.

"Lose something, Witchling?" he asked.

Yeah, my self control. She undid his seatbelt and Finn hopped out of the SUV stumbling into Ivy for the billionth time. He yanked off his boots, throwing them into a nearby bush.

"And good riddance!" he shouted.

Ivy laughed, as he clacked up the porch stairs. Maximus followed, his cute chubby butt waggling.

"Come, Witchling! A storm is brewing!" Finn snapped his fingers, horns reappearing. That's the Finn she wanted. Every single damn day. Pure walking sex with hooves, horns, and a tail. Her hands ached to touch that hard hewed muscle, lips longing to taste the golden knots that traced his spine. *Did you just have that thought?*

Yes, you did, the house sang.

She shot the porch a glare, muttering. "No one asked you."

"Pardon?" Finn asked.

"Um, nothing." She bounded up the stairs, pulling her key from her coat pocket. Finn touched her wrist before she could fit it in the lock.

"Witchling...I..." Ivy waited as his lips parted with uhs and hmms, struggling to find his words. "Thank you. You are brave for what you did for me."

The urge to throw her arms around him and lock lips was overwhelming. "They weren't going to hurt you."

"Still, past experiences make the threat real even if it is not. And regardless, you fought them. For me. No one beyond Callum has done such a thing."

He lifted her hand to his lips, brushing them over her knuckles. Electricity shot through every nerve and she shivered. "I..uh... You're welcome."

He smiled like she had hung the moon in the sky just for his pleasure. A woman could get used to that, could swim in that smile for all eternity. She swallowed, her key missing the lock three times before finally hitting its mark. "I don't know about you, but I need a drink."

"That is the greatest idea you've ever had, Witchling."

Coats and scarves were hung, Maximus prancing to the kitchen, eager for another trash dinner no doubt. Ivy ducked as Finn's sweater sailed over her head.

"I am done playing dress up!" Finn proclaimed, dropping his pants around his ankles. "Have you seen my leathers?" He turned to face Ivy, his dick swinging in the breeze.

"Dammit, Finn!" Ivy spun away from the enticing sight. Looking at his cock was like staring into the gods-damned sun.

"My apologies." He trotted by, that perfect and very naked body only an arm's reach away. She could grab that ass, just squeeze a cheek and wait for delicious retaliation. But she restrained herself, sparing a peek at the glittering knots that rippled down his sculpted back.

He is so. Fucking. Hot!

Her nipples hardened, and she flushed from head to toe. "I'll go get that drink!"

Ivy ran to the kitchen, tripping over Maximus and the overturned trash can. He dropped his half-devoured apple core to expel what she believed to be raccoon curse words.

"Sorry! I didn't see you, okay?" she leaned on the counter, her body throbbing too hard to chastise him over the mess he left. She yanked a bottle of cabernet out of the cabinet, uncorking it and taking a mighty swig for courage. "Relax, horny old lady. He drops trou all the time. It's not a sign."

Oh yes, it was. He'd been hinting that he had been interested in the mattress mambo for days. And she wasn't opposed. Yet she puttered around, fetching glasses, pouring wine, and arranging cheese, fruit, and crackers in a way too elaborate charcuterie board. She emptied her glass and helped herself to another round, still stacking gouda like her life depended on it.

There was a tug at her pant leg. Ivy looked down to see Maximus staring. His tail flipped then he held up his apple core in assistance.

"I'm good. Thanks, Max. Why don't you take the rest of the night off huh?" *Just in case I do end up banging Finn on the couch.*

A racoon in the room would be more awkward than when a cat watched. Maximus chittered and stuffed his apple core back into his maw. She took that as an okay as he waddled to the hall and around the corner. Another gulp of wine was consumed.

"Come on, Ives. He's a satyr. You're a grown woman. If you want to have a one-night stand with an epic sex beast just do it. He'll be down. Hell, even the house wants you to." She looked up to the ceiling. "Right?"

The house was suspiciously silent. She scowled and took another drink. Fuck it. Plotting sexual conquests was never Ivy's forte and there was no point in forcing anything now. Tonight, would either be orgasms or a hangover. She ventured back down the hall. Back to Finn. She really wished her heart wasn't racing like a Ferrari on highway five.

Ivy juggled the board, wine bottle and glasses, hoping that Finn had his loincloth on. No, that was a lie. She was hoping he hadn't found it and was still wandering around sky clad.

"Ah ha!" Finn cried, from behind the couch. He held up his loincloth like a prize. "Victory!"

Dammit.

The board landed with a noisy clatter as she dropped it onto the coffee table. Finn plucked the glasses free before they tumbled to the floor. "You brought us a feast".

"It's not really a feast," Ivy replied. "Just some cheese and crackers. And apples and grapes...and strawberries....and pears... and a banana... and some... salami...and other meats."

Finn examined her half empty wineglass, giving it a sniff. "And you started without me."

Ivy gave him an innocent smile. "I had to taste it. Make sure the blend went well with the cheese...and crackers, apples, grapes, strawberries, pears, the banana, salami, and other meats."

"And do you approve?"

I don't know, I was chugging it too fast to taste it. Judging by how warm her toes were, it was probably a decent blend. "Yep. It all works together."

"Good. Now it's time for leisure, Witchling."

His touch almost made her go off like a firecracker. Instead of realising how long it had been since she had sex with another breathing creature—too long for her liking—she took a hard left towards the fireplace. "Hold on. The fire is getting low. This one is a bitch and a half to keep lit."

Finn struck a melodramatic pose against the couch. "I am so repulsive that you can't sit with me?"

Actually, I want to grind your pelvis into dust. Her nervous laugh sounded like a dying chicken. "Well, hey. A cottage witch's work is never done and... why are you coming at me like that- Aah!" He swept her off her feet, hauling her over his shoulder. "Dammit Finn! You keep doing that!"

"And I will continue until you learn to sit down!" He dumped her on the couch, the cushions squeaking. She struggled to sit up, only to find his finger poking the tip of her nose. "Stay," he commanded like she had to him in the SUV. He snatched up the fire poker, twirling it like a master swordsman before jabbing it into the logs. "Dionysius's cock, Witchling, you work too hard!"

He picked up a huge chunk of firewood—one Ivy would have to use her entire body to lift—and tossed it in one handed. Sparks flew, the fire roaring to life. The house took a deep breath, from the heat and light, then it settled with a creak and went dormant again. Contentment. It was in the walls, in the floor, and now flooding Ivy's heart.

Finn tossed the poker back into its place, lean and powerful in the amber firelight. She longed to taste his kiss, feel his strong fingers slide between her legs and inside her. Panic filled her belly and she poured herself more wine.

Finn tapped his hoof. "Uh, I get some too, yes?"

"Don't sweat it. I have another bottle in the kitchen." She drowned her anxiety in another sip, buzz already rolling.

Finn filled his own glass to the brim, lifting it to admire the color before taking a drink. "I thought I destroyed all your feast ware."

"I went to a thrift store and replaced some essentials." The nudge she gave him spilt wine onto his lap. "And you owe me at least fifty bucks."

"And I will gladly pay you back..." The wink he gave her made her whimper. "Somehow." He snatched a piece of cheese, trying it with the wine. "Hmm, you chose well, Witchling." He sat beside her, rich voice pouring over her like warm caramel. "Open your mouth."

She obeyed, letting him slide the piece of cheese onto her waiting tongue. Gouda. How she loved gouda. On reflex, she let out a mmm and his low growl rumbled through her like a freight train.

"Sip." The cool rim of her glass was lifted to her lips, wine trickling in. It was all so rich. So decadent. And so fucking sexy. She wanted to beg him for more, but Finn returned to his drink.

"See? Sitting is not all bad." He patted his lap. "Come now."

Ivy stared at him. "You... want me to...sit on your lap?" *Yes! Yes! Yes!*

"I would not be opposed, but I was referring to your feet."

"Oh. Oooh!" She slapped her face. "Yeah. Feet. Of course." She swung then onto his lap.

Finn clicked a disapproving tongue at her boots. "Clearly I have to teach you the art of leisure." He unlaced them, tossing them aside, then peeled off her socks. With a grin, he laced his fingers together, stretching them out until his knuckles popped. "Now relax and enjoy."

"Are you giving me a foot rub?"

"Yes, I'm giving you a foot rub. You said you liked them, remember?"

Accept the foot rub, you dumbass! She thrust her toes under his nose. He chuckled, pressing his thumbs into her arch with slow, firm pressure. Knots she didn't even know she had released. The world was forgotten and she liquefied, the warmth of the fire and Finn's hand making her boneless. Eventually, she reached for her wine glass, taking another sip.

Then another.

And another.

Before long she was buzzed, warm, and giggling. "I forgot how good you are at this."

"There are three things that my kind are skilled at. Hunting, brawling, and pleasure in all its forms. Callum is more talented at the previous two." He was upon her, lips a breath away from hers. "I am more talented in the latter."

He was going to kiss her. Finally, he was going to kiss her long and hard and, fuck everything, she was going to let him. Her mouth parted, ready to welcome him in. Thunder cracked and Ivy jumped, almost ramming into his horns as tipsy laugher shook her.

"Never fear!" Finn threw himself over her, caging her against the couch. "I shall protect you from the storm!"

"Oh please." Ivy gave him a push, cackling. "You think a little storm scares me, goat-boy?"

"Honestly, I believe *you* scare the storm more, you frightening and fierce Witchling."

"That is the nicest compliment I've ever gotten." She gave him a poke. "But I'm not a Witchling. I'm forty-fucking-two years old."

Finn blew a raspberry. "A mere child compared to my eight-hundred-and-fifty-two."

"And you don't act a day over twelve."

"It's your ire that keeps me young." He pressed her glass back into her hands, hoof grazing her calf. "I enjoy calling you my little Witchling but if you don't like it, I will refrain."

"It's not a problem." It was far from one, now. Every time he called her Witchling in that smooth honeyed tone she wanted to moan.

He picked up the last of the strawberries, flicking it with his pointed tongue before biting its bright red flesh. A familiar tune flowed from him as he stroked the curve of her jaw, one she knew all too well. Another drunken giggle sputtered out her nose.

"You're humming *Wannabe* by the Spice Girls?"

"I'm humming the song you constantly repeat on your device! Is it not seductive?"

"No, oh Gods, no."

He sat up in frustration, his cock tenting his loincloth. Ivy burst into another peal of giggles and he sighed. "I see this is going nowhere so let's at least sit and finish this cheese and crackers, apples, grapes, strawberries, pears, the banana, and-"

Ivy grabbed his nape, slanting her mouth over his. He was richer than chocolate, more divine than anything her mouth had ever touched. She lapped at the wine staining his lips, greedily and they tumbled to the couch in a tangle of limbs.

"Witchling," Finn snarled, flipping her onto her back. Her wrists were pinned over her head, his gaze pure fire as he tucked his face against the crook of her neck, inhaling deep. "You smell like the Goddess herself. Sweet. Devine."

Fangs grazed her throat, nipping and biting as the rain battered the windows. Her sweater was pulled over her head and tossed it into the darkness. She was a bonfire, legs around his hips, body craving to be filled.

"I wish to spend this night with you." Finn undid her jeans, shoving them down her hips. "With you. Beside you. Around you..." He leaned in and whispered, "...Inside you."

She couldn't think, couldn't breathe. Not while he sucked her swollen nipples through her bra. Not while his cock was hard between her thighs. It had been so long since she had been touched and petted. So long since she had been kissed and brought to come by hands other than her own.

"Your sounds of pleasure are like music." Finn's voice was ragged, his hand sliding into her panties. "I want to make you sing."

A fleeting touch brushed her clit and her cries drowned out the thunder. She needed their bodies naked and covered in sweat. She wanted to fuck him until he was screaming her name. Her vision swam, the room lurching in a sudden kaleidoscope. Her stomach twisted, the taste of wine sharp on her tongue.

Oh yeah, she was drunk, wasn't she? Fuck, he was drunk too. *Dammit, dammit, dammit!* She pressed a hand against Finn's shoulder, pushing him away. "Finn, stop."

He capitulated, worry crinkling his eyes. "What's wrong? Are you hurt?"

"No, not at all it's just..." Ivy managed to untangle herself from him, her vision spinning. "You didn't do anything wrong. I'm just a fucking moron is all."

"What do you mean..." Finn gasped. "By the Goddess's tits, Are you a virgin?!"

A bucket of ice was thrown over her screaming libido. "What?! No!"

"I was far too harsh, wasn't I?" He was up and pacing in a drunken circle around the couch. "Of course, I was! You, having no experience-"

"Finn, I'm not a virgin! I haven't been since I was sixteen! But we're both drunk off our asses and that's a deal breaker!"

Finn blinked then he laughed, waving a hand. "Ooooh. Is that all? Just a moment."

He took a deep breath and with a wail that shook the walls, he bent in two. Oh shit, he was going to hurl. She could hear it in his sickly groans. Ivy crawled to the far side of the couch afraid she'd get caught in the splash zone. The fog of booze lifted from him and he straightened, casually finger combing his hair into place.

"There. Sober now." His voice was as steady as a rock. "Your turn."

Ivy smashed her cheeks in with her palms. "You're sober? Just like that?"

"Well I am a disciple of Dionysus. How else could I get through those weeklong festivals? Can't witches do the same?"

"No!"

"Oh." Finn frowned. "Well then, stopping is for the best."

She stood, yanking her jeans back up. "I can't believe my friggin' luck. This is the first time in forever someone has been remotely close to my vagina! Ugh, why does Lexapro make me such a cheap drunk? I could chug at least two bottles of wine when I was in college!" Finn gestured to the two empty bottles on the coffee table and she stuck her tongue out at him. "Shush! Right now, I could be enjoying your pointed tongue on my clit but noooooo! I had to drink too much!"

Ivy did an angry toddler march around the couch, in search of her sweater. Wait, she should turn the lights on first. It was too dark to find anything by the firelight. Off she went, walking sideways towards... Where was she going again?

"Witchling, what are you doing?" Finn grabbed her elbow and her nipples shot diamond hard, pleading for her to reconsider.

"Trying to find my...thingy!" She sighed dramatically. "You know! That thing! The thing that goes over..." She rubbed her boobs. "This part of me!"

"...Your sweater?"

"Yes! That! It's cold and I need it!"

Finn guided her to the couch, sitting her down. "Do not move!"

He clip-clopped into the darkness. Ivy could hear him moving around her, while her vision wove into swirls of black, green and gold. She was going to pass out, just face-plant into the floor. It was coming. The perfect end to a

perfect disaster. A snicker escaped. Then another. Okay
yeah, maybe it was a little funny.

Finn returned with her sweater then grabbed her
waist, hauling her against him. She flung her arms around
his shoulders, smashing her face into his torso. Her giggle
exploded into a laugh.

"You are going to bed," he said flatly.

"I thought we weren't going to do it while I'm drunk?"

"I said *you*, Witchling. Not us." Finn lifted her into his
arms, cradling her head against his shoulder. "By Dionysius's balls, if this is what Callum had to deal with when I
was drunk, I owe him an apology."

Ivy's temples throbbed as the world rotated again.
Her stomach lurched. Shit, what if she puked on him?
Her heart pitched, acid crawling up her throat. Great,
now that she was worrying about it, she really was going
to puke.

*If you hurl, it will be all over Finn and then you can kiss
sex with him goodbye! Unless he won't mind. Maybe he
won't mind? Of course, he'd mind! No one wants to be vom-
ited on! You're a fucking train wreck, Ives!*

The nausea subsided but her thoughts droned on and
on and on. "Finn? If I throw up on you, would you be
pissed?"

"Are you going to heave?" Abruptly, he changed di-
rections. "If so, we're going to the bathroom before the
bedroom."

"No! I just wanted to know if you'd get upset and like,
I dunno, stop talking to me or use my name against me."

She tucked her face in the crook of his neck and shuddered. "You won't turn me into your mindless slave because I couldn't hold my booze or anything weird like that, would you?"

Finn stopped, his beautiful mouth still swollen from their kisses. Her breath caught and she touched his lips, remembering their softness against her own.

"I would not be mad at you," he replied. "And I will not use your name against you."

Relief cooled her blazing skin. "Good. Because I've been enjoying this. You and me. You make me happy. You make me forget that I'm dying."

He brushed a kiss to her forehead. "I won't let you die, Ivy. That is a promise."

Finn's strong scent enveloped her senses, the wonderful security of his arms calming the building anxiety. A blink later she was tucked into bed, Finn pulling her comforter to her chin. Another kiss was pressed against her forehead and then he was gone, hooves clacking to the door.

"Finn, wait." Ivy sat up, hand to her head to help steady the world. He stopped at the threshold, fists balled. "I'm pretty sure even sober I'll want to finish what we started. Would you?"

The knots down his back rippled as he tensed. He looked over his shoulder, his pointed tongue running over his lips. "In a heartbeat, Witchling."

He winked, then sauntered out the door, closing it behind him with a flick of his tail.

"Fuck, he is so damn hot," she moaned, before falling against the mattress and into the black.

Chapter 20

A crash of thunder jolted Ivy awake; lightning flashing across her room. She ran her tongue across her parched lips. Great, here came the hangover.

She attempted to roll over, but a purring lump was wedged under her arm. Maximus had crawled into her bed sometime during the night and was doing the perfect impression of a fuzzy cinnamon roll, tail covering his snout. She would have cooed "Awwww!" if her head wasn't pounding, and her mouth wasn't like sandpaper.

Careful not to wake her familiar, she groped the nightstand, wincing as the drawer's squeak stabbed her temples. With a triumphant grunt, she retrieved a small bottle of Rowan's hangover potion, unscrewing the cap as fast as her sleep clumsy fingers allowed.

It was vinegary and thick, coating her throat as it went down, threatening to come back up just as fast. Sweat oozed from every pore, probably wine scented. She kicked off her covers, the cool night air soothing her boiling flesh.

"Uuuugh, work potion. Woooork," she muttered into her pillow. "Why couldn't I remember I had this potion earlier?"

This was her penance. If she hadn't over done it, Finn would be in her bed doing wicked, wicked things with that pointed tongue. Now it was her, a racoon, and the wine sweats. Her core ached and she squeezed her thighs, hissing between clenched teeth.

I *wish to spend this night with you.* He had whispered. *Beside you. Around you...Inside you.*

Her tongue darted over her lips, desperate to taste the lingering remains of his kiss. It wasn't enough. It would never be enough. She tossed the blankets off and hauled herself out of bed, stripping off the clothes she still wore from the day before. A shower would help. A cold one.

Maximus's head popped out from one of the comforter's folds. His ears flicked and he chirped, head cocked to the side with questions.

"I'm just taking a shower. I feel gross." *And horny. Oh my Gods, so very horny.*

Her head throbbed as he chittered something back in reply. If only raccoon was a high school language elective.

"Why don't you go check on Finn? Tell him I'm okay." She bit her tongue before she added, *and I'm ready to roll.*

She had no clue were Finn would be now. He could be out doing another search for Callum. Chances were, he was probably asleep.

Or he could be across the hall, touching himself. That beautiful male sprawled across her chair, fangs bared and back arched as he stroked his hard length. Would he moan when he'd come? Would he be thinking of her? Her thighs slammed together.

Maximus's maw practically unhinged as he yawned. He wiggled his way free, squeaked something disgruntled over his shoulder, then pulled the door open with his tiny paws and headed out. Well, at least she didn't have to explain herself to a raccoon.

The shower turned on with a loud hiss and Ivy untied her bun and hopped in. Freezing water slapped her, and she squealed, the shock tensing everything. Rivulets of ice puckered her nipples, stoking the fire that roared inside her.

Your sounds of pleasure are like music. I want to make you sing. His words. His heat. His fangs on her neck. She slid her hand between her legs, fondling herself, praying for release that never came.

Minutes ticked by and her hangover faded. But her desire remained unsatiated. Her hand wasn't going to cut it. This was a job for the battery-operated boyfriend.

As soon as she stepped out of the shower, she was on fire again. She stomped to her closet, unable to ignore how her towel made her already sensitive nipples like diamonds. Thick grey clouds rolled past her window, rain and wind pelting the roof. For a moment she considered running out into the storm, letting its force whisk away the anguish that was making her sex clench.

"What is wrong with me?!"

Her thighs were slick with arousal, hunger beating with its relentless call. Fuck it. She didn't have the patience to rummage through her boxes for her vibrator. She tossed her towel and flopped onto her bed.

Beside you. Around you...Inside you.

She slipped her finger inside her, another circling her swollen clitoris. Her hips churned against her hand, images of Finn's naked body thrusting over her bringing her right to the edge.

Finn sat in his chair, ensconced in his Witchling's scent. Lavender, sage, and desire. The sweet taste of her lips still rested on his own Touching himself would be pointless. It hadn't helped him before and tonight would be no exception. No, the only thing that would satisfy him was Ivy. He longed to run across the hall and wake her, but he knew she would still be slumbering off her drink. *Damn wine to the seven hells.*

The evening had started so promising. She had laughed, she had reveled, she had kissed him with abandon. Tonight, he saw Ivy, all of her; a female who felt deeply, fought fiercely, and loved passionately. Someone he could give his heart too.

You make me forget that I might be dying.

He gritted his teeth. No, she was not going to die. He'd do everything to make sure she lived a long and happy life right here, with him where she belonged. His fists clenched, claws gouging into his palms. He would not let Ivy go. He couldn't. *I need her. I want her.*

His door opened with a low creak. Finn jumped up, His tail slapping the chair. "Ivy?"

Maximus trotted through the door, yawning so wide, all his pointed teeth were visible. Finn flopped back into his seat. "Can't sleep either?"

A series of chitters squeaked from Maximus's cheeks as he sat, giving his tail a little nibble.

"You were with her? And she asked you to check on me? So, she's awake?" An affirmative chirp had him standing once again. "Is she ill?"

For all he knew, she was heaving the contents of her belly and wanted privacy. Vomiting didn't need an audience. Maximus replied around another yawn. She was awake and bathing, pale but otherwise fine. All the confirmation he needed.

"Watch my chair. I'm going to check on our witch."

Finn charged across the hall, Ivy's door still cracked open from Maximus's exit. He was about to push it open when a soft moan perked his ears. That was not a moan of sickness. That was a moan Finn was all too familiar with. He peeked inside.

There she was, bare and bathed in firelight, one hand cupping her breast the other caressing her quim. The scent of her arousal was everywhere; sweet, heady, and so damn seductive. Frustration passed over her face as if unable to get what she wanted.

Finn clutched the door frame, unable to breathe. Her hair was free from its knot, long, thick, and spilling around her shoulders in rivers of molten copper. His fingers twitched, begging to be wrapped around those tresses while his cock was buried in her slick.

Ivy's mouth parted, awaiting phantom kisses, ones he wanted to bring. He should be the one making her dance like that, should open that door and join her. His witch.

His partner.

His mate.

The door slammed shut of its own accord with a hard crack. Finn stared wide eyed, ears twitching to Ivy's panicky buzzes of, "Shit! Dammit! Son of a...!"

"Fear not. It's only me," he called.

"Finn?" There was some shuffling, followed by, "Um, just a second!" and a "Oh fuck me running, where's my robe?!" Eventually the door cracked open and she peeked out clutching her wrap tight. "Everything okay?"

Her eyes were bright and breath heavy. Ropes of her fire kissed mane framed her pinked cheeks. She was more beautiful than any nixie or fae. More beautiful than the Goddess of love herself. His Ivy. His light in his otherwise dark world.

"Are you sober, now?" he growled.

She wetted her mouth and nodded.

"Good." He barged in, took her face in his hands, and kissed her.

She tasted of warmth and autumn. She tasted like home. Her knees buckled and he clutched her against him, taking her weight.

"I don't want you to go." He cut her off with another kiss before she could reply. "You are to stay with me."

This stubborn, clever, and wonderful witch had turned his world upside down. If she left, he'd never be the same. And he'd never want to be. She made him better. Made him whole.

"Finn," Ivy panted. "Are you-?"

"Finnbar An Croí Láidir."

Her eyes widened. "What?"

"My full name is Finnbar An Croí Láidir. And it's yours. *I* am yours." He pressed her forehead to hers. "Keep me. Please. My sweet Witchling. My Ivy."

Ivy's mouth quivered, her gaze growing glassy. "...Yes."

Finn kicked the door closed, pushing her robe from her shoulders. The green silk pooled at her feet, leaving plump beautiful curves dotted with tan freckles and rosy nipples budding before his eyes.

He grabbed her backside, lifting her off her feet and carried her to bed. "Were you thinking of me?"

She kissed him, tugging at his lip with her teeth. "Yes."

He tossed her onto her mattress, crawling up the length of her. "And were you thinking of us, together?" Were we... kissing? ...Touching?"

He flicked a claw over one hardened nipple, and she squirmed. "A lot like this, actually."

"Tell me..." He grazed his thumb through the curls at the apex of her thighs. "Were we fucking?" When she gasped, he took her nape, pulling her close to whisper hard in her ear. "Did I bend you over, ramming inside you until you screamed? Or did I take you slow? Did I kiss every inch of you? Your breasts, your belly, your...quim?" He brushed her swelling bud and she arched against him. "Did I ravage you with my tongue until you were mad with desire? Or did you ride my cock until I howled your name?"

Ivy's eyes rolled back. "Dear Gods, you're filthy."

"You expected less?" He skimmed his tongue over the flat of her nipple. "Whatever you imagined, I believe you rather I be here than in your dreams."

"Yes. Oh, sweet Brigid, yes." Her hips rolled against his, blue eyes glittering with hunger.

He shot rock hard, shifting to untie the knot of his loincloth. "Then part your thighs Ivy Siobhan Bennett and let me worship you properly."

She obeyed.

My Ivy. My beautiful, wonderful witch.

A soft quiver rose from her throat as his fangs grazed her belly. He tasted his way down the length of her, her flesh almost as delicious as her kiss.

His mouth slid along the silk of her sex and she twisted her hands into the sheets, whispering, "Finn," in the faintest of prayers. His name sounded sublime in her pleasure. He had to hear it again, wanted his name like that only from her.

He gave her lick. Ambrosia. Once again, she cried his name. His cock twitched, aching to be inside the forge quivering around his tongue.

Ivy clutched handfuls of her hair, rolling against his mouth. "Oh, thank Brigid for that pointed tongue of yours."

"You like this?"

When she didn't answer, he ran a fang over her clit. Ivy propped herself up onto her elbows with a shout of "Yes!"

He consumed her, sucking, licking, devouring every drop of her arousal. Her cries grew frantic, her climax rising. Quickly he pulled away, sinking his teeth into her thigh before she came. Her annoyed disappointment made him grin.

"In time, my Witchling, in..." His words rose to a shout. Pure ecstasy shot to his groin as she grabbed the rigid lengths of his horns.

She steered him back between her legs. "My aunts lent me some books."

Another stroke made his tail slap the mattress. "They...they have *very* informative books."

He tore from her grasp. Perhaps another time he'd come from just that touch, but now was for her. For them.

He grasped the base of his cock, one stroke bringing a bead of moisture to its tip. Ivy's gaze was branding as her tongue darted across her lips. His tail flicked its brush against her clit, her cries of pleasure pure music. She hooked her knee over his hip, pulling him down, his tail pinned between them.

"Don't stop," she commanded, grasping his shaft, and guiding him inside her.

Tight, velvet fire surrounded him. He thrust before he could stop himself, the headboard thumping against the wall. Her palms returned to his horns, caressing every groove, their bodies grinding. He kept his tail circling her clit, loving every delicious noise he pulled from her.

"My Ivy," he moaned.

"My Finn," she answered.

Something inside him unfurled, releasing emotion he had never felt the likes of before. It filled his heart, flowing through his every breath. Love. By Dionysus he loved her. She was his. And he belonged to her.

He pistoned his hips, unable to slow if he wanted. Their skin was sweat soaked, their muscles aching for release. But he didn't want this to end. He'd wanted to stay in this haze. This is what he was made for. To give his treasured Witchling the pleasure she desired and the love she deserved.

Her core tightened around his shaft. "Oh Gods," she panted. "Finn, I'm... I'm..." She dissolved into a tight scream as she bucked, driving him deeper. She was wild. Unashamed. Perfect.

He thrust harder, desperate to wring every ounce of pleasure from this moment, from his beautiful witch. She fluttered around him one last time and with a roar, he erupted. Their lips met and his heart ached. This was everything, and yet not enough. *Never enough!*

Soon, their bodies slowed, heartbeats falling in sync as they fell into a pile of tangled limbs. Stillness. Silence. Only the steady rhythm of the storm sang as he fell into the summer sky of her eyes, his shaft still pulsing inside her.

Ivy smoothed his hair from his face before nuzzling him. "Fuck, you are so good at sex."

Finn chuckled, still catching his breath. "Centuries of experience, Witchling."

He rolled off her and gathered her in his arms, tucking her head against his shoulder. Lavender and sage soothed him to a place of tranquility as his fingers played in her hair.

"So..." she said. "How did you know I was...um... Pluckin' the banjo, so to speak."

"I could smell your arousal. The room was ripe with it. It was pure paradise, much like your taste." When a blush tinged her cheeks, he fell even deeper under her spell. "Oh, and your door was open."

"What?" Ivy grabbed her pillow, cackling as she gave him a gentle smack. "You pervert!"

Finn shielded himself from the harmless blow. "Your *house* is the culprit! It's the one that slammed the door to get your attention!"

The pillow was returned to the bed. "Fine. You got me on that one. The house *is* a total perv. And okay, maybe it's hot to know you were watching." She gave him a sly smile. "Wait till you see what my vibrator does."

Finn perked with interest. "What, pray tell is that?"

"I'll show you next time." She gave him a wink. "Trust me. You'll love it."

Finn yanked her down on top of him, wrapping an arm around her waist. Another of her sweet kisses was rewarded, and she straddled his hips making him hard all over again. When he rolled against her, she gasped with an incredulous stare.

"Already?"

"I am no mere human, Witchling. My kind were created for pleasure." He ran his tail across her backside before giving her cheek a hardy snap of its brush.

Ivy jerked, then snickered, falling into him. "All right then, goat boy. Let's put you through your paces."

He wrapped himself around her, slanting his mouth over hers. This indeed was his fate, a part he never knew was missing.

And it was perfect.

Chapter 21

T he morning light glowed through her eyelids, wak-
ing Ivy from a deep, exhausted sleep. She yawned,
stretching her arms, and almost getting a horn to
the eye. Finn's head rested on her chest, his arm wrapped
around her waist, his leg slung over her knees, and his tail
coiled around her thigh. She nuzzled his hair with a grin.

Maximus was butted up against her other side, the
softest of snores escaping his little black snoot. Well, neither rain, nor snow, nor countless screaming orgasms
kept a familiar from his cuddles it would seem.

The night had passed in a blur of kisses, caresses, and
insanely hot sex. Finn had taken her four times in a row;
first on her bed, then on the bed again, then on the fur
rug in front of the fireplace, and then shoved against her
dresser with his pointed, and very talented tongue.

She had come multiple times by just him humming
against her clit. The tune was either a lovely renaissance
madrigal or Yankee Doodle Dandy. She was too busy

howling to listen. Eventually, he had shown mercy and let her sleep, the soft whisper of "My Ivy," in her ear before she drifted off.

Raindrops clung to the window before pattering to the ground, thunder growling in the distance. She giggled, burying her face into Finn's thick caramel mane. There was something delightful about waiting out a tempest all cozy with a gorgeous satyr who couldn't get enough of her. The fire roared as if in agreement.

Ivy jabbed a finger towards the ceiling. "You have been way too invested in my sex-life for a half dead house."

Her cellphone rang and she arched around her bedmates for it, the screen flashing Rowan's name. Finn stirred, lifting his head with a drowsy "Huh?"

"It's just my brother calling." She scooped up the limp Maximus, setting him down on Finn's belly. "I'll be right back."

Finn nodded, arm curling around the raccoon. The two snored in tandem, their tails twitching. The cuteness almost did her in. She untangled herself from the cuddle puddle, hitting the answer button.

"You slept with the satyr, didn't you?" Rowan asked.

Ivy gathered her robe from the floor and tiptoed out of her bedroom. "Were my orgasms so powerful that *you* felt them?"

"No, but I'm basking in your afterglow. Damn, he must be good. So, the territorial cock monster claimed you as his territory?"

"You were right all along, Ro! I *can* do hard things!"

Rowan laughed so hard he choked. "Sweet Hecate, Ives! What the hell!"

"Hey, you brought it up." She threaded her arms through her robe sleeves, her body still deliciously sore.

"So, you two like each other now?"

Like? Not strong enough of a word. Ivy glanced into her room. Finn was sprawled on his back, still cradling Maximus in the crook of his arm. He was beautiful even in his sleep; the lines of his face smooth, his mouth relaxed, bliss painting his high cheekbones.

Her heart did a little tap-dance. "He gave me his full name."

There was a loud thump, as if Rowan dropped his phone. After a momentary rustle, he shouted, "Holy shit, you have the full name of a fair folk!?"

Ivy rolled her eyes. "It's not like I'm going to do anything with it!"

"Why not? You have control!"

"Well, it could be because I'm falling for him!"

Another thump followed by Rowan's cursing. "Wait, wait, wait. You're falling in love?"

"Yup."

"With a satyr."

She spared another look to the glorious male spread out on her bed. He yawned, sleep swollen eyes blinking open. A tender smile spread across his beautiful mouth, his tail practically wagging the moment he saw her. Love. That was love in his gaze. And dammit she loved him right back. Loved his humor and his strength. Loved his wonder despite his centuries of age. Loved how he believed in her, supported her, and made her feel safe. She ducked away from the door.

"Yeah," she replied. "I love him, Ro. Absolutely head over heels in love with him."

She could hear Rowan's smile. "Well, as long as he's not dropping anymore chandeliers on you, I think I can approve."

"Pretty sure we're past that phase."

"That's a phase I never want in a relationship." Rowan's heavy pause tied a knot in her belly. "Samhain is only two days away...Does he know about your fade?"

The fade. Shit, she had almost forgotten. For one wonderful night her fade, Aster, and her anxiety were gone while in Finn's arms. Now it all came rushing back to her in a horrendous tidal wave.

Ivy wandered down the hall, her steps mindless. "Yeah, he does. He knows everything. And he said he'll do what he can to help." The worried click of Rowan's tongue made her twitch. "I'm feeling more confident about it, Ro. Auntie Lia and Rosie have finally come around. I have a distant cousin of the fae willing to give power and I've found some things out about the house that lean in my favor. I can do this."

I have to. For me. For Finn. I'm not giving this up after just finding it.

"Good." The worry in his tone was deafening but he chuckled all the same. "I should let you go so you can get back to satyr cuddling. Tell him that he better be nice to you or I rip his lungs out."

Ivy smiled. "Will do. See you in a couple days?"

"Nothing can hold me back." His uncomfortable silence returned then in a rush of quivering words he said, "I love you Ives. I really do. You're...well you're the best sister anyone could ever have."

A cold rush hit her gut as the call went dead. He was saying goodbye, permanently. Her fleeting confidence waned, as she stared at her phone. *I'm not ready to die.*

Her anxious feet took her down the stairs, her mind buzzing. She wandered from room to room, nervous energy building, thoughts warring loud in her skull.

You can't do this. Yes, you can. No, you can't. Even with all this power you think you still can't mess it up? Shut up! You can do this! It's all lining up! Fuck off, anxiety!

She stopped in front of the French-doors leading to the deck, pressing her palm against the cool glass. Rain pooled over its wooden planks, puddles rippling.

"I can do hard things," she whispered. "I can do hard things."

Her fear continued to swell, a screeching discord that made her tug at her hair and a scream push at her lips. She would die. Rowan would feel pain beyond imagining. Her aunts would lose another child. And Finn... Ivy swiped her wet eyes. Finn would be fine. Afterall, he was centuries old and had lived through almost everything imaginable. And yet her emptiness grew. No life with

Finn. After all the shit she had endured, this happiness she earned would disappear in a sad misplaced ritual.

"Is all well?" Finn approached buck naked, the furrow between his brows deep with concern.

Ivy faced him with an artificial smile. "Yep, things are fine."

"Methinks you're lying." He took her hand. "Is it the ritual?"

"No. No, the ritual is all set up. All I need is Samhain to roll in. Her fake grin dropped. "...Which is two days away."

His tail flicked and he frowned. "I had almost forgotten."

"What if I can't do this? What if I mess it all up and fade away? What's going to happen to this house? To you?"

Tears spilt down her cheeks and she growled. She wanted to crawl back into bed and curl up with him, forget that death was only a breath away. He was her anchor. Her lighthouse in the storm of her fear.

Finn cast his gaze out the French-doors. "This weather. It's never been my favorite. I prefer when the sun is hot, and the skies are clear."

The change of subject made her head spin. "I like storms. There's something about them that... I don't know...calms me."

"Whatever it may be, you love it. But eventually it passes into a season you dislike. But that passes on too." He drew a little smiley face in the condensation, then opened the doors, holding his hand out to let the rain pool in his palm and spill between his knuckles. "Good or bad, everything passes. That thought is what got me through those horrors with the coven. The memories overwhelm me, but they always pass. Like your panics. And soon, like your fade."

Ivy shook her head. "No witch has ever survived the fade, Finn."

"Until you. You are clever and strong. The most stubborn creature in this world. If any witch is going to survive this, it's you. Besides, I have your name. I will command you to survive if I have to."

A little smile creeped across her face. "Not that I don't appreciate the sentiment, but I don't think a name has that kind of power."

"I wouldn't underestimate that if I were you, Witchling." His lips brushed hers, his rich taste washing away her dread. Her arms wrapped around him, but he pulled away, tapping the tip of her nose with his claw before looking back out to the deck. "Hmm, let me see what's so special about these storms you like."

He marched out in all his nude glory, hooves splashing through the shallow puddles. Ivy tried to grab him, but he slipped away.

"Finn! It's freezing out there!"

"You are correct. But it's not completely unpleasant."

Rain poured over every muscle, running in thin streams down his belly and around his groin. His caramel locks were plastered to his face, the fur covering his legs turning dark and slick. Ivy's core quivered, her lust springing back to life.

The knots along his spine sparkled, tail swishing over that magnificent ass as he shook like a dog. Crystal droplets flew, catching Ivy in their cold, wild spray. He held out a hand for her, his smile brighter than the flashes of lightning crossing the clouds. "Come join me."

Ivy laughed. "Hell no!"

"You said you liked storms, Witchling. Prove it."

"By freezing my nipples off?"

His low growl liquefied her. "I'll warm you."

That was enough to make her toss her robe and phone to the floor. She shielded her breasts, preparing them for the temperature drop, then slid out onto the deck. As if waiting for her, the clouds unzipped, releasing a gale of icy rain and she screamed.

"Holy Fuck that's cold!"

Finn pulled her against his hot skin. "Better?"

The bite of the storm eased, the apex of her thighs turning to fire. "Oh yeah."

He tucked her face against his neck, hands sliding down her back to take hold of her ass. Moss, earth, and sex, filled her nostrils, topped with the fresh scent of rain.

The cold went forgotten as he backed her against the railing. Droplets thrashed her sensitive skin, every nerve springing to life. She cradled his head while he suckled her nipples with a low groan. Oh, sweet Brigid how he groaned. Like a predator taking his first bite of meat in days.

With gentle hands, he turned her around. His cock pressed against the cleft of her ass, his wicked tail snaking around her foot, tugging it up to rest on the bottom rail.

"I have better ways to warm you," he murmured, fangs grazing her shoulder.

Pleasure stung, skin burning as his tail whipped her backside. Her fingers curled around the railing, and she arched. The brush moved in a gentle circle, soothing her red swollen cheek. Ivy caught her breath only to have it pulled from her by another slap. Then another. Her sex was slick and hot, aching to be filled.

His tail slithered between her thighs. It grazed her clit with the fleetest of touches. "Warm enough now?"

"Not even close," she strained through her teeth.

His seductive chuckle made her tremble. "That was the answer I hoped to hear."

His palms sluiced through the water that poured over her until he was cupping her breasts. The prick of fangs was on her throat and he sucked while he kneaded her.

She pushed her hips back, needing his scalding heat inside her. "Stop playing with me, Finn."

"Where's the fun in that?" He teased her opening with the tip of his cock, his thrusts deliberate and slow.

She grabbed his horns. All his seductive taunts vanished, and he howled from her long, slow caresses. Finn wrestled for control, but she squeezed them harder, stroking faster. He was lost, grinding his steel cock against her ass, panting, "Witchling, what have you done?"

"I told you to stop playing with me."

He bent her over the railing, grasping her hip in one hand and her raised leg in the other. With one smooth thrust, he was inside her. So hard. So perfect. His tail returned to her clitoris, building her pleasure higher. He rutted her like a crazed animal, determined to bring her to full ecstasy.

Ivy lifted her face to the clouds, mouth parted with a soundless cry, the taste of sweet rain on her tongue. In that moment nothing else mattered. Not the fade, not her ritual. Only her and her satyr.

Thunder rumbled, their bodies crashing in wet, forceful slaps. Lightning flashed, reflecting in Finn's carnal mismatched gaze.

One final thrust and she fell over the edge, her scream matching the din of the storm. With a roar he followed her, filling her with his heat. His fang sunk into her shoulder, the mix of pleasure and pain making her come a second time. He bowed over her, lips kissing anything they could touch; her nape, her ear, her back. "My Ivy."

He stared at her, eyes bright. She smiled, loving the wonder of his expression and how his still hard length pulsed inside her. "I love you."

Finn brushed the ropes of wet hair from her face.

"You heard me right," she said.

She'd never forget his elated smile for the rest of her days.

Chapter 22

Finn cradled Ivy in his lap, pulling the blanket tight around their still shoulders. They had a thorough soaking, one that he would gratefully endure again if she asked.

The fire crackled, casting a comforting orange glow on the carpet they were stretched out on. It all made that huge living room so cozy. Actually, *she* made the room cozy. Ivy lifted her mug of tea to her lips, her copper hair drying across her back in soft waves.

He kissed her temple, resting his chin on top of her head. "I suppose I understand your love of storms now."

She chuffed, cupping her mug before her giggle tumbled it to the floor. "Yeah, see? I liked storms for other reasons before that. Not that I'm complaining."

"How could you?" He twisted one of her long locks around a finger. "You just coupled with me. A creature of vast strength, devastating beauty, and learned in the ways of immeasurable pleasure. How fortunate for you."

Ivy gave him a flat look. "Dear Brigid, your ego."

"Is as large as my cock, I know, that is rather enormous." He plucked the mug from her hands, giving it a sip.

Her uproarious laugh made his heart swell. She loved him. He could still hear that wonderful confession in her husky voice. She loved him, loved him deeply. And he felt the same.

Satyrs were never ones to be concerned with something as earthly as love. The hunt, the forest, and sex were all that mattered to his kind. Oh, there would be an occasional mating, but only with those within the herd

But there was no denying the emotion that took hold when he looked at Ivy. The first happiness he had in ages had been waiting in the arms, the kiss, and the smile of a stubborn witch. Hades, Dionysus, and all the Gods be damned if they decided to take her away from him.

He pressed her mug back into her palms, leaning towards her to murmur "I love you too." She looked back at him, her blue eyes sparkling with unshed tears. "My words are true and should have been said earlier."

She sniffled through her quivering smile. "So, I guess we're a thing now, huh?"

"Depends. If by thing you mean I am now endlessly devoted to you, my life is forever in your hands, and yours forever in my heart, even beyond death? Then yes, I suppose we're a thing. My dreams of you were prophetic."

Ivy's eyes widened. "Wait, the house gave you dreams too?"

Finn tilted his head. "The house?"

Her mouth thinned and she shot a suspicious glance to the ceiling. "Yeah. I think it was trying to push us together."

"Well, I suppose I should thank it." He nuzzled her. "Exactly what were these dreams of yours like?"

"Filthy." Ivy grinned, her nose wrinkling as she crooned, "Absolutely, toe curlingly, filthy."

"Only solidifying our thing." He grinned, combing his fingers through her mane. "And as your thing, I've decided you're no longer to keep your hair in that ridiculous knot. It is to flow free so I may enjoy it."

Her elbow jabbed his ribs. "Thing does not equate to boss of me."

Once again, the mug was plucked from her hands, safely placed aside as he pulled her beneath him. He pinned her wrists over her head, running his tongue along her throat.

"Thing may not, but Finnbar An Croí Láidir does." He rumbled a hmm under her ear, making her squirm with giggles. "It translates to Finnbar the Strong Heart, but no one speaks Gaelic in these lands anymore, do they?"

She wiggled free, giving him a gentle push and a playful grin. "Yeah? Well, Finnbar An Croí Láidir, you're not the boss of me."

"Oh no!" He rolled onto his back, gathering her and the blanket to his chest. "You've used my full name! I am

now commanded to never be the boss of you! Such a
tragedy! I had such devious plans!"

Another raucous laugh spilled from her as she laid her
head on his shoulder. "Okay, you can occasionally be the
boss of me." She swirled a finger around his navel.
"Aren't Satyrs Greek in origin? Shouldn't your name be
like, I donno... Spartacus or Biggus Dickus or something?"

"My kind aren't just confined to Greece though we are
most celebrated in the homeland of our God. Our
mother's herd hailed from the Gaelic lands."

"So, you've never seen Greece?"

"Oh no. I've seen it many times when they used to
throw festivals in honor of Dionysus. Herds would mi-
grate through the fae realm moving from country to
country courtesy of our queen who resides there. That's
how Callum and I arrived here." His tail coiled around
her leg, its brush resting on her hip. "My herd considered
this mountain a suitable place. It was strong in magic and
forest. A perfect place to settle."

"What happened to them?"

He stiffened, a chill creeping in. "They were killed...
by a coven."

"Oh..." She fell silent, pressing herself against his side.
"Sorry. I shouldn't have asked. We can change the subject."

He almost said yes, pushed the memories away and
buried himself in his witch. But that would do no good.

For ages, his pain grew inside him like a cancer. Callum couldn't speak of such things without falling into his

rages. So, Finn had suffered in silence, the anguish chipping him down one sliver at a time. Now the Gods had given him someone who knew his pain, and it was time to lance his boil.

He curled around Ivy, tucking himself in her protection. "No. You confided your darkness to me. I... I want to do the same."

Ivy rolled on her side, head propped on her arm, lacing their fingers together. He took a deep breath.

"It had started with a single witch. She was wickedly beautiful with violet eyes and hair as silver as the moon. We don't know where she had come from or when she arrived. Her hovel just appeared on the borders of our territory. At first, we didn't think much of it, after all, a warlock had built this very house of the opposite side of our lands and caused us no trouble. But then others appeared. More hovels. More witches... So many. Our chieftain was wary of their growing numbers. She consulted our queen and was commanded to parley with them."

Fury burned his temples, a growl rumbling his throat. "We met beside the lake in the night, away from human eyes. Our chieftain was so optimistic. This would be the beginning of an alliance of our kinds and would only lead to prosperity. A bargain was to be struck between us. But as soon as she offered her hand... the silver haired witch took her head with a spell. That's when the slaughter began."

The screams of his herd rang in his skull, their warm blood splashing his hooves, the sting of magical bolts as they rained down like arrows. He pulled Ivy's soft body against him.

"It started with their magic, then ended with this... creature. One created from the dying remains of our herd and shadows and...despair. We called it the Hunger. It drained the land, picking us off one by one. In my long life, I've never seen such power.

"We hid, waiting for our queen to save us, to open a portal, anything! Surely, she had felt our suffering. But the portal never came, and our pleas went unanswered." He snorted a sad laugh. "Cal never gave up on her rescue. Pushed me to keep going, to not give up. He was a warrior through and through, never backed down from anything, the stubborn bastard. I'm not sure what scarred him worse, the coven's tortures or the queen's rejection.

"Soon it was only me and Cal. We were desperate for sanctuary and came here. The warlock was an arrogant prick, but magnanimous and sheltered us. The Hunger couldn't cross his wards and I truly thought we would be safe. But even his power couldn't fight the sheer number of witches. Eventually, they stormed the doors."

His throat thickened. "I watched them build the altars we were to be sacrificed upon, watched them drive a blade through the Warlock's belly and use his blood to power their runes. Watched them carve Callum to pieces and bathe in his gore. They drank his essence. And my horror. They drank my fear." Tears poured down his face, as he stared into the fire. "Somehow that damned warlock managed to free me. I fought my way to Callum, but the Hunger gave chase. It would have overcome us if not for the warlock. He performed a spell, combined our blood and what power we still had left inside us...Together we destroyed that creature. With his dying breath, he commanded we hide in the house. And we did...And have been here ever since."

Finn hid his face in the crook of her neck, letting her comforting scent ground him. "Days later we discovered the coven left. No reason, no rhyme. They killed my herd, destroyed all I loved, then walked away as if it were nothing more than a farce. I never saw another witch again... until you."

Ivy paled. "Finn, I...I'm so sorry. No wonder you didn't want me here. If I knew-"

Finn kissed the bridge of her nose. "If you knew, you wouldn't have stayed. And I wouldn't have you now."

She squeezed her eyes shut, face flushing as she bared her teeth. "If those fuckers are still alive, I will find them, and I'll kill them all."

His heart soared out of the ashes of his sorrow. She wanted to fight for him, and may the Gods help anyone that stood in her way. "I'm sure they're long dead."

"If they aren't, magic or no magic, I'll tear their fucking hearts out."

"Spoken like the fierce witch you are. I'm honored you wish to fight for me."

The dread coiling inside him loosened and he kissed her as if there were no tomorrow. It wasn't until the moon was high in the sky when they finally dragged themselves to bed.

Finn curled against her as the storm raged, his tail tangled in her hands. He let sleep take him, wrapped in her aroma of lavender and sage.

A crash of thunder woke him from his nightmare of Callum out in the storm. He could be cold, terrified, and hungry. And here he was, content and well loved in the bed of a witch.

The heavy hand of guilt pressed hard, driving him to push his blankets aside. He had to find him. Had to explain everything that had transpired and beg for him to return.

"Witchling?" He reached to shake Ivy awake, but his palm met nothing. The sheets were strangely cold, as if empty for hours. "Witchling, where are you?"

No light in the bathroom and the door remained closed. Maximus was curled up at the foot of the bed as usual. That's odd. Even in the dead of night, the familiar went wherever Ivy did, much to her chagrin when she needed to relieve herself. Finn frowned, turning to find the blankets still lifted as if someone were under them. He pulled them away. Ivy. She was only the faintest of outlines flickering like a dying candle.

No. No no no! He tried to shake her but only grabbed air that froze him to the bones. He slammed his palms onto the mattress, making it rock.

"Ivy wake up!"

Maximus bolted upright, his tail puffed. One look at Ivy and he let out a screech that pierced Finn's ear drums. Her form returned, eyelids fluttering, mouth open wide with a yawn.

"Is something wrong with Max?" she murmured in a drowsy voice. "I think I heard him scream.".

Seven Hells, she didn't even know she had faded. He bit his lip, tucking the blanket under her chin. "It... was nothing. Just a nightmare. He's fine."

Another yawn and she was out, warmth plumping her skin. Maximus wiggled with a questioning chitter.

"I don't know if it will happen again," Finn whispered in reply. "I'll stand watch in case it does."

He should have told her the truth about her fade. But he couldn't will the words from his lips. *Coward.* Callum would have to wait until morning, until Finn was sure that Ivy would last through the night. He laid down beside her, arms protectively cocooning her. One more sleep left until Samhain. One more sleep until the fade was put behind them.

Dionysus help him, that wasn't soon enough.

Chapter 23

Kitten... what have you done!?" The King of Shadows loomed in the tall tree above, the eddying gloom of his face contorted in horror. "You been feeding behind my back?!"

The deer carcass fell from its claws and exploded in a mess of wet dust. An entire herd lay at its feet, their bodies grey and chalky, eyes clouded over. It had been so easy to take them all, drink their essence, and now their power coursed through its veins. Its body had grown, along with its will.

Devour. Consume. I need. I need!

Its mouth split, tongue running across its pointed teeth. The gargoyle landed and grabbed its shoulders with a fierce shake. "We need to get you back to the den! Now before it's too late!"

It hissed. The bastard only wanted it to starve. He had no idea of its suffering, how it could not rest until all the power in the land resided inside its guts. Well, it would no longer take orders from the likes of him.

Hundreds of red eyes blinked open across its mottled skin, all seeing, all knowing. With a roar, its spine snapped, its bones tearing through its muscles. Thick green ichor splashed, tentacles ripping free. *Yes. Grow. Devour. That is your soul purpose.*

The gargoyle flew into the trees, dodging its sharp claws. It lashed at him, hungry for the life that pulsed through his veins. But he stayed just out of reach of its tentacles. A growl of frustration trembled its throat as it grabbed the tree and shook. Leaves poured down with the pounding rain. Soon so would he. He would be its dinner. He would rest in its belly forever.

"This is not you!" He clung to the branches as the tree swayed. "Fight it! You're stronger than this!"

The slightest yellow glow far in the distance caught one of its many eyes. Lights? No, it was essence, faint and flickering, calling to it with its siren's song.

The house. I must get into the house. It had the strength to defeat its wards now. It could easily get inside for its meal. And what a meal it would be. The gargoyle's puny life would be nothing compared to that prize. Maybe then it will finally be satisfied.

It released the tree, leaving the gargoyle behind. Its appendages drained everything along its path as it kept its many eyes on the glowing essence on the far side of the forest.

"Kitten! Please!" The King of Shadows begged. "Please fight it!"

But it ignored his pleas. It would not be controlled. Not anymore. It had its strength now. It had its will. And it hungered.

The sleepless night was taking its toll on Finn's patience. He had sat vigil over Ivy, praying to his God that she wouldn't fade again before sunrise. Dionysus must have heard him. His Witchling had slept soundly and solidly. When she woke, she sprang from the bed, kissed his cheek then strode to the bathroom.

Finn rubbed his eyes, blinking them into focus. "You seem rather determined this morning."

"I am!" Ivy hopped in an excited circle. "I'm one chalk circle away from my ritual. And I really think I'm going to pull it off! Holy shit, it's been forever since I woke up in a great mood!"

Finn nodded, trying to raise his emotion to her level. But his heavy heart weighed him down.

She finished another pirouette, pausing to flash him a coquettish smile. "Want to join me in the shower?"

Oh, how he longed to. Nothing would please him more than forgetting his troubles by burying himself deep in his Witchling.

A thunderclap shook the room, lightning striking a tree clean down the middle. The two gaped out the window as a pillar of smoke twirled through the raindrops.

Finn's heart shot into his throat. His brother was still out there in the raging storm.

"I need to find Cal." He threw off the blankets, snagging his loincloth from the floor and tying it in place.

"I'll go with you."

"No!" He cleared his throat, calming his tone. "You should stay here and prepare the ritual for tomorrow night."

"I don't have much left to set up. I can do it when we get back." She wiggled into her pants. "You're going to need a second set of eyes out there."

A fang sunk into his tongue, his pulse quickening. "Ivy stay here. It's not safe for you out there in your condition…"

He bit his tongue, but it was too late. That dreaded word had left his lips. Hurt oozed from her, as she twisted the sweater in her hands.

Finn mumbled an oath, raking his claws through his hair. "That's not what I meant."

"Then what do you mean, Finn? Yesterday, you were all rah-rah go team and now I have a condition?"

"The storm is fierce, and you are not as adapt to the elements as I am!"

She narrowed her eyes. "What are you not telling me?"

"Witchling! You have a ritual to do, and I demand that-"

"Tell me Finn!"

Finn shook his head, unable to meet her eyes. "Last night you...you faded in your sleep."

Ivy paled. She pressed a hand to her chest, as if checking to see if she were solid. "H-how bad?"

"I'm not sure." But he was. She had almost disappeared completely. He had almost lost her forever.

Ivy's breath grew short, legs shaking as she stumbled into a sit on the bed. He rushed to her side.

"Breathe, Witchling," he soothed.

She inhaled deep through her nose, then punched the mattress, the springs squeaking from the force. "Why can't things go smooth for me?! Just this once!" She punched again, then again. "Why is it too much to ask that things be fine for a change!"

He wanted to absorb her fear, bring her back to where she was only moments ago. He pulled her into his arms.

"Why didn't you tell me last night that I faded?" she asked.

He winced, clutching her tighter. "The thought of stealing your confidence tore my heart in two. It was a poor choice. Love like this is new to me. And the need to protect you is...overwhelming, even though I know how strong you are." He kissed her forehead. "I'm sorry."

"Thank you." She lay still in his arms. Soon her muscles relaxed, her anxiety passing as it always did. "Callum won't bother talking to you if I was there, would he." When Finn shook his head, she sighed. "Okay then. I'll stay here. But at least put on a coat. It's freezing."

"I don't need one."

"Humor me, okay?"

She went to her closet and yanked out the garment. Her scowl told him she wasn't happy with her capitulation, but she was right. Callum wouldn't dare show himself if Ivy was with him. He didn't fight her, only slid the garment on.

Soon Finn was slogging through the mud, Ivy's coat clutched tight around him. "Callum!" he bellowed into the trees. His quiver bumped his hip as he searched every dark corner that could fit his humungous brother. "Dammit, show yourself! Don't make me shoot you and carry you home trussed like dinner!"

His ears swiveled for a hoof step, a twig snap, any peep. But the rain was too loud. He ventured further into the woods, worry bubbling for both his brother and his witch. Dear Gods above if he lost both of them...

Don't think on that now, Finn. Just get Callum home then help Ivy with her ritual.

"I'm not leaving these woods without you! Not this time!" He kicked at the puddles, muttering a string of curses. "I swear upon Dionysus, the witch is good! And since I know your next accusation, no I'm not under an enchantment!"

A thick arm wrapped around his throat, Callum's voice muttering, "That's exactly what someone under an enchantment would say."

Relief was like a cool sip of water. "By Dionysus's balls, Cal."

Callum released him, giving the heavy blue plaid coat a sneer of disgust. Purple ringed beneath his eyes as if he hadn't slept in days. Mud splattered him from head to toe, his long hair knotted, braids falling free.

"You are enchanted, little brother. But instead of magic, she used her quim." He snorted. "Now you're wearing her garments?"

"Yes. The witch is so wicked that she doesn't wish me to get cold while searching for your ungrateful ass." Callum turned to storm off, but Finn snagged him by the tail. "You're a mess. Did you-?"

"Yes, I took my potions!" Callum shouted. "I always take my potions! Stop constantly asking such asinine questions!"

"Then why do you look as if you haven't slept in days!"

"Because I haven't! The forest keeps me awake!" He slumped against a tree, staring at the dark clouds swarming above. "Their chanting is louder out here Finn. The memories of their blades. It all is amplified amongst the trees."

Finn held out his hand. "Then come home."

Callum hissed, his eyes flashing red. "Where another witch can do the same in my own sanctuary?"

"Ivy is different!"

"How!?" Callum thrust a claw under Finn's chin. "You tell me how you are so sure she is as good as you say!"

"Because I would not love someone evil!"

The confession hung in the air between them. Callum's eyes widened. "What?"

Finn slicked back his soaked hair. "I love her, Cal." Callum's mouth opened but Finn snapped his tail, silencing him. "It's not an enchantment. I love Ivy and she loves me. We are bonded, brother."

"Impossible! Our kind doesn't love like that!"

"Then explain your love of our chieftain, Orlaith! And how her death also contributed to your rages!"

Callum stumbled back as if struck. Regret dug its claws into his heart, but Finn continued, emotion spilling from his lips in a cascade. "The witch is dying, Cal! That's why she's here and needs our house, it will restore her with a ritual! And I'm going to help her! I am going to save her!"

Callum balled his fists shutting his eyes tight. "It's a trick!" he insisted, but his voice shook with uncertainty. "She's trying to steal your essence!"

"A coven stole her powers! She was hurt just like us, but by her own kind!" Finn swallowed his vitriol. "I know you would have moved the heavens to save Orlaith if you had the chance. Well, *I* have that chance with Ivy. Callum, I want you home and safe, but I will not lose her as a compromise."

He expected Callum to roar, to spit on the ground and curse Ivy into the afterlife. But he only stared, mouth quivering.

"Finn," Callum finally said. "I will-"

A howl rolled from the shadows, turning Finn's blood to ice. He knew that sound, remembered it as it echoed over the screeches of his herd as they were devoured. Finn pulled his bow, nocking an arrow as Callum did the same. The two stood back to back, searching the trees.

"It's dead!" Callum whimpered, his hands shaking as he swung his aim in a wide arc. "We watched it die!"

"Easy Cal. It has to be something else."

But there was no mistaking the sound of death as it grew ever closer. Closer. Lightning flashed, outlining the bent back of a massive creature, its long arms dragging it through the mud. Tentacles lashed from its sides, trees turning to ash at their touch.

Finn's throat closed as he desperately tried to take aim. "Oh, seven hells. How? How is it still alive?"

Hundreds of red eyes winked along its leathery mottled skin, setting the two in their sights. The Hunger had returned, and it was taking its vengeance.

Chapter 24

I vy shook out her cramping hand and glared at the chalk runes on the living room floor. It took an hour to draw that circle, and it was crooked. More like an oval, really.

"Son of a..."

She tilted her head. Well, they looked straight like that. Would it matter? *Doesn't matter. Your fade will take you anyway.*

"Fuck off, anxiety." She stormed to her mother's spell book, sitting on the coffee table, its pages wrinkled and musty from its previous swim.

Since Finn's departure, she had buried herself in drawing runes. The ritual was as good as set. All that was left was Samhain and her family's power to charge her circle. And yet dismay continued to run laps inside her belly.

She had faded in her sleep, didn't even feel it happen. Hell, she might not have woken up at all if Finn wasn't there. Her mother's elegant script blurred into incomprehensible lines as she ruminated. *You can't do this.*

"No, you have Finn, Rowan, your aunts, and a powerful house on your side. You did the research. It will work."

In theory it will work. In practice is a whole other thing. Ivy tossed her book down, twisting her hair up into its knot before it became drenched in sweat. "You can do hard things. You can!"

Maximus's chirp pulled her from her spiral. He sat at her feet, a fresh stick of chalk in his teeth. She took it with a grateful smile then looked back out to the window. Lightning flashed, the trees skeletal fingers groping the clouds.

"Shit." She clapped chalk dust from her hands, moving to the window. "Where the hell is he, Max?"

Four hours had passed since Finn went to find Callum. Sure, she hadn't expected the search to be easy. Convincing his brother to come home would involve an insane amount of verbal gymnastics. His time away was perfectly logical. But logic didn't quell her worry.

"I should go find him." She started to the door then did an abrupt U-turn back to the fireplace. "No. Stay here, Ives. Finn was right. You'll only scare Callum off and make things worse." A rumble of thunder turned her path towards the door. "But you can at least call him from the porch, right?" Her hand touched the knob and she groaned, marching back to the fireplace. "No. Just keep working on the ritual..." She swung around. "...after you call for Finn."

Maximus yapped, grabbing her pantleg and tugging her to a stop.

Ivy scrubbed her face. "If you're telling me I'm freaking out, you're absolutely right. After this is done, I'm getting Finn a damn cell phone."

Maximus sighed—if raccoons even could sigh—and scratched his tiny claws against the door, a sign that he was allowing her to go to the porch. Well, she wasn't going to look a gift familiar in the mouth. She threw open the door, wind slapping her in the face as she cupped her hands around her mouth and called, "Finn!"

The storm howled back. Maximus climbed the rail, chirping into the forest for Finn as well. A chill raced up Ivy's back, one not brought on by the cold, Maximus's chirp turned to a hiss and he bared his fangs. His hackles rose as he ran back and forth across the porch rail.

Lightning flashed again, the sudden illumination making the shadows deeper. Movement. Distant but there, through the thick swaying branches. Ivy stepped off the porch, rain matting her sweater to her chest.

"Finn?"

Maximus leapt from the railing, blocking her path. He tried to herd her back to the house with a sweep of his tail. A horned figure stumbled from the trees. It limped and stumbled before crumbling to the ground.

"Finn!" Ivy leapt over the raccoon and ran, rain stinging her eyes. She grabbed the satyr by the waist, hauling him back to his hooves and smoothing his hair from his face. Her heart stopped. That wasn't Finn.

"Callum?"

"Unhand me!" He tried to run but buckled in her arms, howling in agony. His leg was slashed across the thigh but there was no blood. Only ash crumbled from the edges of his wounds.

Ivy's belly lurched. "Callum, what happened to your-?"

A roar shook the ground. Callum stared down the path, shivering until she feared he'd fall apart. His claws dug into her arms. "It's coming."

Eyes as red as blood stared from the shadows, searing her to her very soul. A giant tentacle, leathery and mottled with grey, green, and black splotches, reached for her. It slammed into the dirt beside her feet. Ivy fell, bottom splashing into the mud. She screamed, her belly dropping to her knees.

"Run, witch!" Callum pulled her to her feet and into a slow lumbering gate.

The creature tore after them, gnarled hands at the ends of four long limbs scratching the dirt. Trees withered at its touch, the very earth dying under its talons. Long spine shot from its back, tentacles squirming from where its ribs should be, seeking and tasting.

Adrenaline spiked Ivy's blood. She hauled Callum against her and ran, lungs aching, knees sore. Lights from the house glowed through the sheets of rain. She just had to cross the threshold. Then they would be safe. *Finn? Where the hell is Finn?*

Icy tendrils snatched her ankles. Her feet flew out from under her and she flopped onto her belly, mud splashing up her nose and into her mouth. The cuff of her jeans dissolved, her skin searing from its cold touch.

She shoved Callum away. "Get to the house!" She kicked at the tentacle, nails dragging through the earth for a hold. But it was too strong.

Callum grabbed her wrists, digging in his hooves. Ivy shrieked as she was pulled like a warm piece of taffy. The thing's gaping maw split open, dripping rows of razor-sharp teeth waiting. Her grip slipped from Callum's hands. He dove onto her, arms tight around her waist.

An arrow landed in one of its eyes with a slimy thump. Finn leapt from the trees, rain soaked and battered, shooting arrow after arrow, until many of its eyes were blinded.

"Get her to safety!" A tentacle lashed at him. Finn dodged, sending another arrow into its neck and cursing loud. "Callum!"

"I'm trying!" Callum hollered.

"Callum! Give me your dagger!" Ivy shouted. Callum hesitated. Another yank threatened to tear her apart. "Just do it!"

He pulled his blade free, slapping it into her palm. Ivy slashed the tentacle. Putrid green tar gushed, ripe with the stench of decay. She fought the urge to gag and stabbed over and over until it fell into a squirming severed blob. Finn kicked it aside, leading them up the porch steps and inside. The front door slammed, and they fell to their knees, gasping for air.

"What the hell was that thing?!" Ivy cried.

"The Hunger," Finn panted.

The door blew off its hinges, dark tendrils throwing her across the floor. She slammed into the couch, clutching her belly as the Hunger dragged itself inside, puss and tar trailing from its oozing wounds. Another screech rendered her ears. It made its way towards Callum, drool coating its lips.

"Brother!" he wailed, throwing his arms over his head.

Finn reached for another arrow, swearing as he found his quiver empty. His dagger was drawn. Ivy grabbed her saltbox from the coffee table. With a battle roar she charged, throwing a handful into the Hunger's mouth. Slime bubbled from its maw, a wail of pain making its tentacle's ripple.

She shielded Callum, holding a second round over her head. "Want another? Then come and get it, fucker!"

The Hunger's leathery form swelled, filling the room. It reared up, claws ready to tear her apart. Ivy stood her ground, despite the terror that liquefied her insides. She nudged Callum away with her boot, the salt in her sweaty fist turning to mush.

Its mouth opened but suddenly shut. Red eyes winked out and it settled, shrinking in size. A tentacle slithered to the coffee table, wrapping around the spell book sprawled under it. Ivy wanted to slap it from its hold but couldn't move, could barely breathe as it held the to the light, as if examining it for damage.

It dusted the leather cover with gentle care, then spun towards Ivy, its face splitting open. She staggered back, raising her salt again. Two cloudy eyes peered at her. High cheekbones above pale lips. An all too familiar face she thought she would never see again. The sister she couldn't save.

"...Aster." The salt box fell from Ivy's hands, spilling across her boots. No, this couldn't be real. Aster was dead. And yet here she was.

"Ivy?" Aster's voice was dry and cracked from disuse. The book hit the floor with a crash. With a blood curdling screech, she was consumed, red eyes opening once again.

The Hunger attacked, but an arrow lodged into its gut. Finn surged forward, Callum's quiver now on his hip, his eyes scarlet as he bared his fangs. "Get away from her!"

Tentacles cut the air like javelins. Ivy dove to the floor as they flew over her head. Finn readied another arrow, but his bow clattered from his grip. A dark tendril shot through his chest and out his back.

"Finn!" Ivy screamed.

A wheeze rattled his throat, his color draining, eyes clouding over. Ash flaked from his skin. He fell, a cloud of dust rising around him.

The world faded away as Ivy wailed. She threw her salt box at the Hunger, the granules sizzling its skin. It exploded into thousands of fluttering shadows, circling like bats before fleeing out the door.

Ivy took Finn's slowly crumbling body into her arms. He was so cold, ash coating her clothes. "Come on, say something! Move!" she begged. "Finnbar An Croí Láidir don't you dare leave me!"

She pressed her ear to his chest, listening for a heartbeat. Anything. Silence was her only answer.

Chapter 25

N o! I'm not giving up, Callum!" Ivy gathered blankets and pillows from the couch. She flung the pile at him without a second glance. "Keep him warm. He's cold as ice."

"Of course, he is! He's dead!" Callum snatched her offering and moved Finn's husk to the fire, despite his protests. "My brother is dead, and the Hunger has returned!"

Dust from Finn's drying flesh left a powdery trail. The sight made Ivy's eyes sting, but she balled her fists, forcing her anger to the fore. "I reject your reality!" She picked up the front door, shoving it back into place to block the storm. "I can bring him back and I will!"

"How? You have no powers!"

"I'll figure something out! If I can find a way to cipher the magic of this house to get my powers, I'm sure I can do the same to bring Finn back to life!"

She snatched up her spell book, rifling through the pages. Her eyes wandered to Finn's prone body silhouetted in the firelight. Her chest clenched. She'd never hear his laugh again, never see his smile, or feel his arms around her. *Stop. Stop right there. No spiraling. You don't have time.*

But her mind was filled with Finn's lifeless form and Aster's pleading gaze. Blood filled her mouth as she bit her tongue. She flipped through more pages, reading but not comprehending the words before her. There was only Finn and Aster. The book fell from her grip as she shoved her palms over her eyes to dam the tears. *You failed them both.*

Something rubbed against her leg. Maximus weaved between her ankles, his fur still damp. The poor little guy was thrown from the porch when the Hunger attacked and had returned in the aftermath. Since then, the raccoon hadn't left her side. She reached down to pat his head, the feel of his fur calming her.

Callum grunted, limping to the fireplace to stand vigil beside Finn. His injured leg dragged behind him, lines of pain creasing his brow. Ivy picked up her spell book and sighed, flipping through the pages for healing spells. "Let me fix your leg."

Callum glared. "I'm fine."

"At least let me wrap it."

"If you touch me, Witch, I'll-"

She slammed her book shut. "I'm going to help you no matter what you threaten, you stubborn prick! Now sit!"

She snapped her fingers at the fireplace and Callum plopped down onto his bottom, gaping.

Ivy turned to Maximus. "Get the first aid kit." He chirped and scuttled off to the kitchen. Callum's tail whipped the air as he stared at his brother. She settled beside him, not surprised when he stiffened. "We're going to get him back. Trust me."

"I find it hard to trust witches," he muttered.

"Well, try, okay? Just for the next few hours. Then you can go back to hating me."

Callum shot her a shrewd glare. "Did you love him or was it all a deception?"

"What kind of question-?"

"Answer me, witch! My brother confessed he'd move heaven and earth for you, and I must know if you'd do the same! Did you love him?"

Ivy swallowed a breath, looking at Finn. How did she fall so fast, allowed herself to become so wrapped up in another? In a single month he had changed her life in the best way possible. She knelt beside him, pulling one of the blankets over his exposed shoulder.

"Not did. I do." Her voice cracked. "I *do* love him, with all my heart. And I'm going to keep loving him when he's back. And I *will* bring him back."

Callum tilted his head, mouth opening with a possible objection. It was stalled as Maximus returned, the handle of the first aid kit tight in his jaws.

Ivy popped it open, pulling out her bandages. Callum cringed and she paused. "I'm just going to wrap it.

Nothing more. No spells or potions until I figure out what the hell that thing did to you."

Slowly, he slid his leg towards her. The gashes on his thigh didn't ooze blood, but ashes, as if it had been hollowed out by fire. Instead of heat, a chill as cold as death itself, radiated from his skin.

"Sweet Brigid," Ivy touched the slag that drizzled onto the hearth.

"It drains your essence." Callum grimaced as she wrapped his thigh. "That's what the Hunger does. Takes the very life from you until you are desolate."

"You're leaking your essence out?"

"With luck it will heal with time." Callum's voice hitched. "Unlike my brother."

"Yeah, well I still reject your reality."

"You are both stubborn and insane, Witch."

"I'm also mad as Hell. And Hell hath no fury as the saying goes."

Callum snorted, then went quiet. Silence thickened between them, only rippled by the pops and crackles of the fire.

Ivy squirmed under his dark stare, fumbling with the bandage. "Whatever you want to say, just say it."

"You... you stood up to that monster with only a handful of salt." He swallowed. "You risked your life for mine. Why?"

Well, that's not what she expected. She leaned back, meeting his eyes. "Because you're important to Finn.

And I know he would do the same for my brother if the roles were reversed."

Callum tilted his head, the fear melting from his gaze. "You're not lying, I can tell."

"I never have been." She knotted the bandage, pressing her hand against his knee. A tiny smile touched her mouth when he didn't flinch. "Look, I know you've been through a lot and it's going to take an act from every God and Goddess to get your trust. And I'm so sorry for what they did to you. But you're the brother of the male I'm head over heels in love with. As far as I'm concerned, that makes you family. And I'll always protect my family."

"Family..." Callum's throat bobbed, fingers curling around the edge of the hearth. "You think of me as family?"

Ivy spread her arms wide. "Welcome to the crazy ass Bennett clan, Callum."

He took her hand, the first time they intentionally touched. "Ivy Siobhan Bennett, I accept your invitation for my brother's sake. And my life is now yours."

Ivy arched a brow. "I'm sorry, what?"

"You saved my life. I will spill blood for you."

"Thanks, Callum but that's a little dramatic."

He lifted his chin, determination burning in his stoic gaze. "You need just say the word and I will render your enemies to mere shreds with my bare hands. No one will dare cross you."

"Still very dramatic there but..." she let out an exhausted chuckle. "Thanks."

"And if you can restore him, I will protect you and my brother's *many* sons."

"Oooookay! Let's stop right there! I don't think my kind can even cross breed with-"

"Many, many sons. At least twenty to start a herd."

"Woah! Callum! It's a uterus! Not a clown car!" The tiniest of chuckles curled his lips. Ivy smirked. "You're as big an asshole as your brother."

"Bigger. He learned from me."

The front door creaked then fell to the floor with a crash. Callum dragged himself in front of Ivy, claws flared and dagger ready. "Who goes!"

"Uh...Rowan," her brother's confused voice replied. "Who the hell are you?"

He stood on the porch, his carrot red hair soaked to his scalp, cheeks and nose bright red from the wind. Dead leaves littered his winter coat, a broken broom in one hand, the other still poised to knock. He stepped through the threshold, eyeing the snarling Callum. "...Happy Samhain?"

"Thank Brigid, Ro!" Ivy tried to run to him, but Callum held her back. "Dammit, Cal!"

"I would have been here sooner, but this isn't good weather for broom flying. I almost ended up in a tree more than once. Then I kept getting pinged by your bad feelings and..." Rowan's blue eyes grew as big as dinner plates, a little giggle of wonder sneaking from him.

"Hoooleeeee shit. I never thought I'd see one of you in person and yet here you are! And you're huge! And...gorgeous. Ives, is this the one you had sex with or is this the one that wants to kill you?"

"Begone intruder or I'll rip your head from your shoulders!" Callum shouted.

"With a threat like that, I'm going to guess the latter."

Ivy put a hand on Callum's shoulder, trying to move him. She might as well have tried rolling a boulder up a mountain with her nose.

Rowan backed away from the satyr, hands raised for peace. "Could you put your blade away? I'm wet, cold, and completely terrified of you. I don't want to be full of holes on top of all that."

Callum studied Rowan's lean, tall form not with anger, but with a keen interest. His tail flicked and he wet his lips. "He's trustworthy?"

"He's my twin brother," Ivy replied.

The dagger was sheathed, and he stepped aside, gesturing for Rowan to proceed. "Welcome."

"Thanks?" Rowan crept around Callum, muttering out of the side of his mouth, "Yup. Territorial cock monster all right." He jolted at a vicious shriek, lifting his boot off Maximus's tail. "Holy fuck! It's a zoo in here!"

Ivy threw her arms around her brother as soon as he was close, babbling as her anxiety swelled once again. "Rowan, can you reach beyond the veil? I need you to look! Fuck there is so much to explain!"

"Ives, is this about your ritual? Why is there a raccoon in your house?" Rowan's gaze fell onto Finn's body laying by the fire. "Oh, sweet Hecate. Is *that* Finn? What the hell happened?!"

Ivy wasted no time telling the tale of the last forty-eight hours; the Hunger, what it had done to Finn's herd, and the attack. She sighed, exhaustion taking its hold. "And there's more. That thing, the Hunger. It's... Aster."

"What?" Rowan looked ready to throw up. "How the hell did Aster become a monster in the woods?"

"Because the coven that killed their herd is the same one that stole my power."

"That's insane! You said that coven attacked over eighty years ago. How could a creature that old be Aster?"

"They made a new one." Callum's grave voice interrupted. "The Hunger is comprised from the despair of others, shoved into a single victim. The warlock had killed the first one eighty years ago. The coven made a second using your sister."

"But that would make that coven ancient!" Rowan cried. "And the amount of power it would take just to create a creature like that would be immense. More than any coven has ever produced."

"So, they used Aster's magic too!" Ivy said. "You remember how powerful she was!"

Rowan ran his hands through his mussed hair. "I need a drink."

"I drank all the wine already."

"Typical." He gestured to Callum. "Can I see your wound? Maybe I can get a better idea of how this thing works."

Callum shot a wary look to Ivy. She nodded in reply and with a deep breath he limped to Rowan, sitting on the couch. Moving with extra care, Rowan kneeled beside him, unwrapping the bandage. He whistled low as he took in Callum's putrefying flesh.

"Hoooleeeee shit, It's not even necrotic. It's just empty. It really *does* drain your essence." He looked to Callum, putting on his warm bedside manner. "So, big guy, can I lay hands?"

Callum's tail slapped against the back of the couch and he growled. "It will heal on its own."

"Don't be so sure of that. This goes right to the bone. It might start sucking life if it hits your marrow." Rowan lifted three fingers in a boy scout salute. "I swear on our parents' grave than I won't do you any harm."

That keen interest returned to Callum's mismatched eyes. A fang ran across his lower lip then he nodded. Rowan smiled, pressing his palms over the wound. They glowed a warm, healing gold, illuminating the blood vessels under Callum's fur and flesh. The satyr's painfilled hiss melted into a sigh of relief.

When Rowan pulled away, the gash was gone, replaced with thick brown fur. Callum gaped with wonder. Equal wonder was placed on Rowan, who's cheeks instantly turned red.

"Great! You can heal it!" Ivy cheered. "So, you can heal Finn too, right?"

Rowan rubbed the back of his neck. "Healing a wound is one thing, but his soul is not in there anymore. I can't do anything to a body with no soul." He plopped himself on the floor, stacking his knees. "Let me at least try and find him. We'll go from there."

He lifted his face skyward, chanting in a low whisper. His eyes rolled back, then he was still, not even his chest rising for breath. Maximus crept towards him, sniffing the back of his ear. Rowan didn't budge. He was gone, his soul somewhere in the ether.

Callum crept beside Ivy, staring at Rowan's motionless form. "What is he doing?"

"Crossing the veil," Ivy said. "He's looking for Finn."

The crease between Callum's eyes deepened, but he nodded all the same. Ivy wrung her hands, fighting the urge to pace. If Rowan found Finn floating beyond the veil, there was a chance he could put him back into his body. *Please, oh please, oh please!*

Maximus had settled in Rowan's lap, still sniffing every inch of him. Minutes ticked by, Callum and Ivy watching and waiting. And waiting. And waiting.

After an hour, Rowan convulsed, his eyes flipping back to his bright blues. Maximus sat up, pressing his tiny paws against his cheeks, examining his pupils. Rowan stared at him cross eyed, then patted his head, peeling Maximus from his chest.

"Did you find him?!" Ivy asked.

Her brother's grimace sent her heart crashing to the floor. "There was no sign of him anywhere."

"What do you mean?" Ivy jerked her thumb to Finn's corpse. "He's definitely not in there anymore."

"And he's not beyond the veil, which is just plain bizarre."

"Then he's in a different beyond," Callum insisted. "One that our kind goes to. Check there, witch-boy!"

Rowan dusted off his jeans with a grunt. "Look, Big Guy. I don't know what you've heard but there's only one big beyond and we all end up there. If Finn has a soul, which I'm sure he does, that's where he'd be. But I didn't find him so..."

He paled, transfixed on Ivy. She spun around, half expecting to see the Hunger creeping up on her, but there was only the fireplace and a very puzzled Callum.

"I...I think I found him," Rowan laughed. "Damn, how the hell I missed him in the first place is beyond me. He's like, right there!"

"What is it? What do you see?" Ivy asked.

"It's faint. Just an outline." Rowan rubbed his eyes, then squinted. "Yeah, it's a satyr, all right... And he's anchored to you."

"What?!"

Callum grabbed Rowan's hand, gaze beseeching. "Are you saying my brother is still on this plane?"

"That's exactly what I'm saying," Rowan replied. "My sister anchored a soul to herself without any magic! How the hell did you do that, Ives?"

"I don't know!" Ivy rubbed her temples. "Everything's a blur! I remember after the Hunger attacked, I grabbed him and I...".*...said Finnbar An Croí Láidir don't you dare leave me.* She froze, hands clutched to her chest. "I used his full name. I told him he couldn't leave me. And as a fair folk he had to obey."

"So, his soul is hanging onto you!" Rowan fist pumped. "And that gives us a chance!"

"He gave you his name?" Callum gaped at the two witches in wonder. "I have never been happier in my life for my brother's utter recklessness."

Chapter 26

The new runes looked straighter this time, which was a plus. Ivy tossed her tiny nub of chalk aside, accepting the new stick that Maximus offered. Waves of acid tossed inside her stomach. Dammit, she should have popped an Atarax. "How's it going over there, Ro?"

Rowan placed another candle on the permitter of her circle. He gave her a thumbs up then checked his watch. "Forty minutes to moon rise." A loud scrape of wood on wood made his face screw up tight. "What the hell?"

Callum had kicked the couch out of the way, sending it twirling top over legs. He placed his hoof on the coffee table, giving it a mighty shove, its legs scratching a trail across the floor before it crashed into the wall.

Ivy groaned. "Callum, I know I asked for more room but be nice to the house."

Callum's back rippled as he bent to right the couch and Rowan let out a strained groan. He leaned toward

Ivy, whispering, "Well, he's intense... And hot. So, so, hot."

"Mind on your task, Ro. Not on his ass," Ivy said as she sketched out the last of her runes.

"I can multitask," he teased then grew serious. "Tell me again how you're going to do this?"

She took Rowan's hand, pulling herself up. "I'm going to talk to the house and get its permission to siphon its power into someone other than its owner. Then I'll tap that into Finn, heal him, and his soul can return."

"And you think it will say yes?"

"If it brought Finn and I together, then it will probably want to keep us together."

"But what about you? Will you get your powers back too?"

Ivy swallowed. "I'll uh...I'll figure that out later."

If she *could* figure it out later. There would only be one chance to bring the house back to life. One chance to harness that power. And only one life it could save. *Cross that bridge when you get to it, Ives.*

The front door crashed to the floor, and a gust swept through the room. Like clockwork, Callum threw himself in front of Ivy, dagger drawn. Only this time he included Rowan under his shield.

Dahlia swept inside, a gale of leaves trailing her arrival. "Here we are, Darling! Ready for your ritual!" She untied the clear vinyl kerchief shielding her well quaffed updo, her matching raincoat squeaking noisily as she peeled it off. "We would have been here sooner, but this storm is absolutely ridiculous!"

Rosemary followed sans raincoat. She only pulled her dripping shawl closer to her shoulders, creating her own rain as she tromped inside. "It's a glorious storm, Lia! Absolutely glorious!"

Dahlia patted her soaking head then sighed. "You could have at least brought your umbrella."

"And miss this? You know I love the way rain feels on my skin. Oh, if only this ritual required being sky clad outdoors. I would have stripped down and-"

"Rowan!" Ivy cried, throwing herself over her fragile chalk circle to shield it from the rain.

"On it!" Rowan dashed across the room, struggling to lift the slick door. Callum was instantly beside him, heaving the door one handed back into its frame. "Thanks." Rowan patted Callum's chest, then yanked his hand away, turning beet red.

Rosemary slapped her hands to her cheeks. "Another satyr! How exciting!"

Callum slammed his back to the wall, frozen with fear. Rowan held out a hand to his aunts, holding them at bay. Unlike with Ivy, they obeyed. "It's okay, Big Guy. They may be scary, but they're a good scary. You have my word that you're safe."

The madness in Callum's gaze softened, hands curling tight around Rowan's arm.

"By Demeter's love!" Rosemary gasped. She pointed a shaky finger towards Finn, still laying by the fire. "Ivy, what on earth-?"

"I'll explain everything later, I promise," Ivy shoved a box of matches in Rosemary's hands, her stomach still churning. "But right now, I need you both to light candles and start putting out intention."

Dahlia took the match box. "Rosie, love. You start the intentions. The dry one should light the candles." Her lips tightened, but whatever questions she had locked behind them remained there. With a hiss, the first match was struck.

Ivy puffed out a relieved breath. "Callum, take Finn to the center of the circle. Rowan, help Aunt Rosie get intention growing."

Maximus chirped, his ears perked. Ivy knelt giving his chin a scritch. "Max, you have to stand watch at the window. If you see the Hunger coming back, scream as loud as you can even if I'm mid-ritual. Can you do that?"

Maximus growled in affirmation, dashing to the window, and perching himself on the sill. Callum placed Finn in the center of her runes, chest stained with his powdery remains. He looked up at her, brows knitted over desperate hope. Her throat closed.

"Ives?" She jumped as Rowan placed a hand on her shoulder. "You ready for this?"

Her heart was in her throat. Her hands shook. She forced a smile that he saw right through. "Born ready."

Rowan squeezed her arm. "You can do this. I know you can."

No, she couldn't. She wasn't strong enough, wasn't ready, or stable or anything that was needed to pull this off. Her teeth sunk into her cheek, knees growing weak. Finn was going to die, and she was going to fail him just like she did Aster.

Warmth brushed her nape with the faintest of kisses. *Breathe, Witchling.* Finn's whisper was faint but there, reviving the confidence she had felt in his arms. Ivy took a long breath and knelt before his body, pressing her hands into the floor.

Dahlia, Rosemary, and Rowan positioned themselves around the circle. Callum crept beside Rowan, offering his hand to him. Rowan gave him a smile, clasping it, their fingers lacing together.

Ivy closed her eyes, imagining roots of energy branching from her palms and throughout the house, every crack, plank, and brick. "I know you're here. You've reached out before. Please, reach out again."

Floorboards creaked and walls groaned. A soft hum rose and fell with the rhythm of her breathing. "Feel me. Seek me out. Talk to me," Ivy chanted. "I'm here, I'm here, I'm here."

There was a rumble, distant, ethereal, shaking Ivy to her bones. Then a velvety silence smothered even the beat of her heart. She cracked her eyelids, finding her family motionless as a photograph. The fire in the fireplace was frozen in time, sparks halted in midflight up the flume. What the hell was going on? She had communicated with homes before but always in whispers, never like this.

"H-Hello?" she called.

"Witchling..." Finn's voice was a reverse echo in the thick air. There he was, hovering right beside her as a soft blue mist.

"You're here! Thank Brigid you're here!" Her fingers passed through him, rippling his form in rings of glowing sapphire. In turn, he reached for her, his limbs vanishing each time he tried to wrap them about her. Ivy's teeth sunk into her lip. "I'm bringing you back! I'm not giving up on you!"

An all too familiar giggle surrounded them. A wall bubbled, a body separating from the wood and peeled wallpaper, human shaped yet not. Its legs were too long, its head too big.

It stepped away from its prison, flesh the color of damp wood and moss covering its scalp, dripping down to its extremely narrow ankles. Weak orange ambers flickered where its heart would be. Eyes opened, revealing twin pits of flame, as it tilted its head. "You wished to talk?"

Their voice was as delicate as a windchime. They weren't just one single entity. They were everything; the floor beneath Ivy's feet, the sheltering roof over her head, love, warmth, and protection that surrounded her when she stepped through the threshold.

"You're... the house?" Ivy asked.

"Your house. And you wished to talk. Well, here I am." Their wide mouth split into a grin, their teeth sharp points of stained glass. "And I've been looking forward to actually speaking with my first cottage witch. How are you, my dear?"

"I've been better."

"Ah yes. That creature has returned, that wretched thing. It attacked eighty years ago, when I was strong enough to fight it. I'm sorry I couldn't have held it off for you, my Ivy." Their sigh was the sound of settling wood. "But that coven nearly destroyed me... and they took my Thaddeus."

"The warlock," Finn's echoing voice murmured.

A sad, jagged smile twisted the house's mouth. "I forgot, you knew him as well. Thad was an interesting beast. And he may have been a selfish arrogant bastard, but he was *my* selfish arrogant bastard. He created me, took wonderful care of me." Their flaming eyes skimmed between Ivy and Finn, mossy brows softening their sharpness. "It is a miracle I still live. Partly thanks to you, dear satyr. You and your brother's presence kept my pulse beating. And you, my witch. My Ivy." They cupped the glowing ambers in their chest. "You have fanned the flames."

"So, it's working?" Ivy asked. "This entire crazy plan I had is working and you're coming back?"

"Maybe not in the way you expected. While your work, fires, and runes did much for me, what truly revived me was the love you and your satyr created together."

Ivy's mouth fell open. "That's why you pushed us together?"

"Indeed." Another musical giggle filled the air. "The hearth may be a home's heart but love is what fuels it. Once I felt you, I knew you'd be perfect for this lost, lonely satyr, and that together you both would be unstoppable."

"And the dreams?"

They shrugged. "Honestly, the dreams were just me being naughty. I do enjoy concocting a wicked dream or two."

Ivy smirked. "Such a pervert!"

"I am how my sire made me."

Ivy passed her fingers through Finn's face hope growing. "Then may I siphon your power into Finn's body so his soul can find its way home?"

"Yes." The house sighed. "But there is a price. I can only breathe my power into one being."

"What?" Finn cried.

Ivy shook her head. "Finn, it's the only way."

"No! I won't let you!"

"Your brother needs you!"

"And *I* need *you*! I refuse to go back until you agree not to do this!"

"Don't you dare get stubborn on me, Finn!"

"I won't lose you, Ivy!"

"If you're dead, you already have!"

Finn's strangled cry of frustration made her ache. She tried to cup his chin, her hands, touching only fog.

"Please, Finn," she begged. "This is the only chance we have. Even if I can't figure out how to get my powers, I won't give up any time I have left with you."

His tail flicked in a trail of sapphire vapour. He buried his face into his hands and reluctantly nodded, heartbreak pouring from him.

She wanted to touch him, wanted to pull him close and fall into the comfort of his arms. She tore her eyes from him and turned back to the house. "So, what do we do?"

"Perform your ritual as planned," they said. "When I am revived, press your lips against his."

"A magical kiss? Like a fairy tale?"

"My power will pour through you and into him. Oh, and try to touch tongues."

"Will that strengthen the magic?"

They gave her a jagged smile. "I just like it when you two do that."

Ivy pinched her brow. "Yep. You're a perv."

"This power," Finn asked. "Once I've returned, where does it go?"

The house shrugged. "It goes where it wills."

A thoughtful look passed across Finn's faded eyes. Before Ivy could ask what he was up to, the house curled their lengthy fingers against her jaw. "I've given you all the knowledge you need, my witch. Now go. Revive your love."

Ivy's eyes snapped open to the crackling fire in the hearth, the sounds, and smells of her world returning. Thunder rattled the roof, but it wasn't the storm rocking the house. Magic trembled beneath her, begging for release. All Ivy had to do was grasp it.

She shoved her palms against the floor. "I call upon the powers of this mountain! I call upon the powers of the Goddess Brigid!"

The taste of copper flooded her mouth, electricity crackling inside her. The candles winked out one by one. "I call upon thee to restore life to this house. Please, Goddess! Hear me! Awaken!"

Light shot across the walls in crackling webs, the acidic smell of gunpowder stinging Ivy's nose. Fire exploded from the hearth, scorching the wood and stone black. Power trembled up Ivy's arms, igniting her veins, and shaking her hair free of its knot. Life. Beautiful life. She was a beacon, her vision hallowed in gold, her entire body vibrating.

Ivy cupped Finn's ashen face, slanting her mouth over his. His eyes cleared. Those beautiful, beautiful eyes. One as bright as the sun, the other as dark as the night sky. His color returned, his deteriorating flesh whole again. The sound of Callum's shout was calmed by Rowan's gentle whispers. Her aunts crooned in awe.

With a ragged scream, Finn arched off the floor. His hooves kicked, tail thrashing. Then he collapsed, heaving for air.

"Finn?" Ivy's voice trembled with hope. "Finn, say something. Please."

He sat up, touching her lips. "Ivy Siobhan Bennett, I command you to take back your magic!" He grabbed her by the nape and kissed her. Her fingers curled into his shoulders, the softest of moans against her lips.

Power. Wonderful. Delicious. It flowed from the tip of his pointed tongue, filling the long empty part of her soul. A long-awaited need was satiated, bright and new and filling her with a joy that almost blew her to pieces. Their lips parted and. she fell limp in his arms.

"Ives!" Rowan cried from across the room.

Ivy wanted to answer, wanted to assure him she was fine but could only lay in Finn's secure grip as the world spun in a carousel of color. Hands were upon her, Rowan, Dahlia, Rosemary, even Callum.

She shook her head lifting her exhausted gaze to Finn. "Wha...what happened?"

A smile lit his face. "Witchling, your power has been returned."

Ivy lifted her hand. With one thought, sparks flew from her fingertips. Magic. Her magic. "But the house said they could only syphon power into one of us."

"And they said when I returned the power would go where it willed, and it gave me an idea. I pushed it where in needed to go and commanded you to comply." He grinned, his tail curling around her waist. "They did have a point about our tongue's touching. It is quite nice."

A long-carried weight lifted from her, leaving her as light as a feather and bright as the sun. She flung her arms around him and squeezed him tight. Ivy had done it. She had rescued Finn. And like the stubborn wonderful male he was, he rescued her right back.

Chapter 27

Finn beamed as Ivy was smothered by her family's embrace. No, not just her family. It was his as well. Even if they haven't officially admitted it, he knew he had become part of the Bennett herd. Instead of being terrified like he expected, a comfort he hadn't felt since he roamed the lands with his own kind warmed his belly. Family. More than just he and Callum. A true family.

Callum clasped his shoulder. "I suppose now you're going to gloat about how you returned from the dead?"

"Every chance I get," Finn replied.

Callum yanked Finn into a tight hug, burying his face against his shoulder. "I thought I'd lost you forever. But she never gave up on you. She risked everything to bring you back. ...I was wrong, brother. So wrong. And I'm sorry I caused you grief."

Finn stroked the thick scars that covered Callum's back. "It's all right. I'm sorry I wasn't more truthful with you. No more of this. We stand together going forward."

"Indeed." Callum smiled. "Welcome back, brother."

A blood curdling screech tore their embrace apart. Maximus jumped from the windowsill, chittering wild to him and Ivy. Finn's belly grew cold at what the familiar had to say.

"A male is outside?" Ivy asked Maximus. "Who? What kind of male?" She blinked then looked to Finn. "Holy shit, I can understand him now!"

Finn snagged his bow, tossing Callum his. "Stay inside. I'll investigate."

"You'll need backup." She held up a sparkling hand before he could object. "Trust me. I'll be fine."

A gust of wind blew the door down. Through the pounding rain a booming voice called. "I demand to speak with the residents of this house!"

That voice. It was vaguely familiar.

Finn and Callum barreled out to the porch. They raised their bows toward the large figure in the dirt path. He didn't cringe, only squared his shoulders and great horned head raised towards the storm. "Answer me!" he bellowed.

Huge bat like wings folded against his back. His features were shrouded in a mysterious fog, only revealing his bright golden eyes in any detail.

A King of Shadows. By Dionysus, he couldn't remember the last time he had seen one of his kind. Finn held his breath. *Where in the seven hells had one of his ilk come from?*

The witches stumbled out to the porch, stopping dead in their tracks at the sight. "Is that what I think it is?" Rowan asked.

"A King of Shadows," Callum answered.

"A gargoyle," Finn added.

"Huh." Rowan shook his head. "They looked so different in the cartoon."

"Never mind that, why the hell is it here?" Ivy asked.

Finn pulled his bowstring taut. "Good question."

"Rosie, I believe it's time for a brawl," Dahlia said, raising a lit palm.

"Oh dear. It's been quite some time." Sparks flew from Rosemary's fingertips. "I may be a bit rusty at busting skulls."

"It's like riding a bike, Love."

Finn stepped off the porch, arrow still aimed. "Why are you on our lands, gargoyle?"

The gargoyle sighed. "Ah. Still territorial, I see."

"Speak your peace before I empty my quiver on you."

"You were attacked earlier by the Hunger. Well, she'll return. The house's wards will protect you but not forever. She's not like the ones before her. She's smart. And she has a witch's heart only adding to her power."

"She? Who is she?" Rosemary asked.

Ivy ran a hand through her hair and murmured, "...Aster."

"But Aster is dead!" Dahlia replied.

"That coven... It did something horrible to her."

The gargoyle tilted his head. "Is there a reason she is drawn to this house? Did you summon her?" He snorted. "I thought you satyrs would know better."

"This is her family!" Finn barked. "She's drawn to *them*!"

"Her...family?" The gargoyle's eyes widened, the only sign of emotion under his pall of darkness. "Then if you have any love for her, you will kill her."

"I'm not killing my sister!" Ivy shouted.

A howl echoed from the trees, dark, agonized. Hungry. "You cannot save her," the gargoyle replied. "All she knows now is pain. Pain and the hunger. If you don't kill her, she'll destroy every living creature on this mountain to fill her void."

A whistle climbed on the wind. Something huge soared from the treetops, arcing through the sky towards them.

Rosemary's quivering voice asked, "Lia, is that our truck?"

"Run!" Finn tackled Ivy into the mud, shielding her as the truck sailed over them and crashed into the house. Wood and glass exploded as it slid through the living room with a grinding screech. Everyone scattered, the gargoyle taking to the air.

Finn grabbed Ivy's shoulders. "Are you all right?"

"Yeah. I'm..." Her jaw dropped. With a shaking hand she pointed to the truck's rear end sticking out from the devastated wall. Runes were carved deep into the metal chassis as if by a blade sharp claw. "It's a counter spell! She just broke through our wards!"

Trees tumbled and Aster charged, jaws dripping with saliva and eyes bright as fresh blood. She was bigger now, almost the size of the house itself. The ground beneath her flashed with the briefest of spells then fell dormant, weakened by her trickery. She threw herself at the porch. Finn pushed back his terror, nocking an arrow, and sending it into her thick, leathery hide.

The others stumbled from the wreckage, Callum leading them away from the house, crying "Keep moving!" Aster swiped, knocking him off his hooves. He threw his arms over his head as she brought down her gnarled claws. Rowan threw a net of stars from his hand, shielding Callum from the blow.

The gargoyle swooped down, digging his talons into her back. Puss ran down her sides as he hacked and scratched but she flung him away as if he weighed nothing at all. He vanished into the treetops. Red eyes swiveled, forgetting the previous prey, and settling on the house.

On Ivy.

Finn pulled her to her feet. They climbed past the demolished truck and into the house, ducking from the groaning ceiling. Aster threw herself against its walls and the rafters snapped, the floors above collapsing. Finn hoisted Ivy over his shoulder, running at breakneck speed. They stumbled out onto the back deck. Dust and debris tidal waved behind them, rubble blocking re-entry.

"Come on! We can swim across the pond and run deeper into the forest!" Finn lowered Ivy to her feet, but she turned back to the demolished house. "Witchling!"

Sparks jumped and crackled in her palms, her voice breaking. "I have to try and reach her."

"No!" He tugged at her wrist. "We must run and hide! We need a plan!"

"The plan is to not give up on her! If I can bring you back, I can bring her back too!" Panic danced in her wild gaze, her breaths short and wheezing. "I can't kill her all over again, Finn! I can't!"

Finn released her, his heart breaking. "Breathe, Witchling." She obeyed, closing her eyes tight. He pressed his forehead to hers, lacing their fingers. "Ivy Siobhan Bennett, I'll be right here by your side."

Dark water rose from the pond in a tsunami. Aster emerged, shaking the dregs and debris from her back. She wrapped her bony hands around the porch beams, hauling herself over the side, blocking any escape they might have had. A tentacle lashed out, snaring Ivy. Their hands slipped apart as she was dragged away and towards Aster's hungry maw.

Chapter 28

Sharp splinters tore through Ivy's sweater as she was dragged along the deck. She kicked, slamming her heel into the tentacle to no avail. Aster's jagged teeth grew closer.

An oily, forked tongue grazed over her, turning her flesh to pure ice as it tasted her essence. Ivy grabbed it before it could take more, freezing her fingers to the bone.

Electricity shot through every nerve, emotions flooding her entire being. Guilt. Loneliness. Grief. Pain. So much pain. The hair on her arms rose, her heart shattering to pieces. *My sweet sister! Aster! Make it stop make it stop! Please make it stop!*

"Ivy!"

Finn's voice pulled her from that terrible spiral and back to the world. She released her hold and the darkness faded. With a grunt she clawed her way across the deck, stretching her hand to Finn.

More tentacles sprung from Aster's ribs, cracking like whips. Finn fell with a wail, grey death scoring his chest.

"No!" Ivy cupped her hands, gathering her magic. She threw the bomb into Aster's face, viscera splattering everywhere. It smelt of rotten meat and concentrated sorrow. "Aster, stop! You don't want to do this!"

Aster answered with a roar. She released Ivy, grabbing the railing, and shaking the deck. *Save me,* the house cried. *Save us all.* Ivy slammed her hands against the rough wooden planks. Her body ignited, raindrops turning to steam. Light spilled from her eyes and poured from her lips in a fountain of stars. Her bellow rippled the air, the storm freezing in mid fall. Power scorched Aster's thick hide. The spines of her back stood straight then flattened, her shriek of agony deafening.

Ivy held up her palms in warning, stepping forward. "I know you're in there, Aster. I know you can hear me. I'm not mad at you. I don't want you punished. I want you home."

The beast cringed, snapping its jaws.

"You don't have to feel like this, Aster. We all love you. I love you. I don't blame you for anything."

Aster slapped her hands onto the deck, jaw splitting her head in two. The roar she released blew back Ivy's hair. Panic rose, the voices of doubt screaming inside her, making her want to flee. *No! Get angry! You can do hard things!*

"Stop being a dumb bitch and fight it!" Ivy screamed. "Fight it or kill me!"

"Fuck you!" Aster's voice peeked through the rusty cacophony. Her form shrank an inch, her grip on the deck loosening.

"Anger," Ivy whispered. "That's the key." In the past, Aster had never gotten angry. She barely knew how. Unlike Ivy, she would sooner blame herself than turn her fury on anyone else. And that fucking coven used that to trap her in a cold state of despair. "That's it, Aster! Get pissed off!"

Aster's roar faded into a sad whimper. Her flesh bubbled, growing once again.

"No! Stay mad! Remember that time Rowan and I set fire to your dollhouse?"

Aster shrank another inch, tilting her giant head in an almost comical way.

"Oh! And when Linda Comstock stole your boyfriend at prom? Think about that nasty ho for a while!"

A slit tore across Aster's gut, blood-soaked entrails firing out and ensnaring Ivy.

"Okay! Too much rage Aster! Too much rage!"

There was a disgusting slurp, the bubbling flesh enveloping Ivy's feet, her calves, her hips. Something inside the beast took hold of her leg. Something warm and alive. Finn grabbed her, bracing his hoof on the broken railing.

"Don't let go!" Ivy begged.

"Never!" Finn grunted in pain as he pulled her free of the fleshy mass inch by inch, dragging whatever held her along.

A hand was clasped around her calf, pale and slender. A shoulder followed, then a head of strawberry blonde hair matted with chunks of the Gods only knew what. She looked to Ivy with bloodshot, blue eyes.

"You brought up prom, you bitch!" Aster sobbed.

Ivy half cried, half laughed, reaching down to clasp her forearm. With Finn's final heave, she slid free, and their filthy bodies spilt onto the deck with a wet splat. Ivy flung her arms around her sister.

"Don't hug me," Aster murmured weakly. "I'm covered in goo."

"Too bad." Ivy squeezed her tight, rubbing her ice-cold arms.

"Ivy...Ivy, I'm so sorry."

"There's nothing to be sorry about. I got you, Aster. You're safe now."

Her arms curled around her. "Thank you... Thank you, thank you, thank you." Aster collapsed against her, eyes sliding shut. Her breath was shallow, but she was breathing. That's all that mattered.

Finn smoothed Ivy's hair back, kissing her forehead. The wound on his chest had faded to smooth flawless skin. "My brave little Witchling," he said. "Thank Dionysus, you're all right."

The sound of bones snapping made Ivy jump. The Hunger contorted, folding in on itself as it shrank down to human size. Its flesh went mottled, crumbling to ash and falling bit by bit into the pond. Steam rose from the water, forming a thick cloud before vanishing forever.

The rain returned, washing away the stain of the coven's beast from the earth.

"I got her back." Ivy buried her face in the crook of Finn's neck. "I...I can't believe that worked. I can't believe we did it."

Finn nuzzled her crown. "Of course, it did. I'm strong and you're stubborn. How else was this going to go?"

A sloppy laugh exploded from her. "Even now, your ego..."

"Is as big as my cock."

"Ives! Finn!" Rowan cried. The rubble behind the house shifted and he shimmied out. Callum followed, dagger drawn and ready. Rowan grasped his chest deflating as soon as he spotted them. "Thank Hecate!"

"Auntie Rosie and Lia!" Ivy asked. "Where are they?"

"Out front with your familiar. They're okay too."

Callum was on Finn in a heartbeat, checking him for injuries. When he was satisfied, he bared his fangs. "Taking on the Hunger with only a witch by your side?! You reckless, foolish, idiotic-"

"Brilliant, devastatingly handsome, and well-endowed baby brother," Finn finished.

Callum grunted, snatching him in a bearhug. "If I wasn't so relieved, I'd kill you again."

"Ives?" Rowan knelt beside her with a gasp. "Is that...?"

Ivy nodded, a smile forcing her tears free. She stroked her sister's hair as she slept. "It's Aster. We got her back, Ro."

With careful hands he touched her face, closing his eyes and whispering a chant. "Her heart is steady, and her aura is strong. She's going to be okay... Unlike your house."

"Oh shit, the house!" She handed Aster to Rowan, running to the dilapidated doors. "Are you there? Can you hear me? Shit, I just brought you back and now this!"

Fear not, I still live, the house strained in discomfort.

Ivy pressed her head against a shattered window. "Thank Brigid."

You did well, my witch.

"How can I thank you for all you did for me?"

I suppose asking you to make love to your satyr on my deck again would be asking too much. So I will settle for your healing.

Ivy snorted. Yep, the house was a perv. She closed her eyes. Her body glowed as soft as a candle, power pouring from her and into her home, racing across its surface in webs of life.

Wood and rubble rose, re-forming into walls, floors, and windows. Peeled paint smoothed, dirt blowing away in mini tornados. As soon as the door re-formed, in ran Rosemary and Dahlia, Maximus taking up the rear. They stared at the healed home, their jaws dropping further as they spotted Aster in Rowan's arms.

Ivy collapsed against Finn, the last of her adrenaline draining away. "Well, now that *that's* done, I'm going to pass out for a few days, okay?"

"Sleep as long as you want my Witchling. I'll be here when you wake." He cradled her in her arms. "And for the rest of our days."

Chapter 29

Arabella's cheek was pressed against the floor, desk chair still spinning from her fall. Her head pounded and acid swirled in her gut as her vision wavered in and out of focus. She pushed herself to her hands and knees.

Bile danced upon her tongue and she groped for her waste basket, vomiting until she had nothing left to give. Soon she was drenched in sweat and shaking like a damn child. She wiped the vitriol from her lips, shoving the waste basket away. Death was ripe in her veins, tearing her insides to shreds. Dammit, she hadn't felt this wretched in decades. Not since that damn warlock killed...

Perspiration trickled like ice down her back. "No," she whispered "No, it can't be." She reached out with her mind, groping for the connection with her pet. Nothing was there. It had been severed permanently. She swore an oath. It was foolish of her to leave her alone on that mountain. She was powerful, yes but naïve and could easily fall into greedy hands. Apparently, that was what happened now.

With a scream, Arabella swept her arm across her parlor. Books spilled from their shelves, the fire in her hearth roaring along with her rage. Her masterpiece, her Aster. Gone. Someone powerful had killed her precious little neophyte. Someone who may even have the strength to destroy her as well. Another sweep of her arms sent papers flying and shattered the crystal glasses on her desk.

The door opened, Threnody peering in from the threshold. Her black hair shined in the light of the fire, brown eyes sharp as always. "Mother Arabella, are you sick?"

Arabella hissed, turning her face away. Of all the damn witches in her coven to come to her aid it had to be Threnody, the opportunist who would take this show of weakness and use it to every advantage. She was clever, beautiful, and her youth made her hungry for power. But you didn't live to be Arabella's age without mastering treachery. Luckily Threnody was smart enough to know this, and rarely crossed her.

Don't let her see you weak. Rise above this. Show your power. Arabella stuck out a hand. "Help me up."

Threnody did what she was told, taking on her weight with ease. "Should I call a healer?"

"Not necessary." Arabella wrenched her arm free, pulling her long silver braid over her shoulder.

The young witch's mouth tightened, most likely around words she dare not speak to her coven mother. The scheming bitch was planning to spread word of her collapse, put her weakness out on display for all her children to see, she could feel it. But Threnody was useful despite her deceit. And would be expendable if she just happened to get herself into trouble on a mission.

"Pack your things and clear whatever it is you have the next several weeks," Arabella said. "You are going to Big Bear Mountain."

Threnody arched a thick dark brow. "Why? I thought your business was done there?"

"*Our* business is never done in our territories." Arabella snapped. She took a second to steady her balance then lifted her chin. "Aster is dead."

That gave her the reaction she was hoping for. Threnody paled, her hands twisting the hem of her black tunic. She shook her head wildly. "What? That's not possible!"

"My connection with her was cut. It's why I collapsed."

"You're wrong! Check again! Now! Tell me she's alive!"

"I am never wrong. Someone killed my wayward daughter, your very sister, Threnody. The one you had held dearest. It's why you are the best choice to be my hand of vengeance."

The sorrow that once filled Threnody's dark eyes churned to pure fire. Her fingers lit, deepening the shadows of her angular face. She nodded, tears shimmering down her cheeks. Ah yes, her thirst for vengeance was stronger than her lust for power.

"You want this mission, my daughter?"

"More than anything, Mother." Threnody growled between her teeth. "They hurt my sister!"

"Good." A smile curled Arabella's mouth. "Judith will accompany you."

"Judith?" Threnody stomped her foot. "She isn't as powerful as me! I'll be better off alone!"

While that was true, Judith was also loyal to the coven, and would keep Threnody in line in case she had any second thoughts. The girl had almost gone turncoat and walked away. And that is why Aster had to go. No one left Arabella's coven. They were her children. The only way out was death.

"Judith will accompany you," Arabella repeated firmly.

Threnody sighed, the magic in her hands winking out. She nodded then turned to leave when Arabella caught her arm. Muscles tensed with fear under her grip. Good. That was the way it should be. She pulled the girl close, running her fingers through her hair.

"My beautiful girl, my strongest of all my wayward daughters. I will give you your vengeance for your sister." Arabella twisted her long mane in her fist and yanked, reveling in her hiss of pain. "You know the consequences if you let me down. Don't let me down."

Threnody's gaze only wavered a moment. "Yes, Mother Arabella," she whispered.

She was released, stumbling in her clumsy black boots, and rubbing her scalp. Arabella flicked a hand at her. "Go on. Time is vital."

As soon as the door clicked shut behind Threnody, Arabella's fury returned. Her long skirts swished against the Persian rug as she paced. Aster was destroyed, her beautiful pet that guarded her lands. If she wasn't so sure that damn warlock was dead, she would have blamed him.

This was a challenge of power and territory, one that was given foolishly. That mountain was hers. She had fought for it all those years ago, killed every living fair folk to claim it. She'll be damned if someone tried to take it away.

Chapter 30

I vy's thighs tightened around Finn's hips before she collapsed, gasping for breath. The birds had gone silent, probably scared off by her screams when Finn made her come three times in a row. Damn, he was talented. Her hands were still around his horns as he teased her nipples with that wicked tongue. This had been a great afternoon so far. "Okay. You're right," she panted. "Forest sex is amazing."

A devilish grin made his fangs gleam in the sun. "It only took weeks to convince you."

"Listen, I didn't want dirt wedged in my delicate lady parts."

"Hence why I brought this." Finn patted the blanket under her back before diving into the juncture between her neck and shoulder. His cock twitched inside her, sending a shockwave that made her arch. "When it comes to pleasure, I know what I speak of."

"Fine, fine. I'll be more agreeable when you try to talk me into experimenting."

As if she hadn't been in the past. Ivy had been the most agreeable woman to her satyr's whims, and he never let her regret it. She released his horns and Finn rolled off her, the crisp air biting.

The sky was more grey than blue these days. Soon the first snow would dust the tops of the mountains and winter would be here. And here she was, buck naked and outside. Well, at least the cardio kept her warm. Before she could even shiver, Finn pulled her close, arm around her waist and tail snaked around her thigh. He rested his head on her shoulder with a contented growl.

"We should get back before my aunts hunt us down," she said.

"They're busy prettying up our home and won't even know we're gone."

"Oh, they'll know." Ivy tapped the tip of his nose. "Their satyr sex senses are strong."

Finn's expression turned sour. "Hmm, good point."

He sat up, planting a hot, lingering kiss on her lips. One hot enough to make her reconsider her suggestion. But he pulled away, scooping up their discarded clothing. They dressed, picked the leaves out of their hair, and made their way back home, arm in arm. Rosemary was digging in the herb garden when they arrived, dirt coating her to her elbows.

"Oh, Ivy dear! Just in time. I'm almost done with the winter garden! It will be a prime time for potion brewing during the snowfall and you should be prepared." She sat on her heels, bracing her lower back. "Did you two enjoy your boinking session in the woods?"

Ivy slapped a hand over her blushing face, shooting a look to Finn. "See? I told you they had senses."

Rosemary waved a hand with a good-natured smile. "Oh no extra senses, Dear. I could hear you screaming his name all the way from here." She gave Finn a thumbs up. "Lovely job."

Much to Ivy's chagrin, Finn returned the gesture. "Greetings, Rosemary. Any more questions today?"

Ivy threw up her hands. "Auntie Rosie, really?"

Rosemary batted her eyes innocently. "Darling, I'm writing a book."

"On Satyr sex drives?"

"Finn doesn't mind my questions. And he has so many things to say!"

Ivy thumped Finn's chest. "Don't fill my Aunt's head with lies."

Finn gasped. "Never would I ever!"

"Uh huh. By the way Auntie Rosie, Satyr's cocks aren't made of gold."

"You certainly act like it is," Finn mumbled. He was rewarded with an elbow in his ribs.

"Oh, I know dear," Rosemary laughed. "But he tells the story so well. I like to indulge him."

Finn jerked a thumb to Rosemary. "See? No harm done."

Ivy rubbed her temples with a groan. Rosemary's book was going to be one hellava read. The clack of hooves came down the dirt path as Callum returned from his hunt. Two rabbits hung from his fist, his chin raised proud.

"Ah, there's my brother!" Finn cried. "A fine bounty for your witch-boy, Callum! I'm sure he will swoon over it as much as you swoon over him."

"I am not swooning!" Callum snapped.

"I'm sorry. Not swooning. Mooning." Finn clasped his hands under his chin, batting his eyes. "Mooning like a nixie at an orgy."

Ivy covered her mouth as Callum marched inside, grumbling something about strangling his baby brother in his sleep. As soon as he was gone, she let her laugh fly. "Oh yeah. He's got it bad."

"Indeed," Finn tsked. "Poor fellow. I haven't seen him this far gone since our chieftain."

Ever since they'd met, Callum had been quietly fawning over her twin, giving him longing looks from a distance, and gifting him with various forest goodies like pinecones, flowers... Oh, and dead animals. Lots and lots of dead animals.

"Should I tell him that Rowan is a vegetarian?" Ivy asked.

"And ruin the surprise?" Finn wrapped an arm around her, guiding her through the front door. "Where's the fun in that?"

The fire crackled merrily in its hearth, reflecting off the polished wood floor. Dahlia was gluing a strip antique wallpaper above the polished wainscoting, looking glamourous even in coveralls. Of course, the red pumps with matching belt and earrings helped.

"Ivy, darling. What do you think?" She gestured to the beautiful print of blue, green, and gold leaf like a spokes model. "It's a wonderful replica from the twenties. I had to search five different stores in Los Angeles until I found the perfect one."

Finn tilted his head. "Hmm...it's rather... human don't you think?"

"Says the guy who decorates with dead trees?" Ivy ruffled his hair. "And it's not really up to me. It's up to them." She gestured to the ceiling.

After they rejected every modern print, paint, and fabric by tearing it down and blowing it out the windows, Ivy had gone to Dahlia and her enormous binder of vintage designs for décor choices. So far, all her picks were spot on.

Dahlia clapped her hands. "What say you, house?"

The fire roared, its bright flames reflecting off the polished wood floors. *Approved*, the house told Ivy.

Ivy tapped her finger against the wallpaper. "Another home run, Auntie Dahlia."

"Excellent!" With a snap of Dahlia's fingers, rolls of wallpaper unrolled, and brushes flew from the drop cloth at her feet. Paste was applied and the great room was adorned in its new wardrobe. She wiped her palms

together then looped her arm around Finn's elbow. "Finn
dear, I have to show you what I did with your room. It's
simply divine!"

"But I share chambers with..." He pointed a weak finger at Ivy, which did nothing to detour her aunt.

"Every male needs a den! And that is precisely what
I've created for you and your brother!" She dragged him
up the stairs, either unaware or ignoring the drag of his
hooves. "I even included that ghastly old chair of Ivy's. I
know how you love it so."

"Just roll with it, Finn." Ivy wiggled her fingers in a
tiny wave.

Finn shot her a glare then sighed, resigning to his fate.

Ivy was about to follow when she spotted Aster across
the room, a broom resting in her hands and her stare out
the window towards the forest. She sighed, brows knitted as if looking for someone.

"Hey, you doing okay?" Ivy asked as she made her way
over.

Aster rubbed her chest then nodded with a weak
smile. "Yeah. Never better. Just helping out." She lifted
her broom in confirmation.

"You don't have to. It's been only a week since we got
you back. You're welcome to recover."

"I know. But keeping active is the best thing I can do
now. Or at least that's what Rowan says. So here I am.
Sweeping an already spotless floor." She glanced out the
window again, tucking a long lock of strawberry blonde
behind an ear.

"You're looking for him, aren't you? The King of Shadows?"

"He didn't leave my side for a year... kept me from killing everything around me. He was my moral compass when mine was taken away and now he's gone. What if I killed him Ives?"

"You didn't kill him. I saw him fly into the trees. You threw him sure, but he's a big guy, twice the size of Finn or Callum. Maybe he's just giving you time to readjust to the world?"

"I hope you're right." Aster snorted a sad laugh. 'I'm a hot mess, Ives."

"You've been through a lot," Ivy cupped her face, forcing her to meet her eyes. "It's okay to be a mess right now. Ro and I got your back. And Auntie Rosemary and Auntie Dahlia and Finn. Hell, even Callum...in his own weird way."

Aster wrapped her slender arms around Ivy's middle, resting her chin on her shoulder. "You're a good big sister... even if you pissed me off bringing up prom."

"It was for the greater good." Ivy chuckled. "So... about you looking for things to do..."

"Don't you dare make me clean windows."

"You asked!"

A brief sense of alarm followed by slight nausea tickled her mind. Ivy sighed, pointing to the stairs. "And we have a Rowan in three, two, one..."

Rowan dashed down as predicted, tugging at the collar of his shirt, upper lip dotted with sweat. "Why does

Callum insist on showing me every dead animal he brings home?" He shut his eyes. After a few deep breaths, his color returned. "Doesn't he know I'm a vegetarian?"

"No," Ivy answered.

"Why?!"

"Because it's funny?" Aster replied.

Rowan shot her a glare and she pressed a hand over her mouth, stifling her laugh. "So glad to have my sisters back together under one roof."

"Just tell him you don't want to look at them, Ro," Ivy said. "Remember, you're the one always encouraging communication."

"I know! But...he's so damn proud of them. He gets all smiley and cute when he shows them to me. And that little dimple appears on the left side..." He blushed at his sisters' smug grins. "Telling him to go away would be like kicking a puppy."

Ivy pressed her hands against her cheeks. "And it's not like you don't appreciate that gorgeous hunk of scars and muscle visiting you *every day*."

"Definitely not." Aster added with a bat of her eyes.

Rowan sneered. "*So* glad to be living with both of you! Ecstatic!"

"I like meat," Aster tapped her lower lip. "Think he'd bring *me* a rabbit?"

"Nah." Ivy answered. "No offence, Aster. But your ass isn't as tight as Rowan's."

He gave them both a flat look. "I'm going back up to my office. Away from you. My sisters who I love so dearly." He turned on his heels, marching away. "Hopefully the blood covered carcass has been taken off my desk."

"Rowan!" Ivy called. When he turned she gave him a thumbs up. "Do *hard* things!"

"Soooo *hard!*" Aster chimed.

He snorted, turning beet red before disappearing up the stairs. Aster and Ivy burst into hysterical laughter.

"See, you're already helping me harass Rowan." Ivy chucked Aster on the chin. "You're one step closer to yourself."

Soon the sun set, and Dahlia and Rosemary had headed home. Aster retired to her bedroom upstairs while Rowan headed to the living room to read and probably wait to see if Callum made an evening appearance.

Ivy cuddled Finn in their bed, snuggling under the thick comforter. Maximus was curled at their feet, snoring softly as he did every night. "You don't mind that Rowan and Aster are going to live here for a while?"

"Of course not." Finn replied. "The pandemonium is welcomed. It reminds me of my life with my herd."

"Rowan is planning on reopening his practice here now that he's off assignment. There's going to be witches coming in and out constantly. I'm worried Callum might freak out."

"I as well." He nuzzled her ear. "But your brother calms him. And he seems to have found a kinship with your sister. I...I think he'll be all right. Happy, even."

Ivy brushed her mouth over his, loving how his groan rumbled against her. "And you're happy too, right?"

"The happiest I've been in ages." He rolled her beneath him, the devil in his grin as he pinned her wrists over her head. "How about you make me even happier still?"

Ivy ran the ball of her foot up along the length of his calf. "Forest sex wasn't enough, eh?"

He sighed dramatically. "My work is never done."

"We'll wake up Maximus."

"Hardly. He has slept through most of our romps."

She pressed her lips against the crook of his neck, giggling at his shiver. "Well...since the house enjoys a show, might as well give them, one, eh?"

And if you put on a show, I must reward you, the house replied.

Ivy sat up, staring at the ceiling. "What?"

Windows rattled in their panes, the floor undulating. Ivy was about to scream earthquake and duck under the bed, but nothing cracked apart or fell from its place. The creak of wood upon wood echoed loud then stopped, filling the air with peace.

"What in Dionysus's balls was that?!" Finn cried.

Ivy peered out from Finn's arms. "Something...something happened to the house." She pressed a hand against the wall behind the headboard. Instead of the usual vast echo of the outside, there was life there, familiar, and warm.

Go see what I did, the house whispered, followed by a mischievous giggle. *More for your brothers than you. But then I've grown fond of them as well.*

Ivy spung out of bed, her socks sliding across the floor as she ran into the hallway. Aster, Rowan, and Callum were right outside her door, bombarding her with baffled looks and questions.

"Witchling! Tell me what's going on this instant!" Finn demanded tail twitching.

"Same!" Rowan added. "Did we just have an earth-quake?"

At the end of the hall was a door. One Ivy was positive was never there before. "No," she said. "I think...we just had an addition."

The ornate brass knob turned with a click, opening be-fore she could even touch it. Behind it was another hallway, shiny and clean as the one they stood in. Doors lined either side, the beginnings of a grand staircase at its end.

For your brother, the house murmured. *So, his story may begin.*

"It grew another wing." Ivy laughed. "Holy shit!"

Finn arched a brow. "Why?"

She grinned, shooting Rowan a mischievous wink. "I'm guessing because they want more tongues touch-ing."

Rowan turned puce while Callum peeked into the new wing curiously. Aster laughed, shoving the two males aside. "Well, if you two aren't going to explore, I am!" She marched through the door fearlessly.

"Aster! Wait up!" Rowan dashed after their little sister, Callum dutifully on his heels. Finn started forward as well but Ivy grabbed him by the tail, tugging him back to their bedroom. "Oh no. You're coming back to bed. We have a show to put on."

Finn's mouth split into a wide grin. He scooped her up, carting her across the threshold "My tenacious Witchling is an overachiever, tonight."

Ivy pressed her lips against his. "Well... I *can* do hard things."

Author's Note

Thanks everyone for reading! Its been a blast diving into a new world and playing with a new cast of characters. I've been dying to write more "monster" heroes and well, satyrs seemed to be a good place to dip my toe in. I hope you're excited to follow the Bennett siblings because the next book will follow Rowan navigating his way through the wild world of the satyrs. And Aster? Weeeellll... you'll see.

I started *An Impractical Guide to Satyr Charming* in 2020 right at the beginning of the pandemic. Needless to say, things went extremely pear-shaped for me. I was laid off from my day job, all my author events (which generate decent money) were canceled, and my anxiety disorder got really out of hand. Like, *really* out of hand. Working on my mental health was something that I should have done a while ago and now thanks to medication, therapy, and a load of new coping skills, life is so much better.

I drew a lot from my own experiences with anxiety and poured them into Ivy; the ruminating, the panic attacks, the negative self-talk, and ways to pull yourself out of those spirals. Talk about therapeutic. If you are also suffering from anxiety or other mental health issues, I really encourage you to talk to someone; A friend, a doctor, or someone you trust to get the ball rolling. Its scary as hell but trust me, there is a way through it. As Ivy says, "You can do hard things."

What's coming next? Well, I'm going back to the Wyrd and working on Piper Daniels' story *A Witch's Want*. (Can you tell I'm on a witch kick?) Then its back to Magical Husbandry to tell Rowan and Callum's story in *An Irrational Lesson on Witch-Boy Wooing*. There are a few other surprises coming around the bend, ones that I can't announce just yet, but soon.

If you want to come hang out with me, check out my readers' group, **Cynthia's Wyrdlings** on Facebook. And since we all know how social media algorithms change, sign up for my newsletter, **Wyrd on the Streets** on my website to make sure you get all my updates and new releases. Once again, thank you all for reading and your support! I couldn't have gotten this far without you.

ABOUT THE AUTHOR

Cynthia is an award-winning paranormal romance author that writes for sassy nerds with a sharp sense of humor. Starting her adult life in theater, she earned a Masters of Fine Arts in Costume Design, but her first love was telling stories. After some encouragement, she dove down the writing rabbit hole, creating magical worlds, snarky heroines, and sexy heroes with a dash of "cinnamon roll".

When not telling tales, Cynthia is a geek, a costumer, and an amateur artist. She resides in sunny San Diego, California with her husband Max, two cats of varying intelligence, and a ton of goldfish.

www.CynthiaDiamondAuthor.com

If you like crackling chemistry, sharp wit, and plenty of action, then you'll adore Cynthia Diamond's other luscious stories.

<u>Wyrd Love</u>

Siren's Song
Valkyrie's Spear
Dryad's Vine
Alchemy's Hunger
Starting Fires
Trickster Business

<u>Magical Husbandry</u>

An Impractical Guide to Satyr Charming

(Coming Soon)
An Irrational Lesson on Witch-Boy Wooing
An Impossible Practice of Gargoyle Chasing